The
Man Must Marry

JANET CHAPMAN

The
Man Must Marry

Pocket **Star** Books

New York   London   Toronto   Sydney

Pocket Star Books
A Division of Simon & Schuster, Inc.
1230 Avenue of the Americas
New York, NY 10020

Art by Chris Cocozza

Manufactured in the United States of America

ISBN-13: 978-1-60751-400-8

To Abigail

Prepare yourself, baby girl, for life in a family of over-protective men who love you beyond words.

(Just bat your baby-blues at them, and I promise they'll be yours to command)

Chapter One

*S*am *Sinclair stood beside* Tidewater International's reception desk, waiting for the elevator to reach the thirtieth floor. The bell finally pinged, and whatever expectations Sam had, the woman revealed by the opening doors was . . . she was . . .

Good Lord, Abram had sent them a partridge!

Her hair, which had probably started out as a neat bun, was disassembling around her face. Though she couldn't be a day older than thirty, the shapeless brown suit she was wearing was more appropriate for someone twice her age. Half of her blouse hung out below the jacket. Both of her stockings had runs, the overnight bag at her feet the likely culprit. The woman truly resembled a partridge, her plain brown feathers rumpled and sadly outdated.

She looked exactly like a Willamina.

Frozen in shock, Sam watched as her monstrous purse fell into the lobby when she bent down to pick up her yellow overnight bag. She scrambled out of the elevator with a muttered curse, unsteady on two-inch heels, and retrieved her purse just as the elevator doors closed.

Her overnight bag was still inside.

The straps to it, however, were in her hand.

Instead of the doors reopening as they should have, the elevator softly pinged again, and the handles rose up along the crack in the doors. They stopped at the top, the woman frantically tugging on them. Sam heard the unmistakable sound of cloth ripping, and Willamina Kent fell to the floor with a yelp of surprise, the handles of her bag still in her hands.

Several people in the decidedly stunned audience finally rushed over to help her, and the floor beneath Sam's feet shifted at the sight of the warm, shy, sincere smile she bestowed on her rescuers.

God help them, they'd been invaded by an angelic frump.

This was *not* what they needed right now. The shareholders meeting today, to decide the new CEO of Tidewater International, was going to be a circus.

And it was all Bram's fault.

Abram Sinclair had sent a terse cable from Maine that morning, stating that he was sending Willamina Kent in his stead. Miss Kent held Bram's proxy vote, which would decide who would be succeeding him as chief executive officer.

His grandfather had entrusted the fate of a multibillion-dollar business to a woman who couldn't even exit an elevator without causing an uproar?

Several Tidewater employees were gathered around her as Miss Kent zealously explained the absurd chain of events that had ended with the bag-eating elevator. Sam edged closer.

"I flew in on one of those commuter prop planes. My seat was right between those huge propellers," she explained, tugging her ear, "and now my ears won't stop ringing. You'd think they would have put the airport closer to the city, too. The cab ride was nearly two hours! Heck, I could have rented a car for the fare I paid."

Ten to one, the cabbie also had found Willamina Kent a plump partridge and had given her the scenic tour. What was usually a mere hour's drive in midday traffic could take nearly two hours if the victim didn't know her way around Manhattan.

"Miss Kent," Sam said, moving forward and grasping her elbow. "The meeting is ready to begin, if you are." He ignored her subtle tug for freedom.

"But my luggage . . ."

"Someone will retrieve it for you," he promised, looking at one of the men. "And have maintenance see why the elevator doors didn't reopen," he added, then turned to lead her down the hall.

Sam had to stop when she stumbled. She looked up with intense, curious eyes of an indescribable color. They looked gray at first glance, or maybe blue. They were definitely arresting.

"Who are you?" she asked.

"Sam Sinclair." He dropped his gaze to frown at her shoes, which didn't match her suit. Her skirt and jacket were brown. Her shoes were green. And they looked too big for her feet.

"Abram's grandson," she said.

It wasn't a question. Sam forced a tight smile. "His oldest grandson."

"How do you know who I am?" she asked, giving him a pleased, expectant look.

"A lucky guess," he muttered, once again towing her toward the boardroom, though he did shorten his stride.

"The meeting's starting now? But I'm not . . . I need . . ."

Her voice trailed off as she gave her hair a useless pat, straightened her shoulders, and took a deep breath. Sam hid an involuntary smile. Miss Kent looked like a Christian preparing to enter the Colosseum—which was probably exactly how she felt. The boardroom would be filled with lions today, three of whom where vying for the CEO position. And Sam was one of them.

"We've already held the meeting back an hour," he

told her as he pushed open the door to the inner sanctum of Tidewater.

"Oh. I'm sorry," she whispered, her cheeks flushing a warm pink. "The ride in from the airport was longer than I'd anticipated."

"Had you contacted us with your arrival time, we would have sent the helicopter for you."

"A helicopter," she repeated, sounding intrigued, then gave him a brilliant smile. "I bet it wouldn't have taken me two hours to get here."

He attempted to lead her into the boardroom again. "More like twenty minutes."

She pulled to a stop and peeked inside. Conversations ceased, and all heads turned toward the door. Miss Kent took a step back. "If they've waited this long, they can wait another five minutes. Tell me where the powder room is, please," she demanded, tugging on her elbow again.

Sam turned back into the hall and directed her three doors down. "Five minutes, Miss Kent, and then we start without you," he warned, finally releasing her.

She gave him a smug smile and walked to the bathroom. "Feel free. But you won't be *finishing* without me," she shot back, disappearing inside.

Sam scowled. Damn his grandfather. He held the reins to Tidewater; he should be there. Where was he? In Maine?

Bram had disappeared six weeks ago. He hadn't told

anyone he was leaving and had barely contacted anyone since. The eighty-five-year-old had simply up and vanished into thin air. Once a week for the last six weeks, messages had appeared on an office computer telling everyone that yes, he was still alive, not to worry.

Bram was a wily old wolf. He had complained loud and long about the computerization of his company, but he was not above using the technology to his advantage. Even Tidewater's computer gurus hadn't been able to trace the origin of his messages.

Sam could only guess why his grandfather had disappeared like a thief in the night. It couldn't be easy to step down as head of the company he'd built from scratch with blood, sweat, brain, and guts. Bram obviously hated to relinquish control, though he likely hated growing old even more—a fact that had been resonating with all of them since Grammy Rose had died five years ago.

Sam walked into the boardroom and stood at the head of the table and waited. The twenty or so members of the board quietly took their seats and also waited in silence. Ten minutes later, the large door opened, and Miss Kent walked in, still looking frumpy despite her obvious primping.

Her light brown hair had been brushed out and was gathered in a clip to trail down her back in soft, wavy curls. Her face had been scrubbed clean and glowed with softly tanned freshness. Her shirt was tucked into her skirt, but she still looked more like a child playing dress-up than a woman about to alter the course of an international shipping conglomerate.

"Thank you all for being so patient," she said, walking to the large table. She looked at Sam. "Where should I sit?"

He indicated a seat to his right. The man beside it pulled out her chair.

"Thank you," she told him. As she sat down, she dropped her monstrous purse on the table and immediately started rummaging around in it.

With barely controlled patience, then with growing amazement, Sam watched, along with everyone else, as Miss Kent pulled out the broken straps of her suitcase and set them on the table. Then came an overstuffed wallet, a ring of keys that could sink a cargo ship, three packets of airline peanuts, a packet of tissues, an address book, and a candy bar that was squished beyond recognition. She began to mutter softly, her words lost in the cavern of her purse.

Out came a personal radio and earphones. More tissues. A romance novel, the corners curled, the spine broken, with a pen acting as a bookmark. An eyeglasses case. Finally, a folded mess of papers appeared in her hand.

With a sheepish smile directed at no one in particular, Miss Kent unfolded the papers and pulled one page free, then pushed it toward Sam.

"My letter of proxy." She glanced around the table,

then stood up. "I should introduce myself. I'm Willa-mina Kent, a friend of Abram's. He's asked me to come here today to vote in his stead." She smiled at everyone, then turned expectantly to Sam. "You may begin now," she softly instructed as she took her seat and began stuffing everything back into her purse.

"Thank you," he drawled, picking up the paper and scanning it. Bram had given Miss Kent his proxy, all right. His distinct signature sprawled boldly across the bottom of the notarized paper. Sam narrowed his eyes and read the handwritten note in the right margin: *You boys be nice to the lady.*

Biting back a smile, Sam opened the meeting, telling the board members what they already knew: Abram Sinclair was tired and unable to run the business anymore. Hell, he should have stepped down ten years ago. Sheer stubbornness had gotten him this far, but age had finally caught up with Bram, and Tidewater needed a new CEO.

"Then where is Abram? Why isn't he passing on the reins himself?" one of the members asked with a frown at Miss Kent.

Miss Kent raised her chin. "He's still on vacation. I'm to vote in his place."

"But where the hell *is* he?" Benjamin Sinclair demanded.

Ben was the middle Sinclair brother, and he also wanted the CEO position. He'd been groomed for it, just as Sam had, as well as their younger brother, Jesse. All three were there today, each hoping to persuade the board that he was the best man for the job—even though Miss Kent would have the deciding vote.

Or, rather, Bram's vote, with Miss Kent giving it.

"He's in Maine," she told Ben.

"That certainly pins him down," Ben drawled. "Where in Maine?"

"He asked me not to say."

"How do we know Bram is even alive?" another board member asked, glaring at Willamina.

Sam interceded before she could answer. "Bram sent a cable this morning, telling us Miss Kent would be coming in his place."

"How do we know he sent the cable?"

"He did," Sam assured him. "There's no mistaking Bram's voice in the words. Now, shall we begin?" He turned to the partridge. "Miss Kent. There are three of us in contention for the CEO position. Myself, my brother Benjamin," he offered, nodding to Ben, who nodded to her. "And our brother Jesse."

She smiled at each of them.

"As Bram probably explained to you, the CEO position needs to be filled, at least temporarily until he can decide what he wants to do with Tidewater," Sam explained. "I gather he's taken this little *vacation* to think about just that. Meanwhile, Tidewater is without definitive leadership."

She nodded, her expression intent.

"Jesse, you may begin. Ladies and gentlemen, you may ask questions as we go along," Sam instructed, leaning back in his chair.

While Jesse spoke of his vision for the company, Sam quietly studied the board members. They were all intelligent people, with a lot at stake in the company's future.

Sam's roving gaze narrowed on Miss Kent when he noticed she wasn't scribbling notes as the others were doing. Nor was she paying much attention to what was being said. That's when it hit him: the woman didn't know a damn thing about this business. Those blue-gray eyes of hers, which were sharpened with thoughtful attention, watched Jesse with an intelligence that had nothing whatsoever to do with spread sheets, growth curves, or bottom lines.

Ben spoke next.

And again, Miss Kent studied him with the intensity of a woman attending an auction to buy a horse, not hiring a CEO.

Sam's gut tightened. Their grandfather was at it again, only the old wolf was getting more devious.

He had sent Willamina down to shop for a husband.

Sam was thirty-six years old, Ben thirty-four, Jesse thirty. Since they'd each turned twenty, Bram had been trying to get them married off and settled down. Their grandfather had paraded more women before his grandsons than Sam could even count, much less remember. And now the old man had found another fortune-hunting woman, this time in Maine.

Bram must be getting desperate to sic a gold-digging frump on them, a little brown twit with faerie hair and angelic eyes, possessing all the grace of a newborn filly on ice skates. And from what he'd seen so far, those appeared to be her good qualities.

But as long as she voted as instructed, who cared if she was husband hunting? The three of them had successfully escaped their grandfather's campaigns for sixteen years; they'd send this one scurrying back to Maine two minutes after she voted.

Sam stood up and spoke last, explaining that he didn't intend to make any major changes yet. But he did emphasize his own vision for the company's future, reminding the members that he'd been making most of the daily decisions for the last five years.

Then he called for a vote.

Most of the members had been anticipating this day, and the speeches were more a formality than anything else. All three had their own members in their corners, and as the votes were orally given, each member backed his or her man. Eventually, it came down to Bram's deciding vote, as everyone had known it would.

"Miss Kent," Sam said. "Please tell us what Bram wished."

She looked up at him. "I—ah—I haven't decided."

"You don't have to decide, Miss Kent," Sam told her, his shoulders stiffening. "You just have to give us Bram's vote."

"Um . . . Abram didn't give me a specific vote."

"What?" Ben said in surprise, jumping up from his seat across from her. "What do you mean?"

"He told me the decision was mine," she told Ben, her chin rising defensively.

"Yours?" Jesse repeated, also standing up. "What in hell are you talking about?"

Willamina Kent stood up, though her insignificant height only mocked her attempt to look imposing. "Just what I said. Abram told me the decision was mine."

"He can't do that!"

"Well, he did."

Willamina's gaze moved from one grandson to the other, and she spread her arms wide. "Think about it, gentlemen," she softly implored. "The man's your grandfather, and he loves each of you very much. He couldn't choose one of you over the others."

"Love has nothing to do with this," Sam said tightly. "He just had to name the man best qualified to be his successor."

"He told me you were all equally qualified and that he wouldn't worry about Tidewater if any one of you succeeded him."

Whispered murmurs erupted around the table, along with an underlying tension.

"So what in hell are we suppose to do?" Jesse growled.

Everyone looked at Miss Kent.

She gave them a sheepish smile. "I guess the three of you will take me to dinner."

"But what about the vote?" somebody asked harshly.

Miss Kent darted a wary glance at the table of hostile stares. "I understand the importance of my decision. And frankly, I didn't want to take on this obligation. But I have, and I need some time to decide."

"Why *are* you doing this for Bram?" Sam asked.

"Because he asked me to."

"But why?"

"Abram has been renting a cottage on my property for the last six weeks, and we've become friends. He needed this favor, and I couldn't bring myself to refuse him. I tried all last week to talk him out of this, but he just got . . ."

"Stubborn as hell," Sam finished for her.

"Miss Kent," one of the board members interrupted. "This situation can't go on any longer. Abram Sinclair *is* Tidewater. The business community knows he's gone missing, and we have no leader with the power to make binding decisions. It's imperative that a new CEO be chosen soon."

"I'll decide by tomorrow, after I have dinner with you three tonight," she promised, looking at the three contenders. "But I simply can't vote right now."

"I have a date tonight," Jesse told her.

"Then bring her," she offered. "I just thought if I could get to know each of you a little better, it would help me decide."

"You expect to gamble the future of a multibillion-dollar business over dinner?" Ben asked incredulously.

"I was told the company would be in good hands with any of you."

"If this is a fishing expedition, Miss Kent, then beware," Sam whispered tightly, leaning over the table, watching with satisfaction as her eyes went wide and wary. "The three of us are liable to sink your ship with you still in it."

She blinked up at him. "Fishing expedition?"

"Dammit to hell!" Ben growled, slapping his briefcase shut and storming out of the boardroom.

Sam took her by the elbow again, restraining himself from dragging her to her feet. They didn't need this right now. Not after six weeks of worrying about their grandfather.

"Come on, Ms. Kent," he ground out.

He had to let go of her elbow while she scrambled under the table to retrieve the purse she'd dropped again. While she was there, she patted the floor, looking for her shoes. Sam looked up at the boardroom of equally incredulous people.

She dropped her purse again when she tried to sit down and put on her shoes. Sam picked it up, deciding he would hold on to it for sanity's sake. Finally, he all but dragged her into the hall.

"I've booked a room at the Marriott," she told him as she scrambled to keep up.

"You can stay at the penthouse tonight."

"No. I prefer to stay at the hotel," she said, looking up with unwavering eyes that were nearly the color of slate.

"If you insist." He stopped at the reception desk. "Did you find Miss Kent's luggage?"

"Yes, Mr. Sinclair. It's already in your car."

"Thank you." He started toward the elevator.

"I am quite capable of walking on my own," she quietly told him, tugging on her elbow.

He freed her, then watched with ill-concealed anger as she eyed the elevator doors as if they were going to open up and eat her.

"First time visiting New York?" he asked dryly, forcing his emotions under control. He also had to relax his shoulders forcibly, as they were bunched with the desire to throttle the little twit.

"Actually, it's many firsts for me," she answered, looking up with what Sam could only describe as excitement. "Including my first plane ride."

"Really?"

"Yup. And I can tell you, I'm in no hurry to do it again."

"What do you do for a living in Maine, Miss Kent?"

"I'm a casket maker."

Sam blinked. The elevator doors opened, and without thinking, he took her elbow again and ushered her inside. "Did you say *casket maker?*"

She smiled up at him indulgently, as if she'd been expecting his reaction. "I own a small casket-manufacturing business. I have a few highly skilled craftsmen who do the woodwork and others who do the interiors."

"I see."

"Abram's been working for me," she said, pulling free. She touched Sam's sleeve. "He's been building his own casket."

Sam swayed slightly, as if he'd just taken a blow to the gut.

"It's been comforting for your grandfather," she continued softly. "Abram says he feels good using his hands. And he's proud of his final accomplishment." She moved to stand directly in front of him, looking up with concern. "Your grandfather is dying, Mr. Sinclair," she said gently. "He's come to terms with it, and now you and your brothers have to, too."

"Then he shouldn't have run off!" he snapped. "He should be home with his family. We're all he's got left."

"He'll be back. I think."

"You *think?*"

She canted her head, her countenance calm before the growing storm she must have seen in his eyes. "In some cultures, the elderly go off by themselves into the wilderness to die. In a way, I think that's what Abram has done. I suspect he didn't want the fuss and bother of a deathbed scene," she explained, her voice soothing.

Dammit, he didn't want to be soothed. He wanted to grab this woman and shake her until she rattled. She was a stranger. A twit. And she was saying things he didn't want to hear.

"Tell me where he is," Sam ground out, grabbing her by the shoulders.

Her eyes widened, her sympathy turning to alarm. "I can't. I promised."

Sam glared at her. "I'll find him, you know. There can't be too many casket makers named Willamina Kent in Maine."

"You'll hurt him if you do."

"He belongs at home."

"He'll come back."

"In a box!"

"If that's his choice," she said, her chin rising but not her voice. "We don't have any say in how we enter this world, Mr. Sinclair. But if we have the chance to leave it on our own terms, then we deserve to."

Sam felt the blood drain from his face and tightened his grip on her shoulders.

She winced but didn't try to break free. Instead, she brought one small hand up to his chest. "It's Abram's choice, Sam." Her eyes became beseeching. "Have you thought that maybe he wants your last memories of him to be of a strong man who sat at the helm of his empire? If Abram could have had his way, I think he would have died sitting at his desk."

"Or standing on the deck of a cargo ship, watching the sun rise," Sam whispered. He released her to slam his hand suddenly against the wall of the elevator. "Damn!" He spun back toward her. "He was a sea captain, did you know that? It's how he started. Bram could tell just by the smell of the breeze what tomorrow's weather would be. He loved being at sea, and he and Grammy often traveled on whichever cargo ship was heading where they wanted to go."

"I didn't know that."

Sam closed his eyes against the pain tearing at his insides. He didn't like it, but he understood. Oh, Christ, he really did understand Bram's pilgrimage to Maine. If the old man knew he was dying, he would not want witnesses, especially his grandsons.

Sam took a deep breath. "Okay," he said hoarsely. "Bram is likely coming back in a box."

"I'm sorry."

"The old wolf couldn't live forever," he said with painful resignation, rubbing his temple in an attempt to erase the realization that he would probably never see his grandfather again.

She touched his sleeve, smiling sadly up at him. Just then, the elevator stopped, and the door pinged, and he watched her stiffen. Pushing down his anguish with an iron will, he held up her purse.

"Don't worry, I'll protect it with my life."

She laughed, and the haunting weight of morbidity magically left the elevator. Every muscle in Sam's body involuntarily reacted to the simple, pleasant sound of her gentle laughter.

"You think I'm bad with elevators?" she said, her smile crooked. "You should see me with escalators."

Well, hell. A partridge with the laugh of an angel.

If there was one weakness in Abram Sinclair, it was women. The old man had always liked them plump, laughing, and warm, which was why he was forever preaching to his grandsons that breeding, beauty, and bank accounts didn't matter. Full bosoms were nice, and backsides built to cradle a man were necessary.

Which explained exactly why Willamina Kent was there.

Sam escorted her to the car in the underground parking garage in silence, where Ronald was waiting. He gave his driver instructions to take them to the Marriott, and they rode through Manhattan in silence. Willamina spent the trip with her nose nearly pressed to the window, watching the city go by.

Sam passed the time watching her.

Her shirttail was untucked again. And the suit, which looked as if it had been made in the late seventies, was wrinkled beyond repair. She'd unknowingly knocked over the heavy purse at her feet, and half the contents had spilled out.

Sam silently sighed. He couldn't figure her out. For all of Miss Kent's artlessness, he definitely had seen intelligence in her eyes during the meeting.

A less astute person might only notice her appearance, but Bram always tried to see past the mask a person wore, just as he was always trying to see beyond the ocean's horizon.

Sam felt he'd inherited his grandfather's talent, which was why he would bet there was a lot more to Willamina Kent than first impressions. Abram Sinclair never would have left the fate of Tidewater—or his grandsons—in the hands of a twit.

So, was she merely the dying whimsy of an old man? Bram wouldn't be averse to shaking up his family or his business to achieve an end, which meant the old wolf had an ulterior motive for sending her here.

Marriage, most likely. It wasn't beyond Bram to have fallen in love with Willamina himself; and who better, he would figure, for one of his grandsons to marry? Willamina seemed like a sympathetic creature, if a person could get past her antics.

Although her chosen profession was . . . weird.

Well, hell. He guessed somebody had to build caskets.

But Bram was building his own. Sam still couldn't shake off that macabre vision.

"Do you need help checking in?" he asked when they pulled up to the Marriott.

"No, thank you. I'll be fine." She frowned down at her purse, then started shoving everything back into it. "Will we all be going to dinner tonight?"

"We'll pick you up at seven," Sam told her. He stepped out of the car behind her and watched with wry amusement as Ronald handed her defeated luggage to the porter, noticing some kind soul had wound it shut with packing tape. The porter, bless his training, didn't even bat an eye when he took it.

Once Miss Kent was safely on her way, Sam climbed back into the car and headed back to the office. Maybe he could salvage something of this hellacious day—as well as do an Internet search for a casket company in Maine.

As the elevator doors were closing back at the parking garage, Sam saw a scrap of material caught in the door track. Shoving against the doors to open them again, he reached down and retrieved what turned out to be a pair of iridescent lilac panties.

They were a little larger than he was used to.

With a smile of anticipation for the evening to come, Sam shoved them into his pocket. It appeared the little partridge didn't *always* wear brown.

Chapter Two

*W*illa *dropped her ruined* bag onto the floor of her hotel room, only to watch it break open and spill her laughable wardrobe onto the carpet.

What a mess. And not just her clothes, either, but the bigger mess she was in—including what was sure to be the evening from hell. She was going to have to sit through dinner facing three hostile men who likely wanted to tar and feather her and put her on the first plane north.

After each one tried to charm her vote.

Damn Abram Sinclair. This was all his fault. She didn't belong here. Those people in that boardroom today, and his grandsons, they were all *way* out of her league. She was a small-town girl. The biggest business decisions she made were what new designs she could carve into the covers of her caskets. She had no business deciding who should head a multibillion-dollar company.

Willa moaned in frustration, kicked off her shoes, collapsed onto the bed, and rubbed her forehead. She'd gotten a pounding headache within minutes of sitting between those monstrous props on the plane, and she still had the damned thing, only now it had gone from pounding to splitting. Hell, even her hair hurt.

And her day was not over. Willa opened her eyes and squinted at her watch. In four hours, there would be three angry men taking her to dinner. Oh, they'd be civil enough, considering that each one wanted her vote. They all would probably spread on the charm so thick she'd likely drown in it.

Except maybe Sam Sinclair. He hadn't tried very hard to hide his feelings about the situation—or her.

She didn't blame him. Abram had run away from home, hurting all three of his grandsons. They obviously loved the old man and needed to say good-bye to him. Willa understood both the grandsons' points of view and Abram's; she also understood everyone's pain.

To top everything off, Sam clearly considered her a slap in the face. Abram had brought a stranger onto both the familial scene and the business scene. And not just a stranger but a klutz.

Willa had never worn heels in her life and couldn't seem to get the hang of them. The ones she had on today had belonged to her mother. And she hated elevators. If the boardroom hadn't been on the thirtieth floor, she would have walked up the stairs—though thirty floors was a bit much. Then her luggage had been eaten. And when she'd gone to the bathroom and gotten a look in the mirror, she'd nearly screamed.

She'd laughed instead, until she cried. She'd come to Manhattan, to a high-powered meeting, looking like something her cat had dragged up from the beach. No wonder everyone had been horrified to think she had the tie-breaking vote. She'd been horrified herself.

Now she was simply scared.

And that was unnatural for her. She was twenty-nine years old and considered herself fearless. She had confidence in her ability to read situations and people. She made her own decisions. And even if those decisions turned out to be wrong, she always stood by them.

That was why she was there, facing Abram's three grandsons. When the wild-haired, sharp-eyed old man had appeared on her doorstep, asking to rent her cottage, he'd stolen her heart with his disgraceful charm, atavistic arrogance, and failing body. He'd told her bluntly that he'd come to Maine to die and that he wanted to do it on his own terms. And Willa, being a pushover for anything in need, had taken him in and given him love and understanding—and her promise to come tell his grandsons he was dying.

She should have guessed they would be younger versions of Abram.

All three grandsons were gorgeous—tall, imposing, and downright intimidating. Willa was sorely tempted to write her vote on a piece of paper and leave it at the front desk, so when they came to pick her up that evening, she would already be on a plane back to Maine. She didn't want to be near either of the losers when they realized the results.

With more willpower than ambition, Willa forced herself to crawl off the bed and strip out of the suit she'd borrowed from Maureen, one of her senior employees. Rummaging around in the mess on the floor, Willa found the dress she'd bought for this trip. Shaking it out with a growl of disgust, she fished a hanger from the closet and hung the dress in the bathroom. Then she turned on the shower, hoping the wrinkles would leave the dress while she steamed the wrinkles out of herself.

"Where in hell did Bram find her?"

"In Maine."

"Figures. What did she say? When's he coming home?"

"He's not," Sam said softly.

"Never?"

"He's dying, according to Ms. Kent."

Sam sat quietly in the corner of the car, letting his statement sink in. Jesse was sitting facing him, Ben beside him. All three were dressed in casual evening attire, on their way to pick up their dates for dinner.

Willamina was Sam's date.

"He can't just run off and die on us," Jesse whispered. "Can he?"

"It seems he has. Ms. Kent said he's too proud for us to see him die."

"That's bullshit. The man literally brought us up. He's been more of a father than a grandfather. He has no right to die without us," Ben said, his fists clenched on his knees. "We'll get her to tell us where he is, and then we'll go get him. He belongs home."

"She won't betray him. I tried."

"Maybe you didn't try hard enough."

Sam gave his brothers a wry grin. "Don't underestimate Ms. Kent, gentlemen. She may look like a meek little partridge, but she won't break her promise to Bram."

"We know he's in Maine. We'll track him down," Ben said.

Sam looked at his brothers' anxious faces in the soft interior lights of the limo. "Do we really want to go against Bram's wishes?" he asked, his voice betraying his reservations. "He's of sound mind; it's his body that's failing him. And he doesn't want us to see that."

"Damn. I didn't realize he was sick. I thought we had more time," Jesse choked out, dropping his gaze to stare at his hands.

Ben wouldn't let go of his anger. "Why in hell couldn't he have just faxed us his vote? The woman obviously doesn't know a spreadsheet from a bedsheet."

Sam snorted. "Guess."

Both brothers blinked at him, then started cursing.

"Bram is still trying to marry us off from his death-bed!" Jesse snapped, shaking his head in disgust.

"Yes," Sam agreed. "That, and to prepare us." Sam cocked his head. "I'd guess that Ms. Kent has fallen in love with Bram. Why else would she be doing this for him?"

"To land a rich husband," Ben spat out.

"That woman couldn't land a goldfish, much less a rich husband," Jesse said.

"Don't underestimate her." Sam looked at his brothers with haunted eyes. "She owns a casket-manufacturing business. And she told me Bram's been building his own casket."

"What?"

"She says it's been comforting for him."

"Then she's as sick as he is!"

"No. She's softhearted. And the bravest woman I've ever met," Sam countered.

"Brave?" Ben repeated.

"It was obvious that Tidewater's boardroom was the last place Ms. Kent wanted to be today. And I assure you, she is not looking forward to this evening. It takes a hell of a lot of courage to messenger the imminent death of a man to his family. I honestly can't say that I could do what she's doing."

The car fell silent after that, until they stopped to

pick up Jesse's date for the evening. With legendary Sinclair willpower, the three men forced themselves to throw off their gloom and smile at Darcy as she sat next to Jesse.

Darcy was the epitome of Manhattan womanhood. Tonight she was dressed in elegant black and cultured coolness. She wore three-inch heels, which were necessary if she didn't want to be dwarfed by her escort. Jesse and Darcy had been seeing each other for three months, which was about the limit of Jesse's female attention span.

Sam guessed his brother would soon be moving on, which was probably just as well. For all of Darcy's beauty, she didn't have much depth of character. Traveling, shopping, and spending her trust fund were the extent of her interests.

They picked up Ben's date next. Paula wasn't a steady; Ben enjoyed the company of several different women. He'd been burned badly a couple of times already; first when he was nineteen and then again four years ago.

The last time had been close. Bram had thought he was finally going to get a granddaughter-in-law, and Jesse and Sam had thought they were going to get the pressure lifted from finding their own wives. But just when it had looked as if Ben might propose, he'd broken off the relationship, not telling anyone why.

It would take a stalwart woman to marry a Sinclair. She would have to be intelligent, strong, and forgiving.

She'd also have to be brave. The Sinclair men were not known for their patience. People generally treaded carefully around them, especially Bram. And he'd brought up his grandsons to be just as ruthless, just as relentless, just as driven.

Sam, Ben, and Jesse had been orphaned when Sam was twelve. Their parents had died in a plane crash returning from an overseas meeting that had doubled as a romantic vacation. His shoulders slumped in defeat with the news that his third and last surviving son was dead, Bram had arrived with Grammy Rose at the boys' home and collected them. A powerful bond had been formed that day between the three lost, confused children and their grieving grandparents. Deep, desperate love had blossomed, along with friendship and respect.

That was why Bram hadn't been able to choose among them. He didn't want to turn his business over to just one of his boys; they all owned shares in Tidewater, and they all were wealthy men in their own rights, thanks to the Sinclair drive. To pick one to head his company was clearly too hard for the old man.

The limo pulled up to the Marriott, where Willa was waiting in the lobby. She reminded Sam of an absentminded professor, whose body was having trouble keeping up with her brain. Willamina Kent's head was too far into the clouds to see the everyday details of life. And her heart, apparently, was her own worst enemy.

Why else would she have come on this mission for a man she'd only known for six weeks?

As soon as she saw him get out of the car, she headed for the revolving door. She'd traded her saddle-bag of a purse for a clutch with a long strap that dangled from her fist. Sam watched in stoic resignation as she pushed through the door, snagging her purse in the sweep of the door behind her. The strap snapped, and the purse landed on the ground, unceremoniously pushed along by the door behind her.

Her ankles wobbled as she reached down to get it. Sam grabbed her elbow to steady her, then retrieved the purse himself.

"Thank you," she murmured, clutching the mangled purse, the long strap dangling like a tail as she headed for the car.

Sam settled her into the silent limo. Getting in beside her, he saw her cheeks were flaming red.

They matched her dress.

The dress looked as if it had come from a thrift shop, the style even older than the suit she'd worn earlier, with a high collar in danger of choking her. Ruffles grazed her chin, and the hem was nearly at her ankles.

At least her shoes were better this time. They were black, again with two-inch heels, and matched the wide belt cinching her waist. The purse she was industriously trying to repair was tan.

Sam reached over and took it from her. Upon exam-
ination, he quickly decided the thing was a lost cause
and broke off the strap. "Now you have a hand clutch,"
he said, handing it back to her.

Her gaze, which had widened when he'd popped the
useless strap, lowered to her lap. Turning the small
handbag over and over, she finally looked up at the
others in the car and gave them a shy smile.

"Hello again," she said to Jesse, who couldn't quit
staring.

Ben quietly kicked him.

"Ah . . . hello," Jesse answered. "I guess I should
make the introductions. This is my friend, Darcy. And
this is Paula, Ben's friend. Ladies, this is Willamina."

Everyone smiled graciously, then Willa turned to Sam.
"Are we going to pick up your date next?" she asked.

"No. I drew the short straw."

Her face flushed, and her head bent down, causing
her precarious topknot to loosen.

Aw, hell. He hadn't really meant to say that. He
knew she didn't want to be there any more than they
did. But despite what he had said to his brothers about
Willa's courage, she was also husband hunting. Only
someone hoping to marry into the Sinclair wealth
would agree to come to New York to vote on something she knew nothing about.

Well, by the end of this evening, Willamina Kent
would be more than ready to fly home after a triple

dose of confirmed bachelorism. They'd all sent better women than she down the road shaking their heads. Bram was going to have to go to his grave without getting a granddaughter-in-law.

Sorry for hurting her feelings but determined to stand firm against the threat she posed, Sam turned away and stared out the window.

The man may as well have slapped her face. She didn't *want* to be the arrogant jerk's date. She didn't want to be anyone's date. Especially not one of these three puffed-up baboons parading as men.

They were just like their grandfather—and Willa didn't consider that a compliment. Abram Sinclair was a bossy, arrogant old goat, even if she did love him. But that didn't mean she had to love his grandsons.

She didn't even have to like them.

She was there on a mission of mercy and nothing else, despite what Abram hoped. Oh, she knew he had matchmaking up his sleeve. He'd been blatant enough with his praise and subtle hints that his boys were all lonely, misunderstood men.

Well, they could damn well find their own wives. Which shouldn't be hard; they were gorgeous. But even if they were butt ugly, they were wealthy enough to have women drooling at their feet.

Willa eyed the women in the car. They were beautiful. Elegant. Skinny. Everything she was not. She hated them; she hated New York. And she hated anyone named Sinclair.

The restaurant they arrived at was over-the-top fancy and the only nonlimos pulling up were foreign and expensive. Willa felt like a wren in a house of predatory cats.

Sam Sinclair wasn't helping matters.

"If you take my elbow again, I'm going to drive my heel into your shin," she softly warned when he reached for her.

He drew back as if she'd bitten him, then his eyes narrowed. "If you fall flat on your face, I'm going to leave you there."

Chin raised and with all the dignity she could muster, Willa followed the other women inside—into an Asian country.

Damn. Foreign food. And if they expected her to use two little sticks to eat with, she'd starve first. She was a Maine girl; she ate meat and potatoes and seafood. *Pronounceable* seafood.

They were soon seated around a large circular table in a room so dimly lit she could barely see across it. Not knowing what else to do with her . . . clutch purse, Willa set it on her lap, only to have it slide down her satiny dress, fall onto the floor, and bounce off her foot. She heard Sam sigh.

The damn purse could damn well stay where it was; all it held were some tissues. Willa hated purses. Doing errands at home, she wore jeans and sneakers and a small fanny pack. She didn't have time to chase down a purse whenever she wanted something. Since she'd left Maine, she'd spent more time babysitting her purse than anything else. The floor sweeper could have this one.

They were given menus, and everyone ordered drinks. Willa got stared at again when she ordered a Johnnie Walker Black on the rocks. A double.

Thank God it came quickly. Willa took a large, throat-burning sip, then opened her menu. She didn't recognize anything. She could see the words *shrimp* and *chicken* and *beef*, but there were other, more ominous words associated with them, which everyone pronounced competently as they placed their orders.

The dinner from hell, that's what this was.

"Do you have plain lobster?" she asked the waiter when he looked at her.

He nodded.

"What is today's price?" she asked, knowing it was rude but too curious to care.

He told her, and Willa's eyes nearly crossed. "Shrimp, then. Just sauteed. With steamed rice."

The waiter nodded and left, and Willa looked up to see everyone staring at her again. She gave them her most brilliant smile, no matter how painful it was for her. "I buy lobster off the boat nearly every week. Even during peak season, I don't pay more than five dollars a pound."

"Really?" Darcy commented.

"A hundred years ago in Maine, lobster was considered a poor man's food."

"You don't say," Darcy purred.

Willa sighed. A shallow dish, that one. She looked at Ben. "Abram tells me you all like to sail and that he owns a Sengatti sloop," she offered conversationally.

"That's right," Ben guardedly returned.

"I sail," she told him with waning brightness. "As a matter of fact, I grew up not far from the Sengatti Yacht Yard."

"Have you sailed on one?" Ben asked, looking interested despite himself.

"Oh, sure. My dad was a sea captain. We owned a schooner and plied the tourist trade. Dad often took new owners out for lessons on the Sengatti they'd just purchased, and I went along."

"Bram upgraded his sloop eight years ago," Jesse interjected. "She's forty-two feet long and fast. I believe she was the last boat Emmett Sengatti himself actually built."

Willa smiled at his enthusiasm. "What's her name?"

"Bram christened her the *RoseWind*, after Grammy Rose." Ben's face sobered. "Until Gram died five years ago, the two of them loved to go out sailing."

"Tell us about your father's schooner," Sam interjected.

"She was named *Cat's Tail*, because Dad said she sailed like a cat whose tail had just passed over a candle flame. She was two-masted and sixty-seven feet long. She slept ten, assuming a few couples didn't mind cuddling. In the winter, we sailed her down to the Caribbean and hired out for weeklong charter tours."

"What about school?" Jesse asked.

"Mom taught us."

"Us?" Sam asked.

"My sister and me. We crewed for Dad. Mom cooked."

"You must live fairly close to Prime Point, then," Ben piped up, looking pleased. "That's where Sengatti Yacht is located."

"Not that close," Willa shot back, shooting down his hopes of learning where his grandfather was.

The food arrived, and while Willa eyed hers suspiciously, Darcy tried to continue the conversation.

"So you're a sailor? Is that what you do for a living?"

"No," Willa told her with anticipated relish. "I build caskets."

Bingo. Both Darcy and Paula choked on their first bites of food. The men didn't bat an eyelash, so Sam must have told them already.

"Caskets?" Paula squeaked, her eyes wide in horror.

"Yup, and we do a lot of custom orders. We use local wood and carve beautiful scenes into them." She beamed at her stunned audience, who had set down their forks. "Our caskets hold the remains of some of the world's most eccentric people. We ship all over the world. You'd be amazed at some of the requests we get."

Nobody moved. Nobody spoke. Finally, Sam started to push his food around on his plate.

Okay. That had been a nasty shot, and she was a little ashamed of herself. But dammit, they all deserved it. They all had been looking down their noses at her.

"What do you do, Darcy?" Willa asked.

"Do?"

"For work?"

"Work?"

Willa sighed.

"I'm thinking of going back to school," the woman offered.

"School's important," Willa confirmed, smiling at Jesse, who suddenly started eating.

"I do charity functions," Paula piped up.

"That's important, too," Willa agreed.

Wow. And these intelligent Sinclair men were attracted to them?

"Shouldn't we be discussing Tidewater?" Ben interjected. "That is the reason we're here."

"No, it's not. We're here so I can get to know each of you better."

"We're not biting, Ms. Kent," Sam said softly, leaning closer. "No matter what Bram told you, you're trolling in barren water."

"Fine," Willa shot back. "Then maybe I'll just draw straws tomorrow."

Sam snapped his brows together at Willa's not-so-subtle reminder of his rudeness. If she was fishing, she wasn't baiting her hook. She didn't talk like a woman trying to snag a husband; she talked as if she couldn't wait to be done with the entire lot of them.

Sam repressed a shudder, imagining Willa on a ship full of ropes and pulleys and sails. He wondered how often she unexpectedly went swimming or how many guests she'd drowned. Captain Kent must have the patience of a saint or nerves of steel.

The dinner table returned to silence as everyone ate. Ben and Jesse seemed to be realizing the truth of Sam's earlier warning that Willa was not an easy mark. She had a disarming answer for everything and refused to be trounced on. She wasn't above hitting low, either.

Had Bram realized that? Most likely.

Dinner was interrupted twice by acquaintances who stopped by the table to say hello. Willa always quietly looked on with interest, assessing all of them in that disconcerting way of hers. Finally, the waiter brought over the dessert cart.

Willa eyed the cart with enthusiasm. "Oh, boy! Black Forest cake. I was afraid they'd only have strange desserts."

Darcy and Paula looked askance when the waiter placed a huge, creamy, decadent piece of cake in front of Willa.

"You're going to eat that?" Darcy blurted, only to blush at her own rudeness.

"I sure am. Desserts did me a huge favor once. I owe them."

"What kind of favor?" Paula asked.

"They helped get me a divorce."

Sam, who had just taken a sip of coffee, nearly spit it out. Jesse and Ben set their cups down with a clank.

"Dessert got you a divorce?" Jesse asked.

Willa turned unreadable eyes on him. "I tried for more than a year to talk my husband into a simple, amicable divorce, but he refused to go down without a fight. Finally, though, I got him to give me one."

"How?" Paula asked, leaning over her plate and looking intrigued, not noticing that her scarf was trailing in her food.

"I got fat."

"Fat!"

"David was a rather superficial man," Willa explained. "I got so fat he couldn't stand to be seen in public with me. Bingo. Divorce."

Paula blinked. Several times. "How fat were you?"

"What I am now."

"The man divorced you because of what you weigh now?" Darcy asked, darting a frantic look at Jesse.

Jesse was too busy staring at Willa to notice. Ben had picked up his coffee again, and Sam figured that was to hide his smile behind it; Sam, however, was purely amazed. The partridge had been married?

"Oh, no. I've gotten food on my scarf!" Paula cried. She stood up. "I have to go to the powder room."

"I'll go with you." Darcy offered, standing up.

The men looked at Willa. She stayed sitting.

As soon as the women left, Willa set down her fork. "I wish to clear the air, gentlemen," she said, her smile not quite reaching her eyes. "You do realize your grandfather sent me here hoping one of you would capture my matrimonial eye? And that I might . . . interest one of you?" Her smile widened. "He was looking for a miracle, I'd say."

Sam snorted before he could stop himself.

"I explained to Abram that I never intend to walk down a church aisle again. All three of you could crawl to Maine on your knees, your hearts in your hands, and I wouldn't marry any one of you."

"I don't remember any of us asking," Sam snapped.

"As long as we understand each other," she returned simply, picking up her fork and returning to her cake.

"Then why in hell are you here?" Jesse asked sharply.

"Because your grandfather asked me to do this favor for him," Willa said with tired patience.

"But why, if Bram knew you didn't want to get married?"

She stared at her half-eaten dessert. Finally, she looked around the table. "Abram claims I have an inherent sense of character. He hoped that I could meet you, get to know each of you a little bit, and objectively choose."

"Then choose!" Jesse growled.

"Tomorrow!" Willa growled back, stabbing her cake and making one of the cherries shoot off her plate. It landed on Jesse's white shirt.

Chapter Three

$\mathcal{D}$arcy and $\mathcal{P}$aula wanted to go dancing next.

Would the evening never end?

Willa could dance about as well as she could walk in heels. And her *date* must have realized exactly how she felt about it, because Sam's eyes lit up when everyone agreed they would go to a favorite nightspot.

Well, she'd simply have another drink and watch from the table. She wasn't about to step into his arms naively, because Sam Sinclair downright disconcerted her. He made her palms sweat. He made her arm tingle whenever he took hold of her elbow. And she had a hard time breathing properly whenever he looked directly at her with those impaling ice-blue eyes of his.

He was a good head taller than she was, although that didn't exactly make him a giant. His shoulders did that. But it was his broad, masculine chest that really made her want to throw herself into his arms.

That was why she wouldn't dance with him. She was afraid she'd get wrapped up in his arms, against that chest, and start to drool. He also smelled much too good. She wasn't about to get close to a well-built, handsome, broad-chested, nice-smelling man. It had simply been too long for her.

Since her divorce five years ago, Willa had persuaded her hormones to hibernate, but the damn things had woken up when Sam took her elbow to escort her to the boardroom. Now they were practically jumping up and down in anticipation.

"Where's your purse?" he asked when the car pulled to the curb to pick them up.

Willa looked him right in the eye. "On the floor in the restaurant."

He heaved a mighty sigh and turned to go back in.

She grabbed his sleeve. "Leave it. It's got three tissues and a comb in it."

He looked at her, his blue eyes intent. Suddenly, he grinned and helped her into the car.

Once again, Willa found herself sandwiched between Ben and Sam, across from Jesse, the two women on either side of him. And once again, the silence became awkward.

"What have you and Bram talked about these last six weeks?" Jesse asked.

"Everything," she answered honestly. "About life. And death. About accepting both. He told me that he buried all three of his sons. And he says he misses Rose very much."

"Our father was Bram's middle son. His oldest son, Michael, died in a fire at the age of six. And Peter, his youngest, died at age twenty in a skiing accident," Jesse explained. "Our father and mother died in a plane crash more than twenty years ago."

"He told me Rose passed away five years ago."

"Yes. Our home, Rosebriar, is named for her."

"Bram also talked about you three. About how 'damn proud' he is of you," Willa said with a sincere smile. "And about how stubborn you all are for not getting married," she added, darting an apologetic smile at the two women across from her.

"We'll marry in time," Jesse said. "But on our terms—not Bram's."

"Abram told me he made the mistake of raising you all to be just like him."

Jesse gave Willa a roguish grin. "That's quite a compliment."

"Not really. I think all of you, Abram included, should have been drowned at birth."

Darcy and Paula gasped. Jesse's grin broadened. Ben snorted. Sam's shoulders shook, which shook *her*.

"How long were you married?" Sam asked.

"Three long, long years," she admitted with a sigh.

"And you're sure it was your size that got you divorced?"

"I think, Mr. Sinclair, that ultimately it was the huge rottweiler David found in our bed."

"You didn't!" Jesse sputtered on a choked laugh.

"I was getting desperate. A friend owned a very sweet rottweiler who happened to dislike men. David came home one night a little too late, a little too drunk, and a little too perfumey." Willa smiled. "I think he still walks with a slight limp."

Darcy and Paula looked incredulous, but both sides of Willa started shaking, until Ben and Sam couldn't hold in their laughter any longer.

"A partridge." Jesse snorted. "More like a falcon, Sam."

Willa frowned. "What are you—"

The limo driver suddenly cursed as the car swerved hard to the right, throwing them off balance.

More curses erupted from the men as it swerved again, and Willa was suddenly slammed up against a stone-hard chest. Bands of steel tightened around her as everyone was tossed like clothes in a washing machine, all three women screaming.

The wild ride stopped with unbelievable force, throwing Willa to the floor. A heavy weight landed on top of her. Though her head was protected by the large hand cupping it, her body felt as if a tank had just slammed into it. And she couldn't breathe.

Old ghosts rose in Willa's mind, filling her with terror. She shoved at Sam with all her might. "Out! We have to get out. It's going to burn!" she cried, still shoving. "Everyone out!"

"Easy, Willamina. It's okay. We're not on fire," Sam said close to her ear. Feet and arms and legs poked at her, as more cursing ensued. A back door opened.

Willa shoved at Sam again. "We have to get out! It could still burn. Get off me!"

"Easy, we're getting out," Sam said calmly, trying to quell her panic. "Are you hurt?"

"Just get me out of this car!" she shrieked, scrambling for the open door.

Sam lifted her out, helping her stand as he visually inspected her. She broke free and whirled suddenly, looking at the limo on its side in the ditch. "Is everyone out? Is everyone out?" she shouted, trying to run back to the car.

Sam pulled her against him, walking them away from the limo. "We're all out, Willamina. And the car's not on fire. Take it easy."

Ghost eyes met his; then she started looking around for the others. Ben had taken Paula a short distance away and was sitting with his date on his lap on the grass, cradling her against his shoulder. Jesse was trying to get Darcy to sit on the coat he'd thrown onto the ground for her, but she appeared too unsettled. Finally, he picked her up and simply sat down with her.

Sam looked back at Willamina. She wasn't panicked by just this accident. "Are you okay?" he asked, lifting her face so he could see her eyes.

She didn't answer, shaking silently. Ronald came over with his jacket and put it on her shoulders. Sam wrapped it tightly around her and embraced her again, tucking her head under his chin. "What happened?" he asked Ronald.

Their driver motioned up the road, and Sam saw several cars in the ditch ahead. People were stumbling out of them as other vehicles stopped to help.

"The sports car cut off that blue SUV, which braked suddenly. I could only head for the ditch, boss," Ronald explained.

"Good driving."

"We pretty near rolled," he confessed.

"Like I said, good driving. Have you called it in?"

Just then, Sam heard sirens coming from a distance. Ronald's teeth flashed white in the darkness. "Everyone's got cell phones."

"See if there's a blanket in the trunk."

"There is," Ronald assured him, hurrying to get it.

"Don't let him near the car!" Willamina cried, trying to pull out of Sam's embrace.

"There's no fire, Willamina. Come sit down here with the others. You're shaking. Are you sure you're not hurt?"

"Don't patronize me!" she snapped, shrugging out of Ronald's jacket and letting it fall to the ground. "That car could burst into flames at any minute. It's happened before!"

"It won't happen this time," he promised, grabbing her and sitting down with her on his lap. Hell, if it worked for his brothers . . .

"It—it's happened to me before," she whispered against his chest, shaking uncontrollably. "I barely got her out before it exploded."

"Got who out?" he asked softly.

She wouldn't answer and quietly started sobbing. Ronald returned with a blanket and tried to hand it to Sam. He shook his head, shrugging out of his evening jacket. "Take it to the others. And tell me as soon as an ambulance gets here."

Sam wrapped his jacket around Willamina and simply held her while she fought her ghosts. He rested his chin on her head, liking the feel of her snuggled against him. He remembered how she'd had them all laughing not long ago, telling them how she'd gotten rid of her husband.

Willamina Kent was an enigma. She was sassy and clumsy, short and plump, and apparently contented that way. She was compassionate and empathetic, and she loved Abram Sinclair.

For all of that, Sam admired her. Even in terror, she'd remained level-headed enough to want everyone out of the car. Sam could hear Darcy and Paula wailing about their torn dresses and run stockings.

Sam smiled. Willamina probably had runs in her stockings and rips in her dress, but she wasn't complaining. He ran his fingers through her hair, undoing the last of her topknot. Soft, silken curls cascaded over his hand, making him shiver.

Sam sighed as he looked toward his brothers, who had stood up and were staring down at the two women huddled together on the blanket.

Ronald was back with his beloved car, and Sam could see him muttering to himself as he walked around it. The headlights were still on, and from the expression on Ronald's face, the front end was not a pretty sight. The chauffeur looked as if he was going to cry.

The police arrived, along with several ambulances. Willamina wiped her eyes with the back of her hand, wincing when she moved to get off his lap.

"Where do you hurt?"

"I'm just lame."

"Can you sit here while I talk with the police?"

"Of course," she said, wiping her cheeks again. "I'm fine. Go."

Sam set her on Ronald's coat, taking the time to snug her up in his own jacket. "Stay right here until you can be checked out by the paramedics," he told her, not leaving until she nodded agreement.

As soon as he walked away, Willa stood up and went to Darcy and Paula, keeping Sam's jacket wrapped tightly around herself. Damn, she couldn't stop shaking. It had been five years, but it could have been yesterday for the terror she felt. Last time, it had been just her and her niece, Jennifer, but it had been dark then, too, and Willa had also been forced off the road. Only her car hadn't landed safely in a ditch; it had hit a culvert and rolled, stopping against a ledge and bursting into flames. Bruised and bleeding, Willa had needed all of her strength to get Jennifer out before it had exploded.

Willa still had scars from the incident, but none as deep as the one she carried in her heart for her niece.

"How is everyone?" she asked, sitting on the grass in front of the women.

Jesse and Ben were talking to a policeman nearby. Sam was with another officer and Ronald, looking over the car.

"Nothing's broken, except my bracelet," Darcy answered, holding her arm up.

Willa could tell it was made of diamonds and likely cost more than the car. She'd probably be a little upset herself if she had broken something that expensive. "At least you didn't lose it," she offered.

"That's true. How about you? Did you get burned or something? I heard you yelling about a fire."

"No. I'm fine. And there wasn't any fire."

"Ladies, can you walk to the ambulance?" a young man asked, hunching down to shine a flashlight over them.

"With help," Darcy answered, taking another man's extended hand.

"I think my ankle's sprained," Paula said. "It hurts too much to get up."

"Send a basket down here," the young man called to the man helping Darcy up the slope. "And you, ma'am. Can you walk?" he asked Willa.

"I don't need to be checked. I'm not hurt."

"I'd like to make sure of that," he countered, shining his light over her, smiling as he carefully brushed back her hair. "You have a bump on your forehead."

Willa raised a hand to her forehead. "It's just a small bump."

"Your wrist's bleeding," he said, taking her hand.

"Maybe you can give me a Band-Aid."

"Maybe I should just bring you to the ambulance and see what else I find," he persisted.

"I'm *fine.*"

"Here we go, ma'am," a burly young man said as he and another set a long basket down beside Paula and prepared to put her in it.

"You go help them," Willa suggested to her medic. "I'll go to the ambulance eventually."

He reached into his box and pulled out a large Band-Aid. He carefully put it over the cut on her wrist, then narrowed his eyes at her. "This is just temporary. Until you *eventually* come to the ambulance."

"Thank you."

"Thank me at the ambulance," he shot back, jogging over to another accident victim.

The strobe lights, the sounds of police radios crackling, the smell of gasoline brought back all the painful, horrific memories.

But especially the ambulance.

She couldn't bring herself to go sit inside it. The last time she'd been in one had been with Jennifer, who hadn't been moving and hadn't opened her eyes. Her eleven-year-old niece had become trapped in the car, and her foot was crushed when Willa had pulled her out. Now sixteen years old, the girl wore a prosthesis where her right foot used to be.

No. She couldn't go up to that ambulance.

She walked away from the sights and sounds and smells but couldn't outwalk the piercing strobe lights. She sat down in the grass about a hundred yards from the chaos, her body sore and her bare feet cold. She tucked them beneath her and sat in silence, watching the people running around.

She could see several more vehicles in the ditch past the limousine. There had been no other cars involved five years ago. The driver who'd forced them off the road had continued on, leaving her and Jennifer to their fate.

Sam's angry voice suddenly intruded into her thoughts. "I told you to stay put."

She looked up at him, not blinking.

"You're supposed to be getting checked out."

"I already was," she said, lifting her arm to show him her bandage.

"That's it? They gave you a Band-Aid?"

"Is she hurt?" Ben asked, coming up behind Sam, followed by Jesse.

"I don't know."

"I'm not," she said, looking into the darkness, away from the accident.

"Come to the ambulance and prove it," Sam countered.

"No."

"Willa—"

"Leave me alone, Sinclair. When a ride shows up to take me back to the hotel, you can find me right here."

Sam mouthed an expletive as he looked at his brothers, who'd been helping him search for her. When he'd returned to take her to the ambulance and hadn't been able to find her, he'd become frantic, worried she had a concussion and had wandered off.

He was uncertain what to do. The accident had obviously upset her more than hurt her. Judging by the fact that she'd walked this far by herself and by the tone of voice she was using to get rid of him, Sam guessed she was okay. In fact, she appeared to be in fighting form.

"You're going to the ambulance," he said, hunching down beside her, more than willing to give her a fight if that's what she wanted.

She looked at him again, only she wasn't seeing ghosts now. "Go away."

"No."

"I'm not going to that ambulance, Sinclair."

"If I have to carry you, I will."

Her eyes widened, then she laughed humorlessly. "It will take the three of you."

"You think so?" he asked, getting close to her face, which was lit by the strobe lights. "I think I can handle you, Ms. Kent."

"Aw, hell. Now I've challenged your manly ego, haven't I? Forget it, Sam. Just go away."

He ended the discussion by picking her up and standing. She gasped in surprise, then hissed in outrage, grabbing his neck in a choking grip. "Put me down!"

"In the ambulance."

"I hope you throw your back out!"

Sam strode past his laughing brothers. "Why, Ms. Kent, you don't weigh more than a minute. Certainly not enough for a divorce."

"I hope you *break* your back, you jerk!"

"You think you're fat? You should have seen my date to the senior prom."

Sam thought she was going to hit him—until they reached the ambulance. Then she stiffened and clung to him like a frightened child, her eyes closing tightly.

The accident she'd alluded to earlier must have traumatized her. Sam stepped into the ambulance and sat down, keeping her in his lap. "Here she is. Check her out," he told the attendant. "If you think she should go to the hospital, I'll ride with her."

Willamina opened her eyes, giving him a tight smile, then flinched when the paramedic pulled off the bandage. She sat quietly on Sam's lap while a light was shined in her eyes and her bump was checked. Her wrist was cleaned, and the attendant decided it didn't need stitches. Sam wasn't all that keen on ambulances or hospitals himself, and he gave a sigh of relief when she was pronounced fit to go home.

"That wasn't so bad," he said as he exited the ambulance with her in his arms.

"Will you please put me down?" she asked meekly.

Sam wasn't fooled. She was seething mad. He walked with her to the waiting car Ronald had called. "You aren't wearing shoes. There's glass everywhere."

She heaved a mighty sigh. He set her in the backseat, across from Jesse and Darcy. Jesse had his arm wrapped around his wilted date. Sam got in, and Jesse tapped on the window for the driver.

"Where are Paula and Ben?" Willamina asked.

"Paula sprained her ankle. She and Ben are riding to the hospital in one of the ambulances," Jesse looked at Sam. "What about Ronald?"

"He's staying with the car."

"What happened?" Darcy asked in a sob-worn voice.

"Somebody cut off an SUV, which started a chain

THE MAN MUST MARRY 57

reaction," Sam explained, wrapping his arm around Willamina when he felt her start to tremble again. He lifted her chin with his other hand. "Would you like to stay at Rosebriar tonight?"

"No. I just want to go to my hotel room. I'll be fine in the morning."

Sam guessed she'd be lame as hell come morning. "Jesse, tell the driver to take us to the Marriott."

They rode in silence to the hotel, and Sam insisted on walking Willamina up to her room, ignoring her protests and glowers. It was a damned good thing he had a Herculean ego; Willamina Kent would bludgeon a lesser one to death.

She wouldn't marry any of them if they crawled to Maine on their knees, their hearts in their hands.

Lord, he admired her.

But he also intended to ruffle her feathers a little, just to soothe his Herculean ego. When they reached the door to her room, Sam asked for her key card.

She blinked up at him.

He sighed. "It's in your purse, isn't it?"

"Yes."

"The one you left on the floor of the restaurant."

"Yup."

"Why doesn't that surprise me?"

"Because you've figured out by now that I'm a bit of an airhead," she said without guile.

"Is that how you see yourself?"

"Not as a rule; only when I'm out of my element. Usually, I'm as competent as the next person."

"So, this isn't the you my grandfather knows?"

She frowned up at him. "No. Well, maybe a little. I may be a little clumsy sometimes."

"You must be dead on your feet to admit that," he told her, walking her down the hall to a couch. "Sit here, and I'll go get you a new key."

"Thank you."

Sam went back to the desk, then returned with a new card. He opened the door, and once she had stepped inside, he turned her around in his arms.

"Wh-what are you doing?" she squeaked in alarm.

"Salvaging my pride. And satisfying my curiosity." Then he captured her mouth.

He found sweetness, warmth, softness, and honey.

Willamina froze. Her hands were bunched into fists against his chest, her back was arched away from him, and she'd stopped breathing.

So, the brave little woman was mostly bluster, was she? No, not *little*. Plump. Nicely, nicely plump. She felt damn good in his arms. Sam pulled her closer and slanted his mouth over hers, then ran one a hand up her back to cup her head, patiently laying siege to her resistance. Finally, slowly, she softened. Then she whimpered.

And then she kissed him back.

Yes! Victory.

Her smell, her warmth, her sweet taste suddenly overwhelmed him, and Sam stopped thinking about egos and revenge.

She whimpered again, and he stopped thinking completely.

One or both of them started trembling.

He had to stop. Now.

In a minute. Soon.

She stiffened again, and Sam pulled back to see gunmetal eyes glaring up at him.

He probably shouldn't have smiled just then. The sharp pain from her fingers digging into his chest was a good sign that she wasn't amused.

"What did you do that for?" she sputtered.

Sam stepped away and rubbed his chest. "Because I wanted to."

"That won't get you my vote!" she snapped, wiping her hand across her mouth.

He stepped closer. "You think that kiss was to get your vote?"

"You have a better reason?"

He stared at her flushed face, moist pink lips, and tangled hair. She was angry and utterly enchanting. In all his life, he'd never met a woman like her.

She was driving him crazy. If he didn't get out of there, he was going to kiss her again, just on principle.

"No. Not one good reason," he snarled, turning on his heel and walking out of the room.

"I'm going home and telling Abram that *none* of you deserves to be CEO!" she called out, stalking him down the hall. "I'm going to tell him you should all be written out of his will, too. He should leave his money to charity!"

Sam stepped into the elevator, then turned to face the irate woman standing in the hall: torn dress, wild hair, and barefoot. "Go to bed, Willamina. I'm not going to kiss you again, so stop chasing me down the hall."

The elevator door closed on her shriek. Sam walked to the glass wall so he could watch her stomp back down the open hall, and he broke into booming laughter when she tried to open the door to her room. He'd have to send someone up to rescue her; her key card was on her bed.

She turned and caught sight of him laughing at her as the elevator carried him down. Sam's eyes widened at the gesture she shot him before she started banging on her door.

Sam keeled over in laughter. The woman needed a keeper.

Chapter Four

It took every bit of willpower Willa possessed to get out of bed the next morning. Muscles she'd forgotten she had were complaining, her head felt as if a channel buoy was clanging inside it, and even her teeth hurt.

The hot shower helped. Sliding into old soft jeans felt heavenly. Leaving off her bra and pulling on a fluffy sweatshirt was especially comfy, and her worn-in sneakers were balm to her abused feet.

Feeling older than her geriatric workers, she tried to walk the stiffness out of her muscles by pacing her hotel room. While she walked—and groaned—Willa pondered her predicament.

She'd come there to make a choice that was impossible. As Abram had said, they were all capable. She couldn't find one outstanding difference that that would tell her how to vote.

Even Sam, the kissing fool.

She shouldn't have kissed him back, but her hormones had gone into full riot at the touch of his lips. She'd fought them valiantly but had lost the battle when Sam's heat had slowly permeated her body.

When she'd come to her senses, he'd smiled at her like some triumphant pirate. The jerk. He'd kissed her just to prove that he could get a response.

She should pack what was left of her suitcase, get on a plane this morning, and go back to Maine. And the minute she got home, she would give Abram Sinclair a piece of her mind, then tell him to go find a cave to die in if he was too stubborn to go home where he belonged. He had no right involving her in his personal affairs.

Willa picked up the phone to book a flight just as someone knocked on her door.

Sam leaned his forehead on the hotel door and knocked again. Damn, he hated to be there. He even hated life itself today.

The door opened, and he straightened, only to go still at the sight of Willamina Kent. She looked . . . different. Normal. Even beautiful—until she turned frantic when she saw his face.

"What is it? What's wrong?"

Sam stepped into her room, forcing her to step back. "Is it Abram?"

Sam could only nod.

"Oh!" she cried, whirling toward her bed. "I've got to go to him. I promised to be there. I've got to go *now*."

"Willamina. Willa."

"He promised he'd wait for me to get back," she wailed, throwing her battered bag onto the bed and tossing her clothes into it. She swept past him, going into the bathroom and cramming her cosmetics into a pouch.

"Willa."

She came out and bumped into him, her eyes dark with anguish. "I'll be with him, Sam. I know you want to be, but I promise, I'll be with him," she vowed fiercely.

He said her name again, but she was desperately trying to close her suitcase. The zipper was torn beyond use. "Help me," she pleaded, her face hidden by her hair, tears falling in splotches onto the suitcase.

Sam pulled off his belt, gently pushed her aside, and wrapped it around the overnight bag to cinch it closed. He picked it up and carried it out of the room. "Don't forget your purse."

She grabbed her large purse and went out ahead of him, all but running to the elevator. In silence, they rode down to the street, where Ronald was waiting. Sam gave him the suitcase and opened the back door for Willa, handing her in.

"Can I take your helicopter to the airport? I need to hurry, Sam."

"That won't be necessary."

"Is he at my cottage or in the hospital? Do you know?"

"He was at the hospital," he answered stonily.

Ronald got in and started them on their way. Sam turned to Willa and stared at her hands, which she was wringing.

"Willa—"

"His timing stinks. He was supposed to wait for me to get back," she whispered without looking up. "That was the deal. If he wouldn't let the three of you be with him, he promised me I could." She looked up suddenly. "No one should be alone, Sam. No matter what, Abram shouldn't be alone."

"He wasn't."

"He's made friends of my workers," she told him. "They'll stay with him until I get there."

"They did. Bram wasn't alone."

"You mean *isn't*."

"Willa," Sam said, putting his arm over her shoulder, "Abram died early this morning."

Every drop of blood drained from her face as she looked up at him with wide eyes. Huge tears suddenly spilled down over her cheeks, then she snapped her head down and hid behind the curtain of her hair.

With his own groan of agony, Sam pulled her to him, pressing her wet, hot face against his chest.

"I was supposed to be there. That was the deal," she cried into his shirt. "He *promised*."

"Bram loved you, Willa. He wasn't about to let you see him die, any more than us, honey," Sam crooned hoarsely, rubbing her back. "He was a proud man."

"But he only knew me for six weeks. I'm a stranger to him. It was going to be okay for me to be there."

"I imagine Bram fell in love with you the moment he met you," Sam told her as he stared straight ahead, resting his chin on her hair. "No matter what you thought, he wouldn't have let you be there. It's almost as if he timed this."

She lifted her tear-soaked face, looking up at him with pained eyes. "What happened?"

"He had a heart attack yesterday afternoon, Spencer said."

"I know Spencer. He visited Abram several times."

"He's been Bram's lawyer for forty years. Spencer called this morning."

"He's in Maine?"

"Yes. The doctor contacted him yesterday. Bram had left instructions with one of your workers."

"W-was Spencer there this morning? When . . . when . . ."

"Yes."

"Good."

She rested her head against Sam's chest and gave another harsh sob. He wrapped her tightly in his embrace, and they rode in silence. Finally, she spoke again without lifting her head. "I should probably see to the arrangements. He had things worked out with a local funeral home to prepare him to ship here. His casket's already there." She raised her head and looked at him. "I-I'd like to come back for the funeral."

"Everything's being taken care of, Willa. That's what Spencer is doing now. Bram will be here tomorrow morning. He'll lie in state at Rosebriar, then be buried in the family cemetery on the grounds, next to Rose and his sons."

"Oh." She tried to wriggle away from him.

Sam held her in place. "I'm taking you to Rosebriar now," he said, lifting her chin to look at him. "It's up in Connecticut."

"I can stay at a nearby hotel."

"No. Bram wanted you at Rosebriar."

"I'm not family, and I don't belong there."

"Jesse, Ben, and I want you there."

She thought for a moment. "I could help set everything up."

"You're our guest, Willa. You just have to be there. For us and for Bram. We feel better knowing he had you these last few weeks, you've made his little odyssey easier for us to accept. You've helped us . . . understand."

"He reminded me of my own grandfather," she said, relaxing against him. "Pops was a character right to the end, just like Abram. Your grandfather flirted shamelessly with my help. And he spoiled my cat rotten, bossed me around endlessly, and stuck his nose in every aspect of my business."

"I'm glad."

The rest of the ride to Rosebriar was quiet, Willa sighing occasionally as she fought her tears.

Sam knew that she and Bram had bonded in a simple, elemental way. They had probably perked up at the first sight of each other, assessing each other's mettle. Interest had come next, and shortly after, love had blossomed. That's how it had always been with Bram. Within an hour of meeting someone, either he liked them or he didn't. Sam guessed it hadn't taken the old wolf ten minutes with Willa. The first slip she had made probably endeared her to him; her second would have sealed it.

Sam's hand suddenly stopped stroking up and down her back, to double-check what he was feeling. Nothing. He wasn't feeling anything.

He should be feeling a bra. Willamina Kent had forgotten an important piece of clothing this morning. At least, it should be important to her, if she didn't want to be kissed senseless again.

Hoping she hadn't noticed his delightful discovery, Sam pulled her onto his lap and began rubbing her soothingly again. This time, he put enough pressure against her back to push her chest against his. Yup, the partridge was missing some underwear.

When they turned onto the Sinclair estate, Willa sat up with wide eyes. Sam was afraid he'd been discovered, but she was looking out the window. She turned to him, her face lit with surprise. "Wow."

"Bram's legacy."

"It's beautiful."

"Once you see all of it, you'll really meet the man you've been harboring for the last six weeks," Sam told her, shifting her on his lap a little more comfortably.

She smiled at him. "Your legs go to sleep?"

"I hate to disappoint you, Willa, but you're not fat," he told her dryly.

"I most certainly am."

"No, you're built like a woman."

Just right, upstairs and down. Her expression turned as thunderous as when she'd caught him laughing at her at the Marriott, which reminded him . . . "That was a very unladylike gesture you gave me last night," he said.

"What gesture?" she asked, her expression turning guileless. "When you were in the elevator?"

Sam nodded.

"Why, I was pointing at the cable above your car. It looked frayed. I feared for your life, Sam—I really did."

The only thing that saved her from getting kissed again was the fact that Ronald had stopped the car and was opening the door.

* * *

Holy smokes! She couldn't take much more of this roller coaster. Since she'd arrived in New York, she'd laughed and cried and given Sam an obscene gesture. Her mother in heaven must be hiding in shame. Locking herself out of her hotel room had been the final indignity. She'd still been pounding on her door when one of the hotel staff had arrived with another key.

Now here she was at Sam's home, about to attend the funeral of a man she'd loved briefly but dearly. Abram had touched her heart by laughing at her nunlike existence. He'd claimed she was hiding behind her elderly crew of workers and her dysfunctional cat and that wearing her guilt like a hair shirt wasn't contrition but blasphemy.

So, in what she was discovering was typical fashion, the old goat had thrown her right into the fire by sending her down to his grandsons. And she was afraid Abram wasn't through with her yet; she wouldn't be surprised if he left her one of his "boys" in his will. Well, she could handle that, as long as it wasn't arrogant, sexy-as-hell Samuel Sinclair.

Willa ran from the car, right into another Sinclair.

"Whoa, little partridge," Ben said with a laugh, steadying her by the shoulders. "What sent you bolting?" He looked behind her. "Has Sam been threatening your life and limb?"

"I was just . . ." She looked up at Ben. "I'm so sorry," she said softly.

"Me, too," he said, knowing she meant Abram. "But

it's going to be okay. He couldn't live forever. And we had him when we needed him most. So, what do you think of Rosebriar?" he asked, leading her up the stairs to the mansion.

"It's beautiful. And big," she said, craning her neck to follow the lines of the monstrous stone building.

"Bram liked big things," he said, and Willa looked over to see if he was taking a pot shot at her weight. But he was looking up at the mansion himself. "Our grandfather grew up in a one-room shanty in Texas. Since he made it big, he's been trying to make everything big."

"Just how big is big?"

"Eighteen bedrooms, twenty-four bathrooms, sixty rooms total—all sitting in the middle of twelve hundred acres."

"Wow."

"Forty of those acres are gardens," Sam interjected, coming to stand beside them. "Bram had them built for Rose before the house was even finished."

"It's overwhelming."

"It's home," Jesse added, coming out the door to stand with them. They all turned on the steps and looked down the drive, at the grounds that seemed to stretch into the next state.

Willa eyed the brothers. "He's been living in a two-room cottage on my property."

Abram had come to her like a beggar. She'd taken

him in, not even suspecting how wealthy he was until he'd started talking about a board meeting she had to go to.

"It's okay, Willamina," Jesse said. "Bram was happy in your cottage, wasn't he?"

"He seemed to be."

"He went home to die," Sam murmured.

"You said home was Texas."

"Not in his heart. Bram loved the smell of salt air."

"Both my house and the cottage sit on a bluff, right on the Gulf of Maine."

"Then he was happy," Sam said. "So be happy *for* him, Willa. We are."

"Come on," Ben said, tugging her toward the door. "You should get settled."

"I can stay in a nearby hotel. I don't want to intrude."

Ben stopped and stared down at her, his eyes haggard and his face drawn. "You'll stay here."

"Until you get my vote?" she asked, smiling impishly, hoping to change his expression.

"It's a moot point. Your proxy died with Bram. We won't know who will be CEO until his will is read."

"Oh." Willa felt as bad as Ben looked. If she'd voted yesterday as she was supposed to, things would be settled now.

"It's better this way," Jesse said.

"What will happen to Tidewater International?"

All three men shrugged in unison. "Who knows?" Sam said. "Bram's biggest joy in life was keeping his will a secret, but he likely divided his shares equally among us. Spencer's not been very forthcoming."

"Are you worried?"

"No," Sam said. "Bram will have taken care of the company."

They walked inside and stopped at the foot of a grand staircase straight out of *Gone with the Wind*. The stairs seemed to go on forever, opening at the top onto a gallery that ran right and left to unseen wings of the house. The foyer reached all the way to the roof, which was crowned with a dome of inlaid colored glass. The floor and stairs were marble; the walls were paneled in dark oak. In any direction Willa turned, she encountered lavish, built-to-outlive-a-man money.

"Willamina, you should understand something," Ben said. "It doesn't matter to any of us which one becomes CEO. We're not in competition. Any one of us can lead, and the others will follow. No hard feelings, no jealousy."

"And each of us can walk away anytime," Sam added. "We're not married to the company. Tidewater International was Bram's passion, and it will continue to exist if *none* of us is there. All we have to do is sell out."

"And you would?" she asked. "Just like that?"

"Just like that," Jesse confirmed.

"Then why all the hoopla yesterday?"

"Because yesterday Bram was still alive."

"You're going to just walk away, then?" she repeated, not believing them.

"No. One of us will run Tidewater. But that's not the point, Willa," Sam explained. "The point is, it's not do-or-die for any of us."

Ronald chose that moment to come inside, bearing the tattered remains of her luggage with all the dignity of a man carrying a priceless vase. Willa turned a dull pink and quietly walked up the stairs.

"What in hell is that?" Jesse barked, looking at the suitcase as if it were going to explode.

"Willa's luggage," Sam told him dryly.

"What happened to it?"

"Tidewater's elevator ate it."

"Which room would you like this in, Mr. Sinclair?" Ronald asked.

"Whichever room the lady ends up in," Sam told him, watching Willa climb the stairs. She turned right at the top, her stride stiff as Ronald followed with her luggage.

"She certainly looks different today," Ben said as the three men walked into the parlor, all heading for the bar.

"Yes, she does," Sam agreed.

"What did you say to her in the car?" Ben asked. "She was bolting like a rabbit before the hounds."

"I think it was more the look I gave her."

"And what look would that be?" Jesse asked.

"She knew I was going to kiss her again."

"Again." It wasn't a question from Ben.

"When was the first time you kissed her?" Jesse asked.

"Last night, when I walked her to her room."

"Now, that's low, even for you. She'd just been in an accident. She was vulnerable," Ben said.

"I was defending our honor," Sam explained, taking his drink and sitting in one of the chairs by the hearth. He looked around the room. "We should put Bram up in here. What do you think?"

"I think we were talking about Willamina," Jesse growled. "What in hell do you mean, defending our honor?"

"She said she wouldn't marry any of us if we crawled to Maine on our knees. I was getting her back for that."

"And today, when you were going to kiss her again? Was that also for us?" Jesse asked, taking a seat across from him.

"No, that was for myself. And just so you know, Willa's off limits." Sam gave them a feral grin. "Go hunt your own partridge."

"Are you nuts?" Ben said, standing by the hearth. "You want her?"

"Yes."

"Why?" Jesse asked, looking utterly bewildered.

"I like Willa. It's that simple."

"That woman is not simple."

"No, she's not. She's quite intelligent, and she's got a smart mouth. She also has the heart of an angel. And she's cute."

"She's a disaster waiting to happen," Ben muttered, daring Sam to dispute him.

"I can handle Willa's disasters," Sam said absently. "So, how about this room? Bram liked it enough to have Grammy's wake in here. I think we should do the same for him."

"We'd better get started, then. The obituary will be in tomorrow's papers all over the world. People, flowers, and condolences are going to descend like vultures."

"We'll have the staff move out most of the furniture." Sam smiled at his brothers. "Spencer said Bram wrote his own eulogy. I can't wait to hear it."

"Christ, I miss the old bastard." Jesse sighed. "I thought he'd live to be a hundred."

"Despite the three of us living here, this house has felt empty these last six weeks," Ben lamented.

"Willa will probably take care of that problem," Jesse drawled, standing up and going to call the staff. "Rosebriar's liable to need extensive repairs by the time she leaves."

"I'm eager to see Bram's casket, if you want to know the truth," Ben told Sam. "I know it sounds morbid, but I'm curious as hell. Bram wasn't exactly known for his patience. How could he have done something as painstaking as woodwork?"

"Good God, I hope it doesn't fall apart."

"Maybe Willa can add a few nails or something, just to be certain," Ben suggested.

"Surely, she wouldn't let a casket leave her factory without an inspection?"

"Hell of a business to be in," Ben muttered. "Why do you suppose she's in it?"

"Who knows?"

"I'll have to ask her."

"Are there any clothing stores nearby? I need something to wear for the wake," Willa asked at lunch.

"There's a shopping center not far from here. Ronald can take you," Jesse told her.

"I don't want to put anyone out."

"Maybe someone had better go with you," Ben said. "Just to make sure you . . . um, find what you need."

"That's not necessary."

"But Ben loves shopping," Jesse drawled. "Take him, Willa. Please?"

Willa looked down at her salad. So far, she'd only managed to push it around on her plate. "I suppose. If you're sure you want to," she said, looking at Ben.

"Like my brother said, I enjoy shopping," he said, his smile tight.

Willa saw him dart a killer glare at Jesse, though. Which meant that neither of them thought she was capable of buying a dress by herself. Sam didn't even look up from his lunch to offer an opinion.

"Unless, of course, you'd like to go, Sam," Ben said.

"I've got phone calls to make," Sam said, finally looking up. "No, you go with Willa. Have a good time."

All three men were putting up a valiant front, but Willa guessed none of them would relax until their grandfather was home, until they actually saw him again, even though he'd be lying in a casket.

"It's really weird, not having to cook for myself," she said conversationally, taking a bite of her salad.

"You get used to it," Jesse offered with a smile.

Willa smiled back. "You've all grown up rather spoiled, haven't you?" she said, hoping to get a reaction.

She got three dangerous glowers.

"Spoiled! Because we have a cook?" Ben asked.

Willa waved her fork in the air. "A cook, a mansion, money coming out of your ears. Women hanging on your arms, a chauffeur to drive you places, a helicopter, probably a jet, a Sengatti sloop, a grandfather who loved you to distraction. Shall I go on?"

"Please do, Ms. Kent," Sam said. "And while you're at it, tell us how deprived *your* life has been."

"My life has been just great, Mr. Sinclair," she shot back. "I'm not complaining. I'm just making an observation."

"We have no say in how we enter this world," Sam

countered. "Your words, if I remember correctly. Bram certainly didn't have any say about the poverty he was born into. His choice was how he lived each day." Sam pointed his fork at her, his eyes narrowed. "And our grandparents made sure we weren't spoiled. We work just as hard as the next man. And we take nothing for granted."

"Whew! I can see you got the sense of humor in the family." Willa put some salad in her mouth, chewing it quietly while she watched Sam Sinclair redden with either anger or chagrin, she didn't know which.

"Tell us why you own a casket-manufacturing business," Ben interjected. "How did you get started?"

"I used to work at Grand Point Bluff, a retirement community in Keelstone Cove, where I live. I was the director of entertainment. It was my job to plan all the social activities."

"And you started making coffins during craft hour?" Jesse asked dryly.

"No. This wasn't a nursing home; most of the tenants were still quite active. I set up a woodworking shop in one of the outbuildings." Willa smiled in memory. "Tools began appearing. The men dug them out of the boxes they'd brought from their old homes. They hadn't been able to part with them."

"And . . ." Ben put his fork down to lean his elbows on the table.

"And one man, Levi, began to build a coffin for his

wife. She had cancer and only had a couple of months to live. It was therapy for Levi. He was a master carpenter, and he built a beautiful casket—gorgeously detailed, finer than any furniture I've seen. His wife, Muriel, took a quilt she'd made and fashioned it into a lining for the casket."

Willa stared at her plate. "I was appalled, at first—until I realized that it was comforting for both of them. Muriel knew she'd be resting eternally in a gift her husband had built with loving hands. And Levi felt more at peace because he was seeing to his wife's final comfort, just as he'd done for her all his life."

Silence echoed through the large dining room as Willa looked up at the men, who were staring at her with unblinking, unreadable eyes.

"I decided I wanted to do that for people," she continued softly. "I took some of the money from my divorce settlement, found a silent partner for the rest, and bought an old factory. The residents of the retirement community became my employees. They'd all watched Levi, and they all wanted to do something just as nice. Older people have a wonderful attitude about death and about life in general. And they're really great employees. They've taught me a lot about running a business."

"And you say your caskets go all over the world?" Jesse asked. "That's rather impressive growth for what is basically a cottage industry."

"Yes." Willa gave him a Cheshire cat smile. "There are several retired executives living at Grand Point Bluff as well. I hired them, too."

"That was damn smart of you." Jesse leaned back in his seat and looked over at Sam. "A very intelligent business move, wouldn't you say, Sam?"

"That's what I've been saying all along." Sam gazed at Willa with that look again.

The one he'd given her in the car that had made her bolt.

"Can we go shopping now?" she asked Ben, standing up.

Chapter Five

Willa munched the last bite of toast Peg had made her for breakfast as she headed for the parlor to help the staff prepare for Abram's wake. When she reached the end of the hall leading from the kitchen, she stopped in her tracks.

"Richard!" she exclaimed, taking a step back. "What are you doing here?"

Her brother-in-law stood in the foyer, glowering at her. "Somebody had to drive the old bastard home," he said. "And your sister volunteered me for the job."

"That was thoughtful of Shelby. And you," she quickly tacked on, stepping to the side of the hall when he started toward her. "Um . . . you'll probably want to start back right away, just as soon as you get yourself some coffee," she said, motioning back down the hall. "Peg will fix you up in the kitchen."

He stopped in front of her. "You've been talking to Shelby again," he said through gritted teeth, his eyes cold and accusing. "Trying to persuade her to divorce me."

Willa pressed up against the wall. "What makes you think it's me? Maybe Shelby reached that conclusion by herself."

He snorted and stepped closer. "Women don't just suddenly start talking divorce after sixteen years of marriage unless *somebody* puts the idea in their heads. And you," he growled, grabbing her by the shoulders when she tried to sidestep away, "are the only person with that kind of influence over Shelby."

Willa became alarmed. Richard Bates wasn't merely being his contrary self; he was honestly, truly angry. She ducked under his arm and ran toward the parlor—directly into a hall table holding several vases of flowers.

She managed to stop one of the vases from falling, but the two on the far end toppled over, glass shattering onto the marble floor. Richard lunged after her, grabbing her when she slipped, causing her arms to jerk upward. The vase she was holding broke on impact with Richard's head. She screamed, Richard shouted a succinct curse and let her go, and she fell to the floor with a thud.

With a sudden blur of motion, things went from bad to worse. A roar came from the direction of the stairs, and she was suddenly picked up and tossed against a rock-solid chest.

"Did you get cut?" Ben asked, carrying Willa away.

"I don't think so," she said, looking over his shoulder when she heard another roar.

That one had come from Richard as Sam's fist made contact with her brother-in-law's gut. Willa wriggled to get free, but Ben merely continued to carry her away.

"We have to stop them!" she cried, squirming violently enough that Ben lost his grip, allowing her to stand. But it didn't stop him from dragging her into the parlor, out of sight of the battle she could hear raging in the foyer. "Why is Sam beating him up?"

Ben pulled her over to one of the windows. "He's got this thing about seeing a guest being attacked."

"But Richard was—"

"Hold still," he growled. "I want to make sure you didn't get cut on the broken glass."

The sound of splintering wood came from the foyer, along with the unmistakable thud of a body hitting the wall. Willa flinched, and Ben chuckled as he lifted her wrists to see her hands.

"Check my backside," she said quickly, twisting as if to look behind her. "I think I fell on some glass."

When he let her go so she could turn around, Willa bolted for the foyer. She came to a skidding stop in the doorway, utterly stunned to see Sam throw Richard against the wall, then grab him by the throat.

Richard brought his knee up, and Sam barely deflected a blow to his groin. Richard swung his arms up to break the choking hold and took a swing at Sam's face.

A porcelain statue was knocked over when Richard slammed into a chair and it crashed into another table near the stairway. A picture fell off the wall. Grunts and flesh-bruising blows echoed throughout the grand foyer, accented by heated curses.

"Stop it! Now!" Willa shrieked.

She might as well have been screaming at two rocks. She flinched when Richard's fist connected with Sam's shoulder.

Sam was about the same height as her brother-in-law, but he definitely was the more powerful of the two. Richard, however, was probably more experienced.

When Richard took an obviously painful blow to his stomach, only to give a retaliating kick to Sam's knee, Willa grabbed the only remaining unbroken vase and pulled out the flowers. Just as Richard was about to take another swing, she threw the water, hitting him in the face. He halted in mid-swing, and Sam's fist connected with his jaw, dropping him into a heap on the floor.

"That was a dirty shot," Willa squeaked, horrified.

"But effective," Sam growled, taking a step toward her.

Willa took a step back.

"Get her the hell out of here," he said through gritted teeth, looking past her.

Willa took another step back and bumped into Ben. "No. Wait. What about—"

"Not now," Ben said in a hushed voice, moving her toward the stairs. "Let him calm down."

Willa looked over the railing as she ascended to see that Sam hadn't moved, standing like a cat over his kill. Several of his shirt buttons were missing, exposing his broad, heaving chest. His fists were clenched at his sides, and every muscle in his body was taut, making him appear ready to deal a deathblow should Richard so much as move.

She looked over at Ben. "But—"

"Hush," he said as they reached the top of the staircase, putting a finger to her lips. "You go change into dry clothes and make sure you didn't get cut anywhere, and I'll help Sam clean up the mess downstairs."

Willa looked into Ben's hard eyes, which were in sharp contrast to the softness of his voice. "He's my brother-in-law. He drove Abram down from Maine."

"Sam and I heard you arguing as we came down the stairs, and then you screamed. It looked to us as if he was attacking you."

"Um . . . Richard was trying to argue, and I was trying to get away from him. He was accusing me of trying to talk my sister into divorcing him."

"Are you?"

"Well, yeah. But I don't know how Richard found out. I've been very careful."

"Why do you want her to divorce him?"

"Because he's a jerk."

"What's all the commotion?" Jesse asked, walking from the left wing of the house.

"Just a small misunderstanding," Ben said. He turned Willa toward the guest wing and gave her a nudge. "Go change. We'll send Richard on his way. Come on, Jesse. Let's go help Sam clean up."

Willa silently walked to her bedroom as she heard the steel in Ben's voice again. She'd gotten off easy that day in the boardroom. The Sinclair men were just as ruthless as Abram had alluded to. But they'd been courteous to her and guarded, curious, and compassionate. Ben had been a good host on their shopping expedition yesterday, and despite the gloom hanging over the house, Jesse actually had her laughing last night with stories of their boyhood antics. And other than that kiss two nights ago at the hotel, Sam had been a gentleman with her.

Sort of. Most of the time.

Willa saw now what Abram had tried to explain to her without outright saying it. All three of his grandsons wore a thin veneer of civility. Sometimes it slipped though, as it had when Sam thought Richard was attacking her.

She had learned two very important things this morning. One, Sam Sinclair was not a man she ever wanted mad at her. And two, he had a positively gorgeous chest.

* * *

"Abram Sinclair, you old poop. You promised to wait for me to get back."

Sam stilled when he heard Willa's voice. He was sitting in a high-backed chair pulled around to face the window, his feet propped on the windowsill. It was a dismal day of hard late-May rain. A fire had been set in the hearth, and two lights had been lit over Abram, who was lying peacefully in his own wondrous creation of solid cherry wood and forest-green flannel bedding.

Sam had been sitting in quiet contemplation, the casket across the room at his back, and he was able to see the entire room reflected in the rain-soaked window. Willa had come in carrying a huge bouquet of spring flowers she'd filched from the garden; she was also carrying a rag and what he suspected was wood wax.

"We had a deal," Willa continued. Sam watched in the window as she set down her flowers on a nearby table and walked up to Bram. "I promised to come here and do your dirty work, and you promised to let me be with you, come time. You tricked me, Abram. You planned it," she accused.

Willa slowly reached out and feathered her fingers over Bram's cheek. Sam couldn't see her face, but he'd bet she was smiling and crying at the same time.

Her voice proved him right. "You look damn good, Abram. I bet you left instructions with the undertaker to give you that smile, didn't you? Your grandsons are rascals," she told the old man, touching Bram's hair.

"Right down to their arrogant smiles. Chips off your own block, aren't they?

"I'm sorry you had to come home with Richard as your escort, but your grandsons sent him packing. You should have seen Sam this morning, Abram. He was magnificent. He actually rescued me." She loosened Bram's tie. "I've never been rescued before in my life."

Sam had a pretty good idea that Willa didn't realize Bram had begun rescuing her the moment they met.

It must be Sinclair fate to slay Willa's dragons—whatever they were. Sam knew she had them, and he knew Bram had recognized that fact immediately. He just wished his grandfather had left him a hint to exactly what they were.

Willa was dressed in worn jeans and an oversized sweatshirt this afternoon. Her hair was once again escaping its clip, waving in tendrils around her face, making her look like an angel who had come to help them through this time. Sam thanked God, and Abram, for her, as she was indeed making this easier—though he guessed she didn't realize it.

"Your casket looks good," she continued, opening the can of wax. "Except maybe that ship. I told you to let me transfer my sketch to the wood, instead of your trying to copy it freehand. Your cargo ship is listing, Abram."

Sam silently chuckled to himself.

"I like your rose, though. You did a great job putting

it on your foot cover. I can't believe the inscription, though. You added that when I wasn't watching."

Sam heard Willa snort. "*Been there. Done that. Had fun,*" she read aloud. "*Hope to come back and do it again.*"

Sam held in his own chuckle. All three brothers had had a good laugh when they'd read Bram's little epitaph. And not one of them would put it past the old man to come back and haunt them.

"If you do come back, Abram, it'll likely be as a goat," Willa scolded. "Just so you can keep butting into people's business, like you have mine."

She began polishing Bram's casket, working industriously. "What could you have been thinking, sending me down here?" She stopped and pointed her rag at him. "Your grandsons are first-class rogues, Abram. And I don't care if Sam's kisses *do* curl my toes, either," she hissed.

Sam smiled. Curled her toes, had he?

"I'm on to you, Abram. You've got something up your sleeve, I can feel it. But I'm telling you right now, I'm not going to be part of whatever it is. And I don't care what you think; I'm not ever getting married again. I can't, and you know it. You said you understood."

She was polishing the wood so hard Sam expected it to start smoking.

"I can't ever have children," she blurted. "I explained that to you. And you laughed at me," she finished on a whisper, dropping her forehead onto Bram's chest with a sob.

Bram had laughed at her despair? That wasn't like him at all. If he'd scoffed at whatever she'd told him, it was because Bram considered it baseless.

Another mystery. Or a dragon to slay? A letter would have been nice. Just a note explaining what this dragon looked like, as well as how formidable it might be.

"Oh, Abram. What have you done to me?" Willa cried.

Bram had definitely done something that was going to cause them all a world of trouble. Sam could feel it just as surely as Willa could. The ball would likely drop when the will was read in two days, after the funeral. Knowing Bram, that's where he'd stage his final farewell to them all.

He'd better get Spencer aside and find out what was in that will before it was read to anyone. He had an ominous feeling that Willa might go into shock when she discovered Bram's ultimate plan. He had no doubt Abram Sinclair hadn't gone to his grave peacefully. The old man would be fighting the whole way, as he had his whole life, to win.

And Willa, Sam was beginning to fear, was the prize.

At the sound of someone else entering the room, he looked back into the window's reflection. Spencer was saving him the trouble of hunting him down. The aging lawyer walked up to Willa and gathered her in his arms, rocking her tenderly.

Another man who had fallen for the angel's charm.

"I'm sorry, Willa," Spencer crooned. "I know how much you cared for Bram."

"Yes," she said.

"I also know you wanted to be there for him."

"It's almost like he planned this, Spencer."

"He probably did," Spencer agreed, setting her away. "But he told me to ask your forgiveness. You've been so kind to him these last six weeks. Will you forgive the old man his scheming?"

"Maybe," she whispered, looking at Bram as she wiped her eyes. "I just didn't want him to be alone."

"He wasn't. I was with him."

"How come Richard brought him home? Why not you?"

"I had urgent duties to see to back here."

"For another client?"

"No, Bram's been my only client for years now. The casket's beautiful," Spencer said, running his hand over the shining wood.

"Thanks to my crew," Willa said with a snort, taking a swipe with her rag. "Abram was about as talented at working with wood as I am at cooking."

"That bad, huh?" Spencer teased. "Bram told me about some of your meals."

"Maybe someday I'll be rich enough to hire a cook,"

Willa said with a smile in her voice. "Abram said he certainly hoped so, if I didn't poison myself first."

"I'd say you'll probably realize that dream."

At that foreboding omen, Sam stood and walked over to the casket.

Willa gave a startled gasp. "How long have you been sitting there?" she demanded, her face turning red.

"A couple of hours." He turned to Spencer. "I need to speak with you. Now."

"Certainly," the lawyer agreed, his neck reddening and his eyes going guiltily to Bram. "Shall we go into the office?" he asked, refusing to look at either of them as he turned and hastily walked out of the room.

"You jerk!" Willa hissed before Sam could follow. "You were eavesdropping!"

"I was sitting quietly, contemplating fate."

"You could have coughed or something, to let me know you were here."

"I suppose I could have."

She looked as if she wanted to hit him but contented herself with a glare. Sam captured her face in his hands, kissed her right on her startled mouth, and walked out of the room.

Chapter Six

"*Why the green flannel?*"

"Because it's warm and comfortable. Because Maureen, one of my workers, told Abram it went well with his hair," Willa explained, her cheeks dimpled with a mischievous smile. She reached forward and gently mussed Bram's hair. "There, that's better. Now he looks more like himself, don't you think?" she asked Jesse, who was loosening Bram's tie while he unconsciously pulled at his own.

"Yeah. That's Granddad, all right."

"It was the first thing I noticed about him," Willa told the three brothers, all four of them dressed to greet the guests who would soon be arriving to pay their respects. "When I opened my door, Abram was standing on my porch with my For Rent sign in his hand, his hair looking like he had just come through a hurricane."

Sam was standing to the side, out of sight of Willa's killer glares. She hadn't forgiven him for eavesdropping that afternoon, but he was more amused than repentant. It had been an enlightening deception.

"The casket's really beautiful," Ben said, tugging on his grandfather's collar. "Bram did a fine job."

"I like the sketch on the inside of the cover," Jesse added, undoing the top button of Bram's collar. "Did he draw it?"

"Sort of. He copied one of my sketches," Willa explained. "Levi designs the caskets, and I sketch scenes to be carved into them. The craftsmen do the woodwork, and the women install the lining."

"You're an artist," Ben observed.

"Not formally. I just like to draw. I especially like working up custom orders with clients. You'd be surprised how happy people are to know exactly how their bodies will be spending eternity."

"While his soul is haunting Rosebriar," Jesse exclaimed, ghoulishly raising his hands at Willa, then smiling at Sam. "Trying to protect his home."

"Rosebriar can weather anything," Sam returned, smiling over the top of Willa's head when she wouldn't turn toward him. Yup, she was still in a snit.

At least she was wearing flats this evening, probably at Ben's insistence on their shopping expedition. His brother also must have picked out the dress. Willa actually looked put together. Maybe even stunning.

The dress was appropriately black, with simple, sleek lines that accented her curves very nicely. The only adornment she wore was a small cameo Sam recognized as having belonged to Grammy Rose. Bram must have given it to her, which was telling.

The old wolf had chosen a new Sinclair bride.

But would that bride walk down the aisle of a church willingly, or would she have to be dragged down kicking and screaming?

Sam had finally coerced Spencer into showing him the will. Tomorrow afternoon, after the funeral, the will would be read to one and all. That was when the roof was likely to come off Rosebriar, because if his brothers didn't raise it, Willa certainly would.

After reading Bram's last will and testament, Sam had sat in stunned silence for more than two hours, marveling at the mind of the eighty-five-year-old man. He hoped *he* was still that sharp when he was that old—assuming he lived through tomorrow.

"People will be arriving soon," Willa said, breaking into Sam's thoughts. "I think I'll go see how Peg's doing."

"Peg's been our housekeeper for twenty years," Jesse said, grabbing her arm before she could escape. "Believe me, the woman has entertained more people than the pope has."

"But she's taken Abram's passing hard," Willa said, "and I don't know anyone who'll be here tonight. I'm better off in the kitchen."

"All of the board members will be here," Sam told her with ill-concealed delight. "Don't you want to see them?"

She shot him a glare. "Not particularly."

"If you wish to be helpful, you won't abandon us," Ben said with a ridiculous pout. "We need your support."

Willa tried to stifle a snort as she looked at Ben. "And to think, I was going to choose you to be CEO."

Emerson entered the den to announce the first arrival. Sam caught Willa's elbow and escorted her to the foyer, ignoring her tugs for freedom. Ben and Jesse moved to flank them, making it impossible for her to escape.

"Emerson looks as if he just stepped out of an old Gothic novel," Willa observed, watching the butler take coats and hats and umbrellas. "He looks older than Abram."

"He was sixty-one his last birthday."

"He must have gotten his white hair from living with all of you," she shot back, giving another tug on her arm.

"I'm going to kiss you again if you don't quit squirming," Sam said, leaning closer.

"I suppose you do need the practice," she drawled.

And so began Bram's wake. Friends, enemies, business acquaintances, and foreign dignitaries all passed by Bram's beautiful casket and smiling face; the parade lasted four hours.

Willa lasted nearly three.

By then, her hair had escaped again, she had a small run in one stocking, and she'd spilled tea on her dress. Her forced smile had waned, and her shoulders were drooping. Sam escorted her to the office, sat her down in front of a roaring fire, stole her shoes, and propped her feet on an ottoman. He then placed a full glass of Johnnie Walker Black in her hand, telling her to relax, that they'd join her as soon as they could.

An hour later, the three brothers entered the office in desperate need of something to drink themselves.

"I've been trying to figure out this room," Willa said as she held out her glass for Sam to refill.

Picking up the bottle of scotch, Sam noticed it wasn't her first refill.

"What's to figure out?" Jesse asked.

"Why are there four desks in Bram's office?"

"There are four of us who work here," Ben explained, taking a seat across from her and immediately pulling off his tie.

"This room is bigger than my house. Heck, the desks are bigger than my truck."

Willamina Kent was a little tipsy. She wasn't slurring her words yet, but her eyes were glazed, and her hand was waving at the desks under discussion.

"Bram set this office up when we came to live with him," Jesse explained, pulling up another chair to face her. "He insisted we sit here evenings with him and do our homework. He gave us each a desk, a computer, and a phone," he added, pulling off his own tie with a sigh.

"This room looks like a public library."

"It practically is," Sam agreed, handing her a much-watered-down drink.

Her head was going to hurt come morning. He just hoped she was recovered by the time the will was read. A woman should be . . . all together to hear her fate.

"Was that guy really a duke? The one you introduced me to?" she asked, changing subjects randomly.

"Yup. His Grace, Peter of Kent," Jesse said. "Any relation, Willa?"

"No." She snorted just as she was about to take a sip of her scotch, showering her dress with another stain. Her eyes widened in disbelief.

Tipsy, Willa's eyes turned crystalline blue, making Sam think he was looking deep into the ocean's soul.

"How much have you had to drink tonight?" Jesse asked, studying her with narrowed eyes.

"Not much."

"You're going to have to carry her up the stairs, Sam, if you don't take that glass away from her," Ben warned.

Willa snorted again. "We'd both be killed when his legs gave out halfway up. How *is* your knee?" she asked

Sam, referring to the vicious kick he'd received from Richard Bates.

Then her eyes suddenly widened, and she sat up straight. "Ohmygosh! That reminds me, Shelby called. What happened to Richard?" she asked Ben.

"What do you mean?" He studied the swirl of the ice in his glass.

"He didn't arrive home. What did you do with him?"

"You said you're trying to talk your sister into divorcing him, so Jesse and I bought you a little time alone with her."

Willa's face paled. "How?" she squeaked.

"Richard Bates is on a slow boat to Italy," Jesse said. "You'll have a couple of weeks to talk some sense into your sister, what with the red tape he'll have to go through for not having a passport."

"You *shanghaied* him?"

"Tidewater had a cargo ship leaving port this morning."

"You can't do that!"

"Well, Willa, we did," Ben said with a sigh as he stood up. "So, do you want help to your room or not? I'm beat."

"But what am I going to tell Shelby?"

"Tell her to get the hell out of her marriage. She's got two weeks to start divorce proceedings in peace."

"But she's got two kids!"

"Is Richard Bates a jerk or not?" Sam growled, removing the drink she was clutching in her hands.

"He's a first-class jerk."

"Does she love him?"

"She . . . she might," Willa admitted, her eyes pained.

"Then your interference is unwelcome."

"But he's mean to Shelby—and she just takes it."

"Then *she* will have to deal with him. You can't divorce Richard for her, Willa. Shelby's got to do that herself."

"But what about the kids?"

"Will they be better off with Richard or without him?"

"I don't know," she whispered, looking down at her lap. "I just don't know." She looked back up at Sam. "Shelby's really pretty, and she used to be so full of life. She's six years older than me, and I've always looked up to her. That's why it's so hard to see her like this."

"Like what, exactly?" Ben asked. "Does he abuse her?"

"Emotionally, I think. Shelby's become withdrawn. Especially since . . . the accident."

"What accident?" Sam asked.

"The accident where I crashed my car and maimed my niece for life."

Only the ticking of the mantel clock broke the silence.

Small pieces of what Sam saw as a very complicated puzzle suddenly began falling into place. Willa felt guilty for driving the car that had crashed, for crippling her niece, and for her sister's unhappiness now. Willamina Kent had spent the last five years as crippled as her niece.

A guilty conscience could be a debilitating thing. And of all the dragons to slay, it was probably the hardest.

Abram Sinclair had known exactly that when he'd written his will; when he'd decided to send Willa three knights to rescue her.

Sam blew out a tired sigh. He looked at his brothers, who were staring at the woman they'd all come to care for in only three days. The little partridge from Maine had roosted in their hearts, guilelessly and without intent but packing a small nation of troubles.

No wonder Bram was smiling. The old man had known his bequest would keep all four of them so mad at him they'd be too busy to mourn him.

In just three months, it would be over. Then Sam would take his bride to visit Bram's grave—where, if they listened hard enough, they'd probably hear the old wolf laughing his head off.

Chapter Seven

Apparently unwilling to leave anything to chance, Abram Sinclair had written his own eulogy. It was succinct and as arrogant as the man himself. Spencer read it at graveside before an impressively large assembly.

Some of you here have been waiting for this day to come, while some of you have been dreading it. I may be dead, but I promise I won't be forgotten. Don't any of you cry for me. I'm with my Rose now. And with my sons. Hopefully.

I had a good life and enjoyed myself for the most part. I knew the love of a good woman and the joy of raising my three grandsons to manhood. Just so you'll know, I'll be watching you boys, so don't disappoint me. Take the empire I've built, and triple it. Get married, you rogues. Have lots of babies, and tell them about me.

And you damn well better be kind in the telling.

Smile for me. Hell, laugh if you like. That's what I'll be doing.

And Willamina? You'd better get your thinking straight, girl. I've already started you on the right path; take my gift in the spirit I've given it.

Good-bye. And good luck to you all.

Willa sighed as Spencer's voice trailed off. Oh, how she had come to love Abram Sinclair. Fate, in the form of a white-haired, eccentric old man, had finally caught up with her.

Abram's cryptic last words still echoing through the beautiful little cemetery, the mourners began a slow procession back to the house. She didn't want to go back to that imposing office and listen to Spencer read Abram's will. But the lawyer had told her that she must attend, ignoring her protests.

She just wanted to go home to her safe and simple life. She wanted to put this last month and a half behind her and put the hopes and dreams Abram Sinclair had conjured up behind her.

Willa suddenly realized that she was alone with Jesse, Ben, and Sam. They were looking at her, their faces drawn and their shoulders stiff. "Will you put this on his casket for me, please?" she asked Jesse, holding out the rose.

He set it over the rose Abram had carved in the wood, and they all walked back to the house in silence.

There were several more hours of condolences and handshakes. Willa heard comments on Abram's casket, on the eulogy, and on Rosebriar. Speculation was whispered about what would happen now. The consensus seemed to be that Tidewater International would be divided up among the three grandsons. It was also agreed that an era had ended.

But for all the strain of the afternoon, it went by much too quickly. Within minutes, it seemed, Willa found herself sitting in one of the four chairs Spencer had placed facing a television in the office. Staff, distant relatives, and even some board members of Tidewater were sitting and standing around the room. Ben, Jesse, and Sam were seated beside her.

It was clear that they were going to see Abram Sinclair one last time, in living, breathing color on a video tape. Just what she needed, to hear Abram's voice again, probably in a lecture. She didn't want any bequest beyond the cost of his casket, and even that was unnecessary.

Sam sat in stony silence beside Willa. He knew what was coming, and he didn't like it. He'd decided to keep the contents of the will to himself, giving Bram the pleasure of breaking the news to Jesse and Ben. He'd only read the written terms; he hadn't seen the video. Spencer had somehow "forgotten" to tell him there was one. To the end, Bram's old friend had remained loyal.

Spencer cleared his throat, and Sam grabbed hold of Willa's hands.

She stopped wringing them and looked up at him with a white face. "I want to leave," she whispered.

"It'll be okay, Willa."

"I don't belong here."

"You will," he said, giving her a wink, then turning to nod at Spencer.

"Everyone here today has been asked to be here," Spencer said, going to the television and turning it on.

"Even Warren Cobb?" Jesse asked, glaring at the man leaning against Bram's desk, his cane resting beside him.

Warren Cobb was founder and majority shareholder of Starrtech, Tidewater's closest rival. Warren was also Bram's childhood friend. They had worked their way out of poverty together, but sometime during the building of their separate empires, they'd become enemies. The reason for this had gone to the grave with Bram, and Sam doubted that Warren would be any more forthcoming. But having read the will, he understood Warren's interest in the proceedings today.

"Even Cobb," Spencer acknowledged. "He's here at Bram's request."

"Then let's find out why, Spence. Start the tape." Ben tugged at his tie.

Sam did the same. Not one Sinclair was comfortable in a tie, especially Bram. Which is why Sam had taken his grandfather's tie off just before they'd closed the casket that morning. And, as Bram was wont to do, Sam had balled it up and stuffed it into the old man's jacket pocket, giving it a final pat for Peg. She was forever fishing out those ties and having to press them, and tonight she'd probably be pressing three more. Jesse had already shed his, and by the looks of things, Ben was not far behind him. Sam had loosened his own tie and unbuttoned his top button, but before this meeting was over, he'd want to use his tie to strangle someone.

Or more likely to gag Willa; she was going to scream the plaster off the walls.

Spencer started the tape. The video had been made in Maine, the ocean showing in the window behind Bram as he sat at a battered table in a small, eclectically furnished cottage.

Sam felt Willa tremble, and he wrapped his arm over her shoulders, pulling her snugly against his side. She stared at the television, her eyes misted.

"He looks damn happy," he whispered.

"I'm going to miss him," she whispered back, not taking her eyes off the screen.

Abram cleared his throat, then pointed a finger at them and scowled. "Does that red light mean they can see me?" he asked the cameraman.

"It does, Bram. They can hear you, too," came Spencer's voice from somewhere off camera.

"Then listen up, people," Bram said, still pointing

his finger. "This is my last will and testament. And I'm of sound mind, so don't any of you go trying to change it, you hear?"

"They hear you, Bram," came Spencer's voice again. "Don't worry. Everything is documented."

Sam glanced at Spencer now, sitting off to the side, his shoulders hunched. This was hard for him. Spencer had been a good friend to Bram, as well as a damn good lawyer. And he was still determined to be a good friend, even if he might not agree with Bram's scheme.

Sam would have liked to have been a fly on the wall of that cottage this past month. There must have been some hair-raising arguments over this will.

"Okay, then. Spencer said I should start with the smaller stuff, so listen up," Bram growled. He didn't take his eyes off the camera, giving everyone the uncomfortable feeling that he was looking straight at them. Sam heard more than one body shift nervously behind him.

"Peg. You first, you old mother hen. I'm giving you the deed to that little cabin up on Wagon Wheel Lake you like so much. You've gone on and on enough about it all these years. Well, you can damn well retire there and shrivel away, if that's what you want." Bram pointed his finger. "But not for three months. You'll continue housekeeping for the next three months if you want that cabin."

There was a loud gasp from the back of the room,

but no one turned to see if Peg was blushing or fuming.

"And Ronald. The Stutz Bearcat is yours, lock, stock, and steering wheel. You keep driving for three months, and Spencer will give you the title. You've been drooling over that car since I got it, always pestering me to take it out for a drive. Well, my friend, drive it wherever you want—in three months."

An embarrassed cough came from near the door. Ronald had fallen in love with the Bearcat the day Bram had taken him to the auto auction. Sam figured his grandfather had bought the car more for their chauffeur than for himself. Ronald was one proud puppy when he was behind the wheel, delivering Bram to some meeting.

"Emerson, you fussy old woman," Bram boomed next. "I'm leaving you my antique toy train collection since you can't seem to keep your paws off it." Bram cackled. "In three months, you can sell it for enough to take an honest-to-God *real* train ride around the world, if you want."

Sam turned in his seat, along with Ben and Jesse, to see Emerson slowly walk out of the office, his bearing proud and his face red.

"And now for all you shirttail relatives who've been coming out of the woodwork for the last forty years. Spencer's got the list of the lot of you. I'm giving you each one thousand dollars, which is a hell of a lot more than I had when I started. Go get jobs, you parasites."

Several gasps erupted around the room. Jesse's shoulders began to shake, and Ben barely stifled a snort. The parade of beggars had been endless at Rosebriar. Bram had been generous with some, miserly with others, and downright rude to most of them. In one month, Sam figured, the parade would start again.

"Now for the best part. Can I tell them now, Spencer?"

"No, Bram. You've forgotten the charities," Spencer replied patiently.

Bram waved that away. "I already signed the checks. Just send them out after I'm planted."

"Willamina Kent." Bram's voice shot out from the television, making her jump. "I'm setting up a trust fund for that spitfire niece of yours, so you can just stop worrying about Jennifer."

Willa let out a deep sigh of relief and sagged tiredly. Sam gripped her more firmly. She thought she was off the hook, but there was much more.

"Right now, Jennifer is taking delivery of a brand new SUV that's specially equipped so she can learn to drive. And don't you worry. The title is in Jennifer's and Shelby's names, not Richard's."

Two huge tears fell onto Willa's clasped hands. Sam undid the clip that held her hair, letting it fall around her face to give her privacy. She turned to him and tried to smile, and Sam kissed her forehead.

"Since you three boys already have your trust funds

in place, that leaves Rosebriar, my Tidewater shares, and my bankbook," Bram said. "And I'm bequeathing them all to you, Willamina. Every last acre and every last share and every last dime."

Willamina shot out of her chair as if she'd been electrocuted. "*What?!*" she shouted at Bram, who was leaning back on his creaky chair and smiling.

Snorts, gasps, and shouts of indignation erupted around the office. Only Sam was smiling. Ben and Jesse sat stone still, their faces blank.

"Now, Willa. Don't jump up and down thanking me yet," Bram drawled, his smile widening. "There are some conditions to this little bequest."

Willa stood staring at the television, her fists balled at her sides, her hair all but standing on end.

"Rosebriar's yours, Willa," Bram continued more softly, his expression serious. "The deed's already been put in your name, all of the land, the buildings, and the contents. And Spencer's got a bankbook with your name on it.

"The *RoseWind* is also yours, girl. Enjoy her. All I ask is that you don't rechristen her."

Sam saw Willa sway on her feet, and he jumped up to steady her.

"My stocks in Tidewater are yours, too, Willa. But here's the catch. You own them only for three months. If you haven't married one of my grandsons by then and turned them over to him as a wedding gift, then they will be sold to Warren Cobb for ten cents on the dollar."

Ben and Jesse jumped up and started cursing, but they were hardly heard over the booming laughter coming from the back of the room.

"Over my dead body!" Jesse shouted, turning to glare at Warren Cobb.

Ben stared at Sam. "You're not surprised by this."

"I found out twenty-four hours ago," Sam told him, his arms protectively around Willa, who still hadn't moved.

"Then why didn't we find out twenty-*three* hours ago?" Jesse took a step toward him.

Ben did, too. "How did you find out?"

"I cornered Spencer yesterday. My only reason for wanting to see the will was to protect Willa."

"Protect her from what?"

"Bram."

Jesse kicked one of the chairs, knocking it into another one. Willa flinched, and Sam glared at his brothers.

"Calm down. There's more," he softly told them, nodding to Spencer, who had stopped the tape.

Sam pulled Willa back to her chair. Jesse straightened the chair he'd kicked and sat down. Stone-faced, Ben took his chair again. Sam decided to stand behind Willa, keeping his hands firmly on her shoulders.

Bram began speaking again.

"Warren Cobb," he boomed, "you'll get your hands on my company only if I've raised three worthless grandsons. But I can tell you now, I have not. One of them will marry Willa, and Tidewater will not only remain intact, it will come gunning for you, you old bastard. Starrtech will be dust at your feet to be sprinkled over both of our graves."

Bram shot a sinister smile at the camera. "Like I did sixty years ago, I'll beat you again, old friend. Rose married me, and she died a happy woman.

"Boys," Bram continued, "if I could have found a Willa for each of you, I would have. But only one of you can have her. Win her, and you win Rosebriar and Tidewater." He frowned suddenly. "Lose her, and you'll get just what you deserve."

Then Bram nervously cleared his throat, suddenly looking every one of his eighty-five years. "Willa, honey. There's—ah—one more thing. You've got three months to marry one of my grandsons and one year after the wedding to get pregnant. Otherwise, Tidewater gets sold to Cobb."

Willa jumped up again with a shriek. "What? You can't do that, you old rat! You can't make me get married and then get pregnant!" She grabbed for anything on the desk and hurled it at Bram.

The television screen exploded with a crash. Pandemonium broke out again as Sam lunged for Willa, and Jesse and Ben fell off their chairs in laughter. Warren Cobb was barking with glee, and all of the other guests were shouting in outrage.

"Willa. Calm *down*," Sam growled as she looked for another missile.

"It's not funny, Ben!" she screamed, suddenly heading for him. "It's not one *stinking* bit funny!"

"You broke the television, Willa," Ben sputtered.

"Well, why not?" Jesse drawled. "It's her television."

Willa froze, and her face drained of color as she stared at the two men.

"I think it's time to clear the room," Sam said.

Spencer hastily jumped up and dismissed everyone.

"Get Ronald to bring in another television," Sam told him as the room slowly cleared.

All except for Warren Cobb, that is.

Sam walked over to Bram's desk, picked up the cane leaning against it, and handed it to the man who was grinning at him. "No need to wait around, Cobb. We'll send you an invitation to the wedding."

"You sure there'll be one?" Warren asked.

"There will be."

"To which grandson?"

"I guess you'll have to wait for your invitation to find out." Sam gave Warren a piercing inspection. "So, Rose married Bram instead of you, is that it?"

"Bram stole her from me."

"I'd say *Rose* made her choice."

Warren smiled nastily. "Well, Sinclair, if Willamina Kent decides none of you is worth the trouble, maybe I'll just set my own grandsons after her. If she's been hand-picked by Abram Sinclair, that's good enough for me."

"I've *had* it! Do you hear me? I've had enough!" Willa hollered.

"We hear you, Willa," Sam said, walking over and taking hold of her shoulders. "And so did half of Connecticut. You need to calm down and take a seat. I'm afraid there's probably more."

"More?" she squeaked. "How much more can there be?" She collapsed onto the chair Jesse had thoughtfully placed behind her.

"Just a few details," Sam assured her. "That's all."

She blinked up, looking so confused and defeated that he wanted to whisk her away as fast and as far as he could.

Damn Abram. The interfering old fool had shocked their partridge senseless. She was beyond comprehension; the details would go right over her head.

But not over Jesse's and Ben's. They'd moved their chairs to flank Willa while Ronald hooked up a new television. Sam seemed to be the only one who understood Bram's puppeteering.

This entire fiasco was the old man's attempt to coax a lost little bird out of her hidey-hole and back into life. That, and to get a great-grandchild, even from his grave. Sam couldn't fault Bram's choice of a bride; like his grandfather, he could see the entire woman, ghosts and gifts and gentle soul.

The old man was ensuring the future of his dynasty,

he was giving a special woman the kick in the pants she needed, and he was telling his grandsons that he loved them enough to cut them free of Tidewater International, giving them all a new chance at life. He was telling the four of them to live as wildly and as fully as he had. Eventually, Jesse and Ben would see that, just as he had. Willa, however, would definitely need prodding in the right direction.

"Now, Willa, honey," came Bram's voice again from the television. "I know you're probably steaming mad right now, but you'll get over it."

Sam glanced over at Willa, who had closed her eyes. But she couldn't close her ears.

"Now, you boys listen up if you're interested in marrying Willa. She's got this fool notion that she's too accident-prone to have a baby. She's afraid she'll end up harming her child, just like she thinks she did her niece." Bram snorted. "It's up to you to convince her that she didn't maim Jennifer but saved the girl's life. So, one of you marry Willa, and get her pregnant." He pointed his finger. "After the wedding!"

Abram slumped in his chair at the table, and his eyes filled with moisture. "Someday you'll thank me, Willa," he said softly. "And maybe someday you'll forgive me. I love you, girl, like the daughter I never had. I wish I'd met you sooner." Bram swiped at his eyes.

Then, he looked up, his eyes warm yet piercing. "I want you boys to understand why I've left everything to Willa here and not to you. Sam, Ben, Jesse, you're fine, capable men, and you love one another. I know there's no competition among you for Tidewater. And I know you've stayed with the company only for my sake. But it's a good legacy I've built, and I'd like to see it stay intact. But only one of you should have it. You others can move on now. Find good women, have children, and enjoy yourselves.

"When I thought I could take no more, you boys were there, giving me strength. I have loved you three with all my heart. That's why I couldn't choose one of you, and that's why I still can't. All I can do is say thank you for loving me back. Don't mourn me. Just remember me. Good-bye, boys. Have a grand life."

Chapter Eight

$\mathcal{T}$*he television screen went* to snow.

Ben stood and walked to the office window, his shoulders stiff. Jesse stayed seated, his elbows on his knees as he stared down at the floor. Willa remained utterly still, tears running down her face. Sam pulled the knot of his tie apart and slipped the confining silk free of his neck. He rolled it up with slow deliberation, until he'd formed a neat coil that he placed in his jacket pocket.

"He can't really do what he's done, can he?" Willa asked, her stilted voice intruding into the silence.

"He has," Sam said, washing a worried gaze over her. He reached out and tucked a strand of her hair behind her ear. "It will be okay, honey. We'll work it out together."

"I can't get married, Sam. And I can't ever have children."

"You can't let Warren Cobb have Tidewater, Willa," Ben said from the window, not turning around. "I'd rather destroy it myself than give Cobb the pleasure." He turned to her. "Which is what he'll do. Tidewater will be like Carthage, with not a stone left standing when he's done."

"Warren hates Abram that much?"

"He apparently loved Rose that much."

"And thus makes a sixty-year war between friends," Ben said tonelessly, looking at the snowy television. "Now it's up to us to end the war by winning it."

Spencer cleared his throat and stood up. "I have some papers that need to be signed. I'm sorry to have to do this now, but they're important."

"What are they?" Sam asked.

"Legal transfers of ownership for Rosebriar, the bankbook, and Bram's stocks in Tidewater for Willa to sign."

"What happens if I don't sign them?" she asked, hope in her voice.

Spencer appeared startled. "Well, I guess things will sit in limbo for three months. Bills won't get paid, people won't get their salaries, and Tidewater International will erupt into chaos."

"I see."

"Everything's yours, Willa, whether you want it or not," the lawyer explained. "Bram's will is sound. If you're not married to a Sinclair in three months, Bram's shares in Tidewater get sold to Warren Cobb."

"And what about Rosebriar and the bankbook?" she asked, frowning at the stack of papers on the desk Spencer had been sitting at.

"Everything else is yours to keep."

Willa took a shuddering breath. "And mine to give away?"

"That's complicated," Spencer cautioned. "Bram's will specifically states that you may not turn anything over to his grandsons. Not unless you're married to one of them. And you must get pregnant. Only then can you do whatever you want with everything."

"Is that legal? Can Abram bequeath me a gift and then still control it?"

"He can entail the inheritance. You could try breaking it in court, but it would probably stand. Tying legacies to lineage, thus making it contingent on your conceiving, is a time-honored tradition based in ancient law. Families have been doing it for centuries."

"What happens to all of this if something happens to me in the next three months?" Willa asked.

"Nothing's going to happen," Sam snapped.

"But what if it does?" she shot back, raising her chin.

"There are provisions," Spencer quickly replied. "Legally, Bram had to consider that possibility. If something happens to you, Rosebriar and the money will be equally divided among the three grandsons. But the Tidewater shares will still be sold to Warren Cobb."

Sam gave her a lopsided smile. "You're a wealthy woman now. And would marriage really be so bad?"

"My last one was!" she snapped, glaring at him and then turning her glare on Spencer. "Give me the damn papers to sign. I wouldn't want the electricity cut off for nonpayment of the bill."

"Uh-oh. She's mad now," Jesse chirped, walking to the desk. "We'd better be nice to her, guys, or we're liable to be looking for a place to sleep tonight." He gave Willa a daring grin. "You gonna kick us out of your home, little partridge?"

"What *is* it with this partridge thing?"

Sam shot a warning glare at Jesse.

"It's just something . . . um, Bram said in one of his memos to the office. He mentioned seeing a partridge where he was staying," Jesse quickly prevaricated.

Willa snorted. "Well, Bram still owes me for the casket."

"I think he's paid you in full, Willa," Ben said with a chuckle, holding the open bankbook out to her.

Sam watched Willa read the numbers. "I can't even count all the zeros!"

"Enough to cover the cost of his casket?" Jesse grinned.

Willa slapped the bankbook onto the desk with a

crack. "Each and every one of you can go straight to hell." She spun on her heel and stalked away. "And join your grandfather!"

The windows rattled with the force of the slammed door.

"She's in a bit of a snit," Jesse said, picking up the bankbook and letting out a soft whistle. "Most women would be rather pleased right about now." He waved the book at his brothers. "She could buy a small nation with this kind of money."

"Or a husband," Ben speculated. He looked at the door. "Was her first marriage that bad, do you suppose?"

"I don't think marriage is the problem," Sam offered. "Remember last night, when she told us how she was responsible for maiming her niece? She's scared to have children, because she's afraid she might harm them."

"That's right," Spencer added. "Bram saw it. Willamina does have a tendency to . . . find trouble."

"Only because she's so busy trying to save the world," Sam explained. "She was so worried about doing well for Bram at the board meeting she couldn't even get off the elevator without causing a commotion." Sam turned serious. "Does Warren Cobb know the specifics of the will? Did either you or Bram consider all of the different scenarios?"

"We did. And Warren Cobb is a smart man," Spencer answered softly. "He'll figure it out."

"Then we may have a problem."

"What?" Ben asked, stiffening.

"If Willa doesn't get married in three months to one of us, or if she doesn't get pregnant within fifteen months, or if she dies, Warren wins."

"Cobb wouldn't do anything drastic," Jesse said.

"Sixty years is a long time for hate to fester."

Ben cursed. "Then you shouldn't wait three months to marry her. Unless you'd rather one of us gets the partridge pregnant? I suppose I could volunteer."

"For the good of Tidewater?" Sam asked, stepping toward his brother.

"Tidewater can go straight to hell with Bram, for all I care," Ben said with a laugh. "Just as long as Cobb doesn't get it, I don't care if the whole damn business explodes."

"You seem to be the only one of us *kissing* Willa," Jesse said, moving between his brothers. "So, what's the problem?"

"There is none!" Sam snapped. "Maybe I'll just ask her to marry me right now. 'And while you're signing the marriage license, would you please sign over the Tidewater shares while you're at it?' " he finished scathingly.

"But that's the plan," Spencer piped up.

Sam growled, "Did you or Bram consider how Willa will feel, thinking she's merely a prize? She's going to think I'm marrying her only to get Tidewater."

"But you will be," Spencer pointed out.

"Dammit! It's not the business I want!"

"You'll be getting Willa, too!" Spencer shouted.

"That's enough. Calm down, both of you," Ben said. "We'll figure something out. Together we'll find a way to convince Willa it's *her* you want."

"You really want her?" Spencer had the nerve to ask.

"Yes," Sam snapped. "And like my brothers, I don't care if Tidewater rots."

"But Bram worked his whole life to build that company."

"He needed it. We don't."

"What about Rosebriar? Don't you want it?"

"We can build elsewhere on the estate," Jesse said. "Sam will probably be busy making caskets in Maine most of the time, anyway."

"Just as long as Warren Cobb and his damned grandsons are out of the picture," Sam growled.

"Have you met any of his grandsons?" Spencer asked.

"Yup. And if you think Warren's bad, you should see them."

"He's got four, hasn't he?" Ben asked.

"Warren had six children," Spencer told them. "Four daughters and two sons. And several grandchildren now. I don't remember the exact number."

"The old bastard didn't pine for Rose long," Jesse drawled.

"He married about four years after Bram did," Spencer said. "And he married money. That's how he got his start."

"Then I can't imagine them holding a grudge for sixty years."

"It was heated at first, until they both got busy building their empires. It's only been minor skirmishes for the last thirty years."

"Then Willa shouldn't be in any danger," Jesse speculated.

"Don't bank on it," Spencer offered. "One of his grandsons, Barry Cobb, is ten times worse than old man Warren. And he hopes to gain his grandfather's favor. It would be my guess that most of the battles Tidewater has fought lately have been because of Barry."

"But why? The feud's two generations removed from him."

"All of the children were raised on stories tainted with Warren's bitterness," Spencer explained. "Most of them could care less, but with Barry, it took. He'd like nothing better than to bring down Bram's company for his grandfather."

"So, now we know where to look for trouble," Sam said. "We keep Willa safe, and we keep a close eye on Barry Cobb."

"We'll do the watching, brother—you concentrate on wooing your bride. Then you can start making a baby. Fifteen months isn't all that long," Ben said.

Sam gave his brother a challenging grin. "One million bucks says I get her pregnant within two months of our wedding."

Ben's eyebrows climbed into his hairline. "A million?"

"Each."

Jesse's eyebrows went the way of his brother's. "Pretty cock sure, aren't you?"

"Eleven months from the wedding, I'll consider accepting your christening gifts."

"You're on!" Jesse said. "One million each, to be set in trust for your kid. One day past eleven months, though, and you set up trusts for *our* future offspring."

"Fair enough."

"Deal."

"Deal."

Three hours of crying hadn't helped, and the laughter Willa heard coming from the office only added to her anger. It had begun drifting up the stairs two hours ago in increasingly boisterous waves.

It was obvious that those three pitiful excuses for grandsons were getting roaring drunk. They'd put Abram in the ground not ten hours ago, and now they were carrying on like uncivilized baboons. The ungrateful wretches.

Bram included.

The old goat had trapped her smartly. He'd known

she wouldn't be able to turn her back on a company full of people who depended on it for survival. Just as he'd known she was too damned softhearted to let Tidewater fall into the hands of a man whose lifelong ambition was to make anyone named Sinclair suffer.

If she married one of the grandsons, it would become her name too, and her war. But if she walked away, everyone suffered. Warren Cobb would destroy Tidewater. Jobs would be lost. Sam and Ben and Jesse would have lost not only their grandfather but their heritage. And if that happened, she would never be able to live with herself.

She had spent the last three hours feeling sorry for herself, crying, raging, and worrying. She'd packed twice and was now making her third attempt to leave. This time, she'd actually reached the top of the stairs.

Now she was sitting on them. Listening.

And crying again—but for a different reason.

The door to the office was closed, but she could still hear what was going on inside. The laughter was interspersed with stories, outrageous memories of three boys growing up in a home filled with love and plenty of pranks.

Each tale began with "Do you remember when we" and ended in laughter. Abram had been the butt of most of the boys' escapades, and of course, he had retaliated, sometimes with well-deserved punishments, sometimes with even more devious pranks. Abram's "boys" were giving their own eulogy as they came to terms with their grandfather's death.

That was why she was sitting there, undecided. She'd dearly love to get to know Sam and Ben and Jesse better, to understand what made them tick. Not one of them had batted an eyelash when they'd learned Abram was leaving his entire fortune to her. They'd definitely been surprised, but they hadn't been outraged or hurled accusations at her or threatened reprisal.

They'd simply accepted it.

As if they'd *expected* Abram to do something outrageous.

As if they didn't care.

Abram actually expected her to marry one of them?

They scared her spitless. Not physically—even though she suspected each of them had a formidable temper, she also knew they'd never use it against a woman. No, what scared her was their fortitude, their confidence, and their arrogance. All three of them overwhelmed her without even trying. Their very ability to walk away from Tidewater and start over left her speechless.

Willa had realized years ago that she was a little more clumsy than most people. About the only place she felt confident was surrounded by the sea and her senior citizens. Take her out of her element, and she turned klutzy. She'd embarrassed David so many times in the three years they'd been married it was a wonder he hadn't considered putting her out of her misery.

Most likely, he'd been waiting for her to do it herself.

And she almost had, the day she'd stopped by David's office and found a red-headed bombshell missing some clothes sitting on his lap. Willa had taken Jennifer's hand, turned and walked away, and gotten into her car and driven off. At least she'd remembered to fasten Jennifer's seat belt. Otherwise, her niece would likely be dead.

A normal woman would have screamed and torn that bimbo off her husband's lap, then sued David for divorce, along with every dime she could get from the slimy worm. Instead, she had maimed her innocent niece.

Recovering in the same hospital as Jennifer, only to walk out eventually, had made Willa realize that her own children were better off unborn. She'd been known to poison people with her cooking, she'd broken more dishes than she could count, and she'd gotten into enough mishaps as a child to gray her mother's hair prematurely.

She couldn't do it again. She couldn't marry a man and watch him grow exasperated, then impatient, and eventually angry. Indifference would follow shortly, and the marriage would finally die a bitter death. And this time, with a man as good and strong as any of the Sinclair men, Willa would die with it.

She stood up finally and squared her shoulders for the coming battle. She was leaving Rosebriar. Tonight.

She was going home, locking all the doors, and keeping the world at bay. Maybe next week, she'd be able to think clearly enough to find a way to make sure Tidewater International remained intact and the grandsons got their rightful inheritance.

Yes. She would fix this mess or die trying.

Chapter Nine

Willa's nose woke up before her eyes did, to the pungent aroma of a sour-mash distillery. She tried to wipe the odor away but couldn't seem to move her hand. Nor could she feel her arms. Apparently, they didn't want to wake up, either.

She finally forced her eyes open, only to snap them shut with a groan. Oh, Lord, she was waking up in bed with the grandsons. Thank God she was fully dressed.

Still, Willa was reluctant to open her eyes again and find out exactly whose arm was pinning her down. And whose leg was thrown over her thighs. No wonder most of her body was asleep; the man weighed a ton.

Oh, God, was it Sam?

The men had led her up to Abram's room, pulling her into the celebration of their grandfather's life with drunken charm. Another bottle of brandy had come upstairs with them, but she had refused to drink any, still queasy from her previous night's scotch marathon.

Instead, she had climbed onto Abram's massive bed and leaned against the headboard while the men had sprawled around her, and she'd listened to their tales of a strong man who had lived every one of his eighty-five years to the fullest. Sometime around two in the morning, she'd fallen asleep. A short while later, she'd half awakened to see somebody stumble out of the bed with a curse and go over and stop the pendulum on the clock on the opposite wall. She'd slept more peacefully then. She'd actually snuggled into the closest man with a sigh, feeling warm and protected and utterly content.

Now, though, nature was calling. She was also mad that she had so easily been talked out of leaving last night. She wasn't any closer to a solution to her problems, either. If anything, she had one more.

She was falling in love with the Sinclairs, every damn last one of them.

Finally finding the courage to open her eyes, Willa lifted her head to see Jesse on the far side of the bed, his mouth open and one arm thrown over his eyes. Ben was snoring beside him.

Which meant it was Sam's chest she was snuggled against.

Figures. He volunteered to be the one to marry me. That's what they'd told her last night. For the good of Tidewater, Sam Sinclair would sacrifice himself to a dead man. He was even up to the task of getting her pregnant, too.

How noble of him.

Well, he could damn well walk down the aisle by himself. She was going to find a bathroom, then the kitchen, and then she was stealing a car and driving to Maine. She wasn't flying on one of those commuter planes again.

Praying he wouldn't wake up, Willa carefully tried to move Sam's hand. It immediately tightened, then started kneading her softly. Despite herself, she moaned.

Dear Lord, she had to get out of there!

She tossed his hand away, scrambling off the bed before any of the men could get their bearings. Sam shouted when she pushed off his chest. He bumped into Ben, pushing Jesse off the bed with a yelp of alarm. Ben sat bolt upright, his eyes wild, his hair standing on end, his fists raised for battle.

Then all three of them grabbed their heads and started cursing.

Willa couldn't help but smile. Hangovers were such just rewards—and really handy when a woman wanted everyone to overlook the fact that she'd just spent the night with them.

"What in hell is all the hollering?" Sam hissed with obvious restraint, slits of blue fire escaping his bloodshot eyes.

Bolstered by the fact that she couldn't possibly look

any worse than he did, Willa gave him a smug smile. "Go back to sleep. It's still early," she said, determined to brazen her way out of this. At the very least, she hoped to buy herself time.

Sam dropped his head into his hands with a groan. Ben flopped back onto the pillow, whimpering in agony. Jesse remained sitting on the floor and simply laid his head on his knees, quietly cursing.

Willa escaped.

Realizing she was limping because she was wearing only one shoe, she slipped it off when she reached the hallway, then tried to decide which direction to go. She was in the family wing, which meant her room was at the opposite end of the house. She headed down the hall at a run, determined to be long gone before anyone realized she was missing. She smiled again, thinking about the shoe she must have lost in Abram's bed, and she wondered if Sam would show up on her doorstep in Maine, seeking the princess it would fit.

Willa suddenly scowled. As fantasies went, Abram Sinclair was the fairy godmother from hell—and Sam was *not* her Prince Charming!

Standing under a hot shower until the water ran cold went a long way toward making Sam feel human again. He had even greater hope that the coffee he smelled would go just as far toward restoring his memory. He was more than a little ashamed of getting so drunk last

night and even more worried about what he might
have said.

"Please, God, don't let me have proposed to Willa,"
he whispered. "And if I did, let her be so hung over
that she doesn't remember."

Sam stopped at the kitchen door and slowly cracked
it open. Ben and Jesse were seated at the staff table,
their hands curled around mugs of steaming coffee,
staring at nothing. Peg was just setting a large platter of
dry toast on the table, and Emerson was perched on a
stool at his desk, scribbling in his journal.

Emerson took more notes than a field scientist, and
Sam suspected the man saw his employers more as a social experiment than a job. Either that, or he was planning to write an exposé when he retired.

"It's safe to come in," Ben said, his voice sounding as
haggard as he looked. "Willa hasn't come down yet."

Sam entered the restaurant-style kitchen and took a
seat at the table. They'd given everyone the next few
days off, but Peg, Emerson, and Ronald lived at Rosebriar.

Peg immediately set down a mug of coffee in front of
Sam—black, steaming, and smelling less strongly of
maple syrup than he usually liked. "Thank you," he
said, wrapping his hands around it and blowing on the
surface. He eyed the platter of toast. "Do you have any
maple spread?" he asked as Peg walked to the stainless-
steel island that ran the length of the kitchen.

"You slather that toast with anything sweet, and you'll throw up." Peg picked up a piece of paper and glanced at it briefly, then reached under the island, grabbed a couple of jars of spices, and placed them in a box on the counter. "That's why I only put a drop of syrup in your coffee. It's going to take a whole loaf of dry toast to sop up all that brandy you boys drank last night." She headed into the pantry, returned with an armful of canisters, and set them in the box with the spices.

"What are you doing?" Sam asked, picking up some toast when his stomach growled.

"I'm packing what supplies I want to take with me."

Jesse and Ben came out of their stupors and frowned at her. "Um, Peg," Ben said. "You're supposed to stay working for the next three months before you go to your cottage."

She turned to look at the table of men. "I will be working, just not here. I only have four, maybe five days to get myself up to Maine and get familiar with my new digs."

"Maine?" Jesse said. "What are you talking about?"

"Miss Kent became my boss when she inherited Rosebriar," Peg said, placing some packets in the box, then picking up the box and setting it by the door that led to the garage. She walked back to the island with an empty box in her hand and looked at her list again.

"You're going to Maine with Willa?" Sam asked, confused as well as surprised.

"Then who's going to take care of us?" Jesse asked before Peg could answer.

She smiled. "Poor babies," she said with mock sympathy. "The kitchen staff is capable of feeding you, and I'm not taking any of the house staff with me, so you don't have to worry about dust bunnies attacking in your sleep. Emerson will watch over everything here. Willa said her house is too small for more than just me to take care of, so I'm going to Maine alone."

"You've spoken to Willa about this already? When?" Sam asked.

"This morning. She got all flustered when I said I intended to go keep house for her and tried to talk me out of it. But when I started listing some of the dishes I can cook and told her that I've always wanted to see the Maine coast, she finally relented." Peg's face reddened slightly. "I might have bullied her a bit, but that poor thing needs looking after right now. She's had quite a shock. She was in such a hurry to leave before you boys came down, she finally just scribbled her address on a paper, told me to be in Maine in five days, then left."

"She's gone!" Sam yelped, standing up.

"When did she leave?" Ben asked.

"*How* did she leave?" Sam asked right behind him.

"Ronald took her," Emerson interjected, swiveling his stool to face them. "They left in the Stutz Bearcat. Ronald told Willa she had only three months to enjoy it."

Jesse strode over to the desk and picked up the phone. "I'm calling him to bring her back here this minute."

"When did they leave?" Ben asked.

"Nearly three hours ago."

"And you guys just let her?" Jesse said, angrily punching numbers on the phone.

"What were we supposed to do?" Peg asked. "Lock her in the pantry until you boys sobered up?"

"It wouldn't be the first time you've done that to one of us," Sam drawled. "Hold up, Jesse," he said, going over and hitting the off button on the phone. "We knew Willa would likely leave today. Maybe we should let her. It's going to take her some time to come to terms with what's happened, and we're probably the last people she wants to see this morning."

"But what about Cobb?" Jesse asked.

Sam shrugged. "Willa's as safe with Ronald as she would be with any of us. And we know where she's going and how she's getting there. I'll give her a few days to calm down, then show up on her doorstep and tell her that I'd like to rent her cottage." Sam warmed to his idea as he formed it on the fly. "I'll tell her I need a little vacation myself and that I want to use up whatever remaining rent Bram had."

"That's perfect," Ben said, grabbing a piece of toast. "It'll be easier courting her on her own turf."

Sam was thinking the same thing, until Ronald walked in the back door.

"Where's Ms. Kent?" Sam asked. "I thought you were driving her to Maine."

Ronald's face took on a dark tinge. "She's on her way home."

"On her way *how?*"

"I'm not at liberty to say. She asked me not to."

Sam took a step toward him. "But I'm asking you *to.*"

"I'm sorry, Sam, but I work for Willa now."

Sam gritted his teeth against the throbbing in his head. "Ronald, there's a chance one of Cobb's grandsons might bother Willa because of Bram's bequest. How about you go back to wherever you left her, pick her up, and drive her to Maine yourself?"

Ronald's face paled. "I never considered Cobb or his grandsons might bother her." He suddenly brightened. "It's okay, though. Nobody can get to Willa for the next few days. By then, I can be in Maine to look after her."

"*I'm* going to look after her in Maine," Sam growled. "And what do you mean, nobody can get to her for the next few days? Where the hell is she?"

"I promised Willa I wouldn't say. I can only assure you she's safe."

The phone suddenly rang, and Jesse answered it. "Sinclair residence," he said. He listened to what the caller had to say. "What!"

Jesse paled as the caller repeated what he'd just said. "How long ago? And nobody stopped her? Where in hell was security?"

Sam made a lunge for the phone, but Jesse hit the off button. "That was the marina," he said. "They said that when they went to move the *RoseWind* to its summer mooring just now, they were told a lone woman had taken her out."

All three brothers turned in unison to glare at Ronald.

Ronald took a step back, his hands raised in supplication. "She's a world-class sailor. She told me she grew up on a schooner."

"She can't get off an elevator without tripping over her own feet," Sam snapped. "She's probably hanging from the rigging by now, if she hasn't fallen overboard!"

"I went down to the dock and helped her get under way," Ronald said. "She was as nimble as a cat from the moment her feet hit the deck. And she sure as hell knows her way around a sailboat." He actually stepped closer. "She told me she needed to spend a few days at sea, alone, to think. I think it was cruel, what Abram did to her. The woman was nothing but nice to him, and he blindsided her on that video tape. I really feel sorry for her."

Sam's anger instantly evaporated. "Yeah. Bram may have thought he was helping Willa, but he really screwed up her life. And that's why I'm going to fix this." He looked at Jesse. "Call our helicopter pilot, and have him pick me up on the front lawn in an hour."

"You're flying to Maine?" Jesse asked. "But it'll take Willa several days to get home."

Sam headed to the back staircase leading to the family wing. "I'm not flying to Maine, I'm sailing."

"How? Willa took the boat," Ben said.

Sam stopped with his foot on the bottom step. "She'll only be a few hours out by the time I find her. I'll board the *RoseWind* and sail up with her."

"And just how are you going to board from a helicopter?" Ben asked in alarm.

"I'll have our pilot get as close and as low as he can, and I'll jump into the water."

Jesse snorted. "You're assuming Willa will stop and fish you out. She'll more likely throw you the anchor."

"She won't let me drown," Sam assured the five incredulous people gaping at him. "She's too softhearted."

Chapter Ten

Willa was so involved plotting her course on the nautical chart that it took her a while to realize the comforting drone of the radio she'd tuned to the NOAA weather station was being drowned out by a familiar noise she couldn't immediately identify. She scanned the horizon behind her from west to east, noticed some boats scattered several miles away, and finally decided the source of the sound was the helicopter in the distance. It seemed to be on a zigzag course, flying from one boat to the other, then moving on to the next one as if searching for something. Only it wasn't orange, nor was it large enough to be a Coast Guard helicopter.

The sleek black aircraft reminded her of the fancy one she'd seen on Donald Trump's *Apprentice* show. But then, probably half the corporations in Manhattan had helicopters. But this one was working its way out to sea, and Willa didn't think such helicopters had a very far range. It would either have to rendezvous with a large ship or head for land soon, she decided, as she glanced at her sails to make sure they were catching the maximum breeze. She checked her compass heading, then stood and adjusted the wheel to a more northeasterly course. She sighed, wishing she had gotten a ride in Tidewater International's helicopter before she'd left.

But wait—she *owned* a good portion of Tidewater now. For the next three months, she probably had the authority to call the office and ask them to send the helicopter up to Keelstone Cove!

She could take Shelby and Jennifer and Cody for a ride in it, and they'd buzz all around town, and the kids could wave to all their friends. Ten-year-old Cody would think she was the coolest aunt in the world.

Even better, instead of having Ronald drive Jennifer and her date to the homecoming dance in the Bearcat, as she and Ronald had discussed on the way to the marina, she could let her niece use the helicopter. How extra-cool would that be?

Whew! This being rich was heady stuff.

But the way she figured it, how many people got to be stinking rich for three whole months? Abram had cursed her with this outrageous bequest, so why not take advantage of it while she tried to find a way out of it? Thus the brilliant idea of sailing the *RoseWind* to Maine instead of driving home.

That's also why she'd agreed to let Peg come keep house for her. With any luck, Peg's cooking would put another ten or fifteen pounds on her, and then she'd see if Sam Sinclair still wanted to marry her. A cook, a chauffeur, a helicopter, a sailboat, a mansion, mountains of money—what more could a girl ask for?

"Don't get caught up in your daydreams, Willamina, or you'll forget the price of keeping everything is a husband," she reminded herself, only to have her words get lost in the *thump-thump-thump* of the fast-approaching helicopter.

Holy smokes, it was coming right at her!

Willa scrambled to catch her chart before it blew away, then lunged for the wheel, turning the *RoseWind* to keep the sails from slapping in the turbulence. The helicopter swung in a wide arch and flew over her again, and she frantically waved it away with one hand while adjusting the wheel with the other.

"Get away!" she shouted, despite knowing that the pilot couldn't hear her. "If you get any closer, you're going to shred my sails!"

The helicopter returned and settled into a hover just off her starboard side. "Break sail and pull about," came a booming voice over its loudspeaker. "I want to come aboard."

Willa went stone still and gaped at the helicopter. That's when she noticed "Tidewater International" in broad gold letters on the fuselage. They had chased her down?

"Turn your radio to six-three," the voice boomed over the *thump* of the spinning blades.

Willa checked the set of her sails, then went to the radio, turned the dial to six-three, and keyed the mike. "Don't get any closer than you are. You'll shred my sails."

"Come about, Willa. I want to come aboard."

"Sam?" she squeaked in surprise, only to forget to key the mike. She pushed the button. "Sam?"

"Stop the boat, Willa."

She shaded her eyes with her hand, scowling at the helicopter keeping pace beside her. "Sam, you can't land here. The mast is in the way."

"Just stop, and I'll jump in and swim to you."

"Are you nuts? No—go away."

"I'm coming aboard, Willa."

"You jump, and it's a long swim home. I am *not* letting you onboard this boat."

"The *RoseWind* isn't set up for solo sailing."

"She is now. Go away, Sam. I don't want to talk to you, your brothers, or anyone else for the next five days. When I get home, I'll call to let you know I made it okay."

"And if you don't make it okay?"

"Then you and your brothers become very wealthy men. I can't do anything about the Tidewater shares, though. Sorry, but you'll have to blame Abram for that one."

"Stop the boat, Willa."

"No can do, Sinclair. And you're going to run out of fuel before I run out of wind. So go away."

Willa set down the mike, grabbed hold of the wheel with both hands, and stared straight ahead, pointedly ignoring the lunatic. Or she tried to, until the chopper got close enough to make her sails flutter again. She scrambled to the winches and tightened the mainsail down even further, then did the same to the jib.

Just as she turned, she heard a loud splash. Willa looked over to see Sam break the surface of the water with a shout and grab hold of a dry sack he'd obviously thrown down first.

"You idiot!" she screamed, rushing to the rail. "You're going to drown!"

The helicopter pulled away, going several hundred yards east before hovering again. Willa quickly ran to the wheel and turned the *RoseWind* into a stall, then broke both sails to let them flutter in the breeze.

"You get right back on that helicopter!" she shouted to Sam, who was a good hundred yards away.

He simply kept swimming through the gentle swells toward her. He was having a difficult time of it, though, with his bulky life vest and having to tow his dry sack.

"You are certifiably insane!"

He kept swimming toward her.

"I mean it, Sam! I don't allow idiots on my boat."

He stopped about ten yards from the *RoseWind* and treaded water. "Goddamn, the water's cold. Th-throw me a line, Willa."

She pointed at the hovering helicopter. "Go back."

Teeth chattering, he gave her an incredulous look. "How? I have no way of getting back in the helicopter. If you don't throw me a line, I'll drown."

"You should have thought of that before you jumped."

His head disappeared below the surface.

"Sam!" She ran to the stern, grabbed the throw buoy with the attached rope, and tossed it at the dry sack and the bobbing orange vest. *"Sam!"*

He reached out and grabbed the buoy just as his head popped up. He sputtered, sucking in large gulps of air. "P-pull me in," he said, his voice faint as he looped his arm through the buoy ring and rolled onto his back. "I'm fading fast."

She immediately began pulling him in, alarmed at how difficult it was. If Sam got so cold he lost the use of his muscles, there was no way she'd get him into the boat by herself. "Hang in there, Sam!" she urged. "Help me by kicking your feet."

He made a weak attempt to move his feet.

"Oh, Sam, what have you done?" she cried, straining

to pull him in. "I won't let you drown. You're going to be okay. Keep kicking."

He began floundering like a hooked marlin.

"Maybe you'd better save your energy instead," she told him. He bumped into the side of the boat, immediately turned upright, and smiled up at her like the idiot he was. "Easy, Sam. Don't get all slap-happy on me," she warned, worried that he was getting hypothermia. "Let go of the bag."

"P-pull it in f-first," he sputtered, making a weak attempt to lift it toward her.

"Let it go! I'll get it later."

He finally let go of the sack and grabbed the rope with both hands. "Pull me to the back of the boat. There's a ladder there," he said, kicking his feet to send him in that direction.

Willa hauled him to the stern, glancing at the helicopter that was still hovering about two hundred yards away. "That pilot should have his license revoked," she growled, dragging Sam around to the ladder. "He's as much of an idiot as you are for letting you jump."

"You're starting to hurt my feelings," Sam said, grabbing the ladder and quickly climbing out of the water.

He stepped onto the deck and immediately pulled her into a cold, wet, and surprisingly powerful embrace. He kissed her full on her gaping mouth, then gave her a lopsided smile. "I knew you wouldn't let me drown."

She gave him a hard shove with every intention of pushing him back into the ocean. "You faker! You weren't drowning!"

He spun away before she could shove him again and waved at the helicopter. "I would have been in trouble in another ten minutes," he said, signaling the helicopter to leave.

"Enjoy your sail, boss," the pilot's voice boomed over the loudspeaker as he arched around the *RoseWind* and headed back toward land.

Sam unfastened his life vest and let it fall to the deck with a soggy plop. Then he grabbed the gaff hook clipped to the rail and snagged his dry sack. "Damn, that water was colder than I expected," he said with a shiver. He headed down the stairway leading below. "Your sails are flapping, Captain. You might want to reset them and get us under way."

Willa stood frozen, watching him disappear below.

What in hell had just happened?

"You were conned is what happened," she muttered, going to the wheel, turning the *RoseWind* back onto her course. "Another Sinclair just pulled the wool over your eyes!" She stomped to the winch and furiously cranked until the mainsail snapped taut and the boat strained forward. "Because you have the word 'sucker' written across your forehead," she continued, resetting the jib. "First Abram and now Sam. And people wonder why you don't want to get married again!"

She stomped back to the wheel, checked her compass heading, and plopped down onto the bench. "Now what am I supposed to do? I am not spending the next five days cooped up on this boat with that . . . that . . . lunatic." She shook her head, unable to believe he'd actually jumped.

"Here's a jacket," Sam said when he appeared on deck, dressed in dry clothes and with a towel covering his wet hair. "Sorry I got you wet when I hugged you, but I was just so damned glad to be alive. You'd better put this on before you catch a chill."

"And you'd better put on a life vest, in case you *accidentally* fall overboard," she shot back, taking the jacket and setting it on the bench.

He sat down beside her and began rubbing his hair dry. "This boat's too small for us to wage war on, Willa."

"You should have thought of that before you bullied your way onboard." She gave him an angry glare. "You and your brothers talk big about walking away from Tidewater International, but that's obviously a big fat lie if you're willing to jump out of a helicopter to get those shares."

He stopped drying and glared right back at her. "I'm not here because of Tidewater. I came to save *you*. You can't get off an elevator without nearly killing yourself—I half expected to find you hanging from the rigging."

She lifted her chin. "I am a damn good sailor."

"So you say." He started drying his hair again but

then suddenly dropped the towel around his neck and eyed her suspiciously. "Unless it's all been an act." He smiled—not very nicely, either. "I'm beginning to suspect you aren't a klutz at all. You knew exactly what Bram was hoping for when he sent you down here, so instead of hurting the old man's feelings, you made sure the three of us wouldn't 'crawl to Maine on our knees' for you. That's why you dressed like a bag lady and got into one mess after another."

"Bag lady? I'll have you know that was Maureen's best business suit, and she was nice enough to lend it to me. You and your grandfather are the duplicitous ones, not me."

He narrowed his eyes. "When have I been anything but up front with you? From the moment you stumbled off that elevator, you've known exactly where I stand."

"I certainly have—right up until Abram left all his worldly possessions to me. Then you were suddenly more than willing to kiss klutzy little me."

He leaned in close, his face only inches from hers. "You are about to go swimming yourself, lady," he said with lethal softness. "I kissed you *before* any of us knew what was in Bram's will."

Willa refused to lean away. "You are getting off *my* boat in Bristol, Mr. Sinclair."

"You and what army are going to make me?"

"Me and the Coast Guard."

He kissed her.

Again!

Before Willa could even gasp in surprise, he pulled her against his chest and had her in a lip lock. Man, oh, man, if he thought he was going to spend the next five days kissing her and . . . and . . .

By God, she'd show him duplicitous.

Willa kissed him back. She leaned into him with the most feminine purr of delight she could muster, kneaded her fingers into his beautifully broad chest, and parted her lips. Willa's hormones started jumping up and down in joy, and she knew—she *knew*—that if she kept this up too long, she was asking for trouble. Spending five days alone at sea with Sam's beautiful chest and her raging hormones in such close proximity might be more than she could handle.

The arms around her tightened, and the mouth exploring hers got aggressive. Drat the man, he was calling her bluff!

Now what? If she got more aggressive herself, they'd both be naked in two minutes.

She'd kiss him as if he was God's gift to women for ninety more seconds, and if he didn't pull away in abject surrender, *then* she'd . . . think of something else. She could endure anything for ninety seconds.

But she hadn't counted on his equally talented hands, especially the one he slid under her sweater to cup her breast.

She moaned in pleasure.

She'd have to remember not to go braless around him, and just as soon as he stopped kissing her, she was putting one on.

What had she been doing again? Oh, yeah, *she* was kissing *Sam* until he cried uncle. So the faker had better back off pretty soon, if he knew what was good for him. And she would have told him exactly that if her mouth wasn't so busy making him sorry he was even born.

Sam ran his thumb over her nipple. Willa arched her back, pressing her breast into his palm as she tried to remember her mission. She didn't think sprawling out on the bench seat, with Sam's wonderful body sprawled on top of her, was what she'd had in mind. But Lord, his weight felt wonderful. It had been so long since she'd been in this position, and it felt so *right*.

What was she supposed to be doing again?

Something about ninety seconds . . .

The cool air suddenly blowing across her breasts brought her back to her senses, but the incredibly warm mouth that covered one of her nipples sent her right back over the edge.

Yup, Sam Sinclair was going to cry uncle any moment now.

"Oh, God, please don't stop," Willa said as she slid her hands under his sweater. She thought she'd died and gone to heaven when her fingers found his soft, deliriously sexy chest hair.

Boy, did she love it when a plan came together.

The bow of the boat suddenly dipped, sending a rogue wave splashing over the side and drenching them both. They slid off the bench and landed on the deck with a thud. Willa thoughtfully broke their fall with her body, though Sam did make a halfhearted attempt to keep from crushing her.

The smile he gave her was not one of abject surrender.

In fact, it looked perversely triumphant.

"I'm giving you a choice," he said, his voice guttural and his eyes sharp with desire. "Either you go below and put on a bra, or *we* go below together, take off all our clothes, and crawl into bed."

If she acted affronted, he would likely smile triumphantly again, and if she showed even a hint of how disconcerted his offer made her, he would probably press his advantage and carry her below himself. But if she did what her hormones were screaming for her to do, they'd *both* be naked, right here on the deck, in front of God and the seagulls.

Dammit, her ex-husband hadn't given her this much trouble.

Willa sensed the *RoseWind* rising on a wave and timed her move accordingly. At the exact moment the boat crested, she shoved Sam with all her might, using the boat's downward dive to her advantage. Sam went rolling into the rail with a yelp of surprise when they hit the bottom of the trough, and Willa scrambled to her feet, ran to the steps, and simply grabbed the jamb and swung herself below.

She turned to close the doors but stopped long enough to watch Sam try to get back on his feet as the *RoseWind* leaped into another swell. "Hey, landlubber," she called to him. "Why don't you see if you can remember how to rig the spinnaker while I'm changing? We've reached the open ocean, so we'll let this beautiful lady run the wind." She paused for effect. "That is, if you're up for some real sailing."

She closed the doors with a laugh and went hunting for some dry clothes—including a bra.

When he wasn't scrambling, cranking, or hoisting his butt off, Sam spent his much-needed rests gaping at Willa. He just couldn't believe the woman he'd known for the last four days and the woman standing at the helm were one and the same. She appeared determined to push the *RoseWind* right to the edge of the boat's limits, utilizing every last centimeter of sail. Sam was beginning to realize that his knowledge of sailing was just a footnote compared with hers. She hadn't been boasting when she'd told him she was a damn fine sailor, and as soon as he got over his amazement, he would tell her so.

They were both tethered with safety lines, wearing life vests and dressed in rain gear—not because it was storming but because Willa was attacking the swells like a woman possessed.

Or a woman determined to redirect her passion?

She'd blindsided him with her response to his kiss. He'd only been trying to shut her up, and she had turned the tables on him. He hadn't been bluffing when he'd asked her to go below and get undressed; he'd wanted to bury himself inside her so badly he'd almost taken her right there on the deck.

Sam staggered to the helm and plopped down onto the bench in utter exhaustion. "This has been a hell of a run, but can we please call it a day, Captain? I'm bruised and beat and in need of sustenance."

She looked down her cute little nose at him, smiled in satisfaction, and nodded toward the bow. "I'll slack off the wind, and you haul in the spinnaker. *Then* you can go below and start supper."

"You expect me to crew *and* cook?"

"I expect you to take orders like the stowaway you are."

Sam braced himself against a giant swell that crashed over the side and drenched them both. Willa laughed with delight, and he violently shivered. The crazy woman was having the time of her life.

"Do you own a sailboat, Willa?"

"I do now. And she's a beauty."

"Does your father still own the schooner you grew up on?"

She didn't look at him. "No, the *Cat's Tail* went down in a violent squall a hundred miles off St. Maarten seven years ago. The crew survived, but my mother and father didn't. The first mate told Shelby and me that Daddy died trying to save Mom."

"I'm sorry. I would have liked to have met Captain Kent and your mom. So," he said, gritting his teeth against the pain of standing up, "do we sail all night or find a place to set anchor?"

"We sail. I'll take the first watch. There's a storm forming off the Carolinas and coming up the coast, and I'm hoping to ride this wind ahead of it and be tucked into Keelstone Cove before it hits."

Sam staggered to the spinnaker winch. Another day like today would surely kill him. He doubted he'd be able to get out of bed in the morning, much less hoist a sail. He called up the very last of his reserves, released the spinnaker line when he felt the sail slacken, and started gathering it up as it fell to the deck, fighting the wind for control of the cloth.

Mutiny was beginning to look like a viable option.

But another mind-blowing kiss might be equally effective. It would definitely go farther toward gaining Willa's affections than setting her adrift in a lifeboat.

Chapter Eleven

Yesterday's kiss must have been even more mind-blowing than he realized, because he was having one hell of a dream. Sam actually stopped breathing, afraid the naked woman crammed into the small bunk beside him, running her fingers through his chest hair, would disappear if he woke up. Either this was *really* wishful thinking, or it had been way too long since he'd been laid.

When she started licking his nipple, Sam sat up with a shout of surprise, only to slam into the bulkhead and fall back onto his pillow with a groaned curse.

"Sorry. Didn't mean to startle you," his naked dream woman said in an amused whisper. She brushed her fingers lightly over his temple. "Want me to kiss it and make it better?"

"Willamina?" Sam choked out. "What are you doing?"

"Accepting the offer you made. I don't like wearing a bra if I don't have to, so I decided to take off all my clothes and crawl into bed with you."

Had he died jumping out of the helicopter, and this was heaven? Or had he landed in hell? She definitely was naked, and he burned to accept her offer, but he worried that making love to Willa right now might actually hurt their chance of having a future together.

"You've changed your mind," she said, her voice suddenly distant. She started backing out of the bunk. "Sorry. Go back to sleep. It's half an hour or so to sunrise."

"No, wait!" Sam said, sitting up and reaching for her. He managed to catch her wrist and pull her back on top of him. "I haven't changed my mind." He wrapped his arms around her when she continued to try wriggling away. "I'm just surprised, is all. I thought you didn't like me very much."

"I don't."

He smiled at that. "Then what's going on here, Willa?"

"To put it bluntly, I'm using you. Sometime around three this morning, I finally made a deal with my hormones. I promised to give them free rein for the next four days, if they'll go back into hibernation the moment we drop anchor in Keelstone Cove." She shifted on top of him, sliding her naked breasts across his chest—snapping *his* hormones to attention. "I thought we could use each other for the rest of the voyage. I would put an end to my sexual drought, and you would finally rid yourself of this foolish notion of marrying me."

"I see."

"And then we'll both be free to spend the next three months figuring out how to break Abram's will."

"Let me get this straight. You've decided that a four-day sex marathon will give us our fill of each other, and when we reach Maine, we'll go back to . . . business as usual?"

"Right. You have a shipping empire to run, and I have caskets to make. But in the meantime," she said, trailing her fingers in maddening circles over his chest, "we might as well have a bit of fun."

Now what in hell was she up to? "I packed clothes and food in my dry sack, but I don't believe I packed any condoms."

Her fingers started dancing across his chest again. "No problem. I've got that covered."

"You travel with a box of condoms?"

"No. I've simply taken care of it on my end." She gave his chest hair a gentle tug. "Yes or no, Sinclair. My offer expires in exactly sixty seconds."

A warning growl was the only answer he gave, rolling them over until she was lying beneath him. He captured her maddening fingers and pinned her hands above her head, then brought his mouth down on hers when she started to protest.

He was done trying to figure her out. The lady wanted some fun for the next four days, did she? Either he was the luckiest bastard ever born, or Willamina Kent was even more naive than she was cute. Whether she knew it or not, she had just jumped out of the frying pan and into the fire—and sealed her fate.

Sam used his knees to spread hers, nestling himself between her thighs, and dove his tongue into her mouth when she gasped at the realization that he was also naked.

And ready. And willing. And definitely able.

It was all he could do not to slide inside her right then. She tasted sweet, of jam and peanut butter. Willa had obviously eaten a sandwich before she'd crawled into bed with him, apparently in preparation for the upcoming marathon.

Was there anything sexier than a woman who went after what she wanted?

Sam broke the kiss and rose onto one elbow, which was as far as their cramped quarters would allow. He moved his free hand over her body while gently rocking his hips into hers. She made soft mewling sounds, wiggling beneath him, and he wished there were more light so he could see her face.

Giving her a taste of her own sweet torture, he traced a finger up her torso, first over one breast and then the other—paying particular attention to her nipples—and then up over her chin to her lips. She wriggled frantically, her breathing growing labored as she tried to position herself so he was poised to enter her.

"Patience," he whispered.

"Oh, God," she groaned, trying to tug free as she arched into him. "You're one of *those* guys."

His hand stopped. "One of what guys?"

"Methodical. Slow. All touchy-feely."

Sam forced himself to relax. He had to remember that this was Willamina; anything could come blurting out of that mouth of hers. "Is there some sort of Maine trick I haven't heard about, where people can make love without touching?"

Her chest rose on an exasperated sigh, causing her nipples to brush his forearm. "It's been five *years*. Get on with it already, Sin—"

He kissed her to shut her up.

She tried to push his tongue out, apparently not happy with his kissing, either.

"Now what?" he asked, wondering if this was ever going to happen.

"I want you to stop kissing me every time you don't like what—ooohhh." She moaned as he eased inside her. "Oh, God, yes! Ohmygod, that feels so good."

Finally, something she liked.

He rather liked it, too.

He released her hands to prop himself up on both his arms, which in turned freed *her* to touch *him*. Apparently, the no-touching rule only applied to him. She dug her fingers into his chest, arching her spine and throwing back her head on another moan of pleasure.

She was warm and tight, and she screamed so loudly when Sam started moving inside her that he went utterly still.

"Don't stop!" she cried, lifting her hips and straining against him. "Move!"

He moved.

She screamed again.

He stopped again. It was taking a toll on him; beads of sweat broke out on his forehead.

She actually punched him in the shoulder. "Don't stop!"

"I'm hurting you!"

"No, you're driving me crazy! *Move*, Sinclair."

Okay, she was a screamer. He kind of liked that, as it gave him immediate feedback on how he was doing.

Apparently, he was doing quite well, because the moment he started moving again, Willa started in again, her unabashed cries of bliss bouncing around the cramped bunk.

Sam started to grin, but his own bliss finally caught up with him, and he turned his attention to concentrating on how wonderful she felt beneath him. They fit together perfectly, her beautifully curvy body cradling his, her uninhibited passion making his heart race. He could feel her coiling around him, straining into each thrust, lost in the grip of her building release.

It arrived on a tidal wave of convulsing heat, her inner muscles tugging Sam to the edge of restraint. He thrust into her hard and fast and deep, gritting his teeth to hold off his own release for as long as possible.

Willa carried on for what seemed like forever, and when Sam finally lost his control, he pulled out and came on her belly. He collapsed beside her with a groan of satisfaction, cupped her buttocks, and pulled her body snugly against him.

She stiffened, bringing her hands up to his chest, to push him away. Sam gave a long-suffering sigh. Honest to God, the woman's moods changed direction more often than the wind.

"What?" he asked, refusing to let her wriggle away. "Is it also against the rules to cuddle? I thought women liked to enjoy the afterglow. You'll have to give me a play book so I know what's expected of me."

"I have to go check the sails. They're fluttering."

He lifted himself up slightly and listened, then relaxed back onto the pillow. "They sound fine to me."

"And that's why I'm the captain, and you're not."

He splayed his fingers across her back, still refusing to release her, and toyed with the dimple at the base of her spine.

She immediately arched to get away from his touch— which pushed her beautifully plump breasts into his chest. Sam kissed the tip of her nose. At least, that's where he'd been aiming, but he ended up kissing her hair when she ducked to bury her face in his neck. Her cheeks felt unusually hot, and he suspected she was blushing.

"You're not fat, Willa."

She muttered something against his throat.

"What was that?" he asked loudly. "Sorry, but my ears are still ringing."

She popped up, glaring at him. "Look, I get a bit loud sometimes, okay? It's not like we disturbed the neighbors or anything. You got a problem with a little noise, Sinclair?"

His aim was dead-on this time when he kissed her nose. "Nope," He gave her lush behind a gentle squeeze. "I like that sort of noise. It lets me know I'm doing my job."

She snorted, but when she buried her face in his neck again, Sam realized her blush had kicked up several notches. Maybe he shouldn't tease her, but damn it to hell, she was driving him crazy. Ending her sexual drought didn't seem to have done a damn thing to mellow her out.

The *RoseWind* took a sharp dip into a trough, and Sam cupped Willa's head to protect her just as his own head slammed into the end of the bunk. "Cuddle time's over." He rolled onto his hands and knees above her, straining to see her face in the first shafts of sunrise filtering through the portal. "I've never sailed at night before. It feels like driving with blindfolds on."

"That's why they put alarms on the navigational equipment. They would have sounded if we'd strayed off course," she said. "You get dressed and go check that sail. I'll be up in a minute." '

He bumped his head again, since the bunk was no taller than it was wide. "If I'd been expecting company, I would have chosen one of the bigger back bunks."

There was enough light for him to see that Willa could sit up without her head touching. She had the blanket tucked under her chin, leaving only her tangled hair and her huge eyes exposed. He was just reaching for his dry sack when he heard her sigh.

"Do you know why they call it making love missionary-style?"

What in hell was she up to? One minute, she was sending him away; the next, she was suddenly chatty. It must have something to do with those hormones. "No, why is it called missionary-style?"

"Because in colonial days, young couples heading out to do missionary work often got married just before they left to sail abroad. Their bunks were no bigger than this one, and the only way they could consummate their marriages was in that position—thus, it became known as the missionary style."

"Who told you that?"

"Shelby."

"And who told her?"

"One of the crew Dad had hired for our autumn run down to the Caribbean." She canted her head in thought. "She was eighteen, I think. I was twelve."

"And you knew what she was talking about at age twelve?"

She lifted that cute little chin of hers. "I might have been home-schooled, but I had plenty of friends in town. And, I'll have you know, I lost my virginity at fourteen."

"You did not."

Her chin inched up. "Well, I would have, if Dad hadn't come below when he did." She grinned. "Daddy and I were both surprised that Kevin couldn't swim. Though I don't think that would have stopped Dad from throwing him overboard in the middle of the Gulf of Maine."

Her eyes were focused not on his face but on his chest. He also noticed that her gaze dropped a bit lower every so often.

The little witch! She was sitting there covered up like a nun, telling him tall tales so she could ogle his body!

She must have realized the jig was up, for she frowned suddenly, her face bright pink. "I hear the jib flapping. You'd better go winch it down."

"Before or after I dress?" he drawled, slowly reaching for his dry sack. Still facing her, he dug around inside the sack, found some clean underwear and pants, and, just as slowly, slid them on. He heard her sigh when he slipped a heavy jersey over his head and tucked it into his pants.

He turned away so she wouldn't see his smile and stepped over to the galley sink. He ran a cloth under the water, wrung it out, then tossed it to her. "Here, so you can clean up," he said, turning to head up the stairs.

"Wait."

He stopped on the step and ducked his head to see her.

"Why did you pull out at the last minute? I told you I had the contraceptive thing covered."

"Let's just call me cautious, okay?"

She nodded. "So, you really *don't* want to marry me and get me pregnant." She sighed with obvious relief. "That's good, because we both know it would never work, anyway."

Sam turned to face her. "You don't think so? Why not?"

"Because we don't really like each other," she said, sounding exasperated that he couldn't see the obvious.

"I never said I didn't like you."

"Only because you're too polite to come right out and say it." She lifted her chin. "Since we've met, you've spent half the time laughing at me and the other half wanting to strangle me."

He took a step toward her. "What about now, Willa? Can you sense which way I'm leaning right now?"

Her eyes grew huge, and she clutched the blanket to her throat. She suddenly pointed at the deck over her head. "Something is definitely wrong with that jib," she said quickly. "Hurry, Sam! If you don't get it winched down, we're going to lose it."

He hesitated just long enough to glare at her, then turned and slowly climbed the stairs up to the deck. Honest to God, if he didn't strangle her before they reached Maine, it would only be because he'd thrown her overboard instead.

Willa slapped the wet cloth to her burning cheeks. Sweet mother of God, was she suicidal? Crawling into bed with Sam Sinclair had been as bright as a four-watt light bulb.

But who knew hormones were capable of throwing their weight around like that? She'd spent half the night sitting at the helm, dozing off and on, daydreaming *and* sleep dreaming about Sam's mouth on her breast. All she'd been able to think about was his offer to go below yesterday. She knew he'd kissed her only to shut her up, but she never should have tried to prove to herself that she was immune to his . . . his chest.

She was in such big trouble. Maybe if she hadn't been living like a nun for the last five years, she could handle a brief, casual affair. But jeez Louise, making love after such a long drought had felt unbelievably, wonderfully good. Hot and heart-poundingly fulfilling.

She couldn't remember ever having an orgasm that intense before. It had been . . . it had . . . damn, she wanted to do it again right now. But she had to get through the entire day first, because she sure as heck wasn't getting naked in the daylight, when Mr. Touchy-Feely could also *see* her. Next time, she intended to cop a few more feels of her own, and not just of his chest, either. The guy had an amazing butt as well.

That was, assuming there would be a next time. Maybe he wouldn't be in such a hurry to get naked with her again. Willa knew she wasn't any man's idea of a dream lover; she was a tad loud, in a rush most of the time, and worried about her body to the point that the less a guy felt her up, the better she liked it.

Willa scrubbed her face with the cloth, then reached under the blanket and wiped her belly. Imagine him not believing her about having taken care of the contraceptive. He knew she never wanted children, so why hadn't he taken her at her word?

Unless he was only trying to make her *think* he no longer wanted to marry her and get her pregnant. Or maybe he'd been lied to before by women hoping to buy their way into the Sinclair empire with a baby.

"Don't you dare start making excuses for him," she muttered, crawling off the bunk. "Remember what he has at stake here. You're only a means to an end."

"Willa?" Sam called down. "You might want to get up here sooner rather than later."

What was wrong? "I'm coming!" she called back, pulling on jeans and slipping a baggy sweatshirt over her head as she ran to the stairs, barefoot.

"What does that look like to you?" he asked the moment she stepped on deck and looked at where he was pointing.

"It's a water spout." She pointed to the east of it. "And there's another one." She studied them for several seconds to discern their direction of travel, a bit surprised to see the natural phenomenon this far north this early in the season. She smiled at the ocean's version of a tornado, then headed below to find her socks and shoes.

"Wait!" Sam said. "What are we supposed to do?"

She held on to the sides of the hatchway and stared at him. "I thought you and your brothers sailed with Abram all the time."

"In the sound," he growled, glancing over his shoulder at the spouts, which were a good fifteen miles away. "And only in fair weather. The *RoseWind* was Bram's and Grammy's passion, not ours."

She nodded. "Then I suggest you keep a close eye on them. That thunderstorm is traveling faster than we are, and if it suddenly decides to turn north, we just might find ourselves on some yellow brick road in Kansas."

His eyes narrowed, but at the sound of distant thunder, he turned to face the squall heading out to sea to their south.

Willa backed down the steps and went hunting for her shoes with a giggle. Man, oh, man, was this going to be a fun four days or what?

Chapter Twelve

As impromptu voyages went, Willa supposed this one had no more problems than could be expected; the nights were absolutely heaven, and her hormones definitely were getting plenty of exercise. But during the daylight hours . . . Well, for her sailing-challenged stowaway, this was probably the voyage from hell.

To begin with, Sam was always either eating or looking for something to eat. He *was* burning an awful lot of calories—both during the day and well into the night. But he'd already gone through the small supply of food she'd brought, as well as what little food he'd packed in his dry sack. They were still at least a day from home, and Willa figured she would have to start fishing.

When he wasn't eating, Sam was tripping over the rigging, slamming into the boom, or nearly falling overboard. He just couldn't seem to find his sea legs.

He had a small cut on his left cheek and a knot the size of an egg on his temple, and three of his fingers were taped together because he'd caught them in the mainsail winch yesterday.

If this trip ended up killing Sam, Ben and Jesse would be forced to draw straws to see which of *them* would have to marry her, and then she'd have to find a way to ditch each of them. Though she could claim it wasn't her fault that Sam couldn't sail his way out of a wet paper bag, she didn't think she could explain three unexplained deaths. Four if she included Abram. After all, the old man had died while in her employ.

They'd all be buried in really nice caskets, though.

"How did you find that can of sardines?" she asked when Sam plopped down with a groan beside the wheel. "I hid it in the oven because I knew you'd already checked there. Did you think the food fairy had paid a visit since the last time you looked?"

He popped the top off the can and held it up with a smile. "She obviously did."

"I was saving those sardines to use for bait."

He snorted. "You can use the dead flesh hanging off me instead. I haven't been this sore since Andy Simmons beat me up in kindergarten."

"I hope you've noticed that I've refrained from laughing at your klutziness," she said, working hard not to smile. He looked positively pathetic.

When he finally finished draining the last drop of

oil from the can, he eyed her speculatively. "I just figured out why you're always tripping over yourself. If the
floor's not moving, you can't function. You grew up on
a swaying deck."

"The floor of my factory doesn't move, and I'm not a
klutz at work. I've never met anyone with such a huge
appetite."

"For food or . . ." His gaze dropped to her chest.

Willa immediately reached for her jacket. "We're
definitely in the Gulf of Maine. It's getting downright
cold."

"We could put the *RoseWind* on autopilot and go
below," he suggested, his deep blue eyes snagging her
gaze. "And share our body heat."

"The deal is we sail by day and share our body heat
only at night." Not that she wouldn't love to see him
naked in daylight. But that would mean Sam could also
see her, and her mama always told Willa that a smart
woman kept the mystery alive in a relationship.

Not that she and Sam *had* a relationship.

He sighed and actually started licking the empty sar-
dine can clean, a drop of oil glistening on his four-day
growth of beard. "How far are we from Keelstone Cove?"
he asked, eyeing the tin forlornly.

"We'll be there this time tomorrow, if the wind
holds."

"Who were you talking to on the radio a few minutes ago?"

"Clark Kent."

Sam blinked. "As in Superman?"

"He's my cousin." Willa smiled. "And when he's not out saving the world, you'll find him on his boat, the *Lois Lane*, hauling lobster traps." She nodded at the expanse of ocean off their starboard side. "He's fishing about seventy miles northeast of us."

"What sort of twisted parents name their kid Clark with the last name Kent? Your cousin must have spent his childhood having to live up to his namesake."

"Not many people challenge Clark. He was always big for his age and didn't stop growing until his mid-twenties. He finally topped out at six-foot-three and two hundred and fifty pounds." She shot Sam a smile. "He was a year ahead of me in school, and I had to go to his senior prom with him because the girls wouldn't date him."

"I thought high school girls liked big, strong boys."

"They like jocks. Clark was like the fictional Clark Kent, only more so. He was shy, geeky, and, um . . . a bit of a klutz."

"It runs in the family?" Sam drawled.

Willa shot him a glare. "Clark finally grew into his size his junior year of college and came home that summer a completely new man. That was also the summer his father died. He was forced to quit school when he inherited his dad's federal lobster license and had to support his three younger sisters and his mother."

"Did he ever finish college?"

"No. He decided he actually prefers fishing to veterinary work. He says lobster bites aren't nearly as painful as getting kicked by a horse."

"I'm looking forward to meeting your cousin."

Willa shrugged. "You probably won't get the chance. He heads out before dawn and doesn't get back until real late. He's busy this week moving his traps to deeper water, and you'll be heading back to New York once we drop anchor."

Sam shook his head, eyeing her speculatively. "This little trip has shown me that I'm long overdue for a vacation. I thought I'd take over Bram's remaining two weeks of rent on your cottage. From what I saw of it on the video tape, the place looks downright peaceful."

Willa's hormones immediately started doing a happy dance. He was planning on hanging around *two more weeks?* How in heck was she going to stop herself from walking over to that cottage in the middle of the night and crawling into bed with him?

"Oh, no you don't. There's only a few days of rent left, and the lease is nontransferable."

"Then I'll find another place in Keelstone Cove to stay. Maybe a bed and breakfast—that way I won't have to do my own cooking."

Dammit dammit dammit. "You will not! We had a deal. Five days of fun, then we both get on with our separate lives."

"*We* didn't have a deal, Willa. *You* set the rules for this trip, and I followed your orders. But once we dock, you're no longer the captain." He shrugged. "I was just hoping to see why Bram thought Keelstone Cove was a good place to die." His gaze locked on hers again. "I don't understand why my staying for a couple of weeks would be a problem for you."

"You don't understa—" She took a calming breath. No need to get excited; she just had to explain the situation to him. "We just spent the last four nights making love like monkeys, and you expect to live next door for two weeks and . . . and . . ." She threw up her hands when he gave her a blank look. "Dammit," she growled. "You can't turn hormones on and off like a water faucet!"

"Then let's keep them turned on for two more weeks."

"No! We can't sleep together once I reach home!"

He frowned at her obvious alarm. "Why not? Is there a local ordinance that says two consenting adults can't share a bed?" He shook his head. "You Mainers have some really weird notions about lovemaking, you know that?" He gave her his infamous Sam Sinclair smile, which started her hormones dancing again. "We just have to be discreet, Willa."

"In Keelstone Cove?" She snorted and plopped down onto the bench beside him. She never should have fished him out of the ocean in the first place.

Sam immediately threw his arm around her, hauled

her up against his side, and kissed her hair. Willa cringed. She was going to smell like sardines all day.

"Since Peg will be staying with you," he said, "you'll have to sneak over to my cottage after she turns in for the night." He kissed her on her cheek this time, his beard catching her hair. "I promise to kick you out before daylight, so you can sneak back home."

Willa straightened away when she heard the amusement in his voice. "Keelstone Cove has a population of twelve hundred and forty-six people, and everyone knows everyone's business. And if they don't, they're just as liable to make up something."

She leaned forward and turned the wheel slightly to adjust their course, then pivoted on the bench to face him. "Just last year, the coffee-shop club decided Mary-Jane Simpson had a thing for Rory Peterson, even though Mary-Jane had just married Chad six months earlier. Rumors of their affair spread all over town within a week."

"And Mary-Jane didn't have a thing for Rory?"

"He was old enough to be her father!"

"So the town gossips hurt her new marriage?"

"It turned out that a week after the rumors began, Mary-Jane and Rory ran off together," she muttered. She grabbed the front of his jacket and gave it a tug. "The coffee clubbers are notoriously good, Sam. They can sniff out a scandal before the participants themselves even know they're involved."

"And my renting your cottage is scandalous?"

"For me—a single, eligible woman—to have an equally eligible man living in my dooryard is going to start a tidal wave of rumors."

"So what?" He peeled her hand off his jacket and held it in his. "You're how old?"

"Twenty-nine."

"Okay. You're a twenty-nine-year-old, totally independent woman who has the right to rent to anyone she chooses, as well as the right to *sleep* with whoever she chooses. You can't stop the rumors, but you can rise above them. So don't even try to be discreet. What can they possibly do to you?"

She stood up, glaring at him. "Since my parents died, the entire town has felt it's their duty to take over parenting me. I have endured everyone in town trying to marry me off for the last *five years*. I swear, they didn't even wait until the ink was dry on my divorce. I can't tell you the men they've thrown at me—even tourists! Some poor unsuspecting guy will walk into the coffee shop, and if he's not wearing a ring, he's fair game. Before he knows it, they're persuading him that Keelstone Cove is a great place to live—especially if he were to fall in love with a wonderful woman who just happens to own a thriving business. Then they drag the poor schmuck out to Kent Caskets, because every perverse tourist wants to see a casket factory, and then they suggest wouldn't it be nice if the two of us had dinner together."

Sam was laughing so hard he was holding his belly. "You're kidding, right?"

"No, I'm not! Sam, if you spend even one night in Keelstone Cove, you're going to find yourself facing down the marriage posse. And I'm only one of five eligible women in town they might decide you're perfect for." She scrunched up her nose. "Although I *am* considered the spinster in the group, so they're trying to get me married off first. Only they keep telling me to sell my business, because no one wants to be married to a casket maker!" she finished loudly, since Sam was laughing so hard he actually fell off the bench.

"It's not one stinking bit funny, Sinclair! How would you like to have a bunch of busybodies butting into your love life?"

He leaned against the bench and grinned up at her. "I already have, Willa. Bram could have given lessons to your marriage posse." His eyes suddenly widened. "Hell, I wouldn't be surprised if he had been *leading* your posse for the last six weeks. Your coffee clubbers probably helped him draft that bequest."

Willa was so horrified by that possibility that her knees buckled, and she landed on the deck beside Sam. "Come to think of it, Abram never showed up at Kent Caskets until after ten every morning," she said, staring off at the horizon. "And he did smell of coffee and bacon. He must have been going to the diner before he came to my factory." She turned to Sam. "What are we going to do? If we show up in Keelstone Cove together, they're going to make my life hell. I probably can't even go home now! If anyone knows about Abram's will, I'm toast."

He pulled her against his side again and leaned back against the bench. "We could get married. That would shut them up."

She shuddered.

He chuckled and gave her a squeeze. "Then stand up to the bastards, Willa. Sail straight into Keelstone Cove as if you own the damn town—which you probably *could* if you wanted, considering your new net worth." He used his finger to lift her chin to look at him. "No-body can make you do anything you don't want to, Willa. Not your neighbors, not Bram, and not me."

She eyed him suspiciously. "So you'll stop bugging me to marry you and help me break Abram's will?"

"I only said I can't *make* you marry me. I didn't say I wouldn't keep asking."

"But why?" she cried, pulling away. "Why would you even consider marrying me?"

"Because I love you."

She gaped at him for several seconds, then scrambled to her feet. "You can't fall in love with someone in only a week! You're just saying that because you don't want Warren Cobb to get those shares."

He stood up and faced her, his feet planted against the sway of the deck, his hands shoved into his jacket pockets. "There isn't a damn thing I can do or say that will make you believe I couldn't care less what happens to Tidewater International. But I swear, Willa, my heart hasn't been in that business for years."

"Then why were you so hot to be the new CEO?"

"I told you, and so did Ben and Jesse, that we all wanted it because Bram was still alive. But Ben is the only one who has any genuine interest in Tidewater. So even if you and I do get married and you turn your shares over to me, I will use them to vote Ben in as CEO."

"Then why didn't Ben offer to marry me?"

"Because he doesn't love you."

Willa drew in a shaky breath. This was getting them exactly nowhere. She turned her back to him and silently walked to the bow of the boat. *Nobody* fell in love in eight days, and nobody as handsome and rich and self-assured as Sam Sinclair was going to fall in love with her.

Which was perfectly fine, because she sure as heck wasn't ever falling in love with anyone ever again. It was bad enough that she loved Shelby and Jennifer and Cody with all her heart.

Not for the first time since the accident, Willa was tempted to sail into the sunset and find a deserted island. She could drop Sam off on the town dock, go home to pack some clothes and supplies, and point the *RoseWind* toward the southern horizon. Shelby and Jennifer and Cody would miss her at first, but they'd eventually get over it. And Sam could clean up the mess Abram had made and eventually find someone he could *really* love and get on with his own life.

She stared out at the ocean and sighed, wondering why that was such a depressing thought.

Since he'd grown accustomed to going to bed and making love to Willa for half the night, Sam was unable to sleep despite being utterly exhausted. He was back up in the front bunk, alone, and thoroughly at odds with himself.

He'd been more surprised than Willa that morning when he'd told her that he loved her. He wasn't sure when he'd fallen in love with her, but he'd said the words out loud, by God, and he wasn't taking them back. Hell, why else would he have volunteered to be the one to marry her? He wasn't into self-sacrifice, so it must be love—or something real close to it. And considering the position his grandfather had put her in, the truth was the best he could offer Willa and the least she deserved.

Abram Sinclair had been able to accomplish what the marriage posse hadn't in just six short weeks, proving that money and power were amazing tools in the hands of someone who knew how to use them.

Dammit, he was a successful, intelligent business-man in his own right—so why couldn't he find a solution to this mess? Willa had asked him to help her

break Bram's will, but he'd dismissed the idea because . . . because . . .

Probably because he didn't want to. Because if he
found a loophole, where would that leave him with
Willa?

He snorted. "Exactly where you are right now, you
idiot—sleeping alone."

But breaking the will *would* solve one major problem: without the Tidewater shares hanging over their
heads, Willa couldn't accuse him of wanting to marry
her only to get them.

"Then find the loophole," he muttered. "Secure Tidewater, then go after the woman with everything you've
got, Mr. Badass Businessman."

Acquiring a wife couldn't be any different from acquiring a company. He just had to concentrate on finding a loophole, while spending every available minute
showing Willa he really did love her.

Chapter Thirteen

Sam stood at the bow as Willa guided the engine-powered *RoseWind* through a maze of moored boats. He was supposed to be securing the sails, but after getting his thumb eaten by a winch for the third time in three days, he'd had enough. What could she do to him, anyway? Fire him? Throw him overboard? Starve him to death?

He'd already taken an unexpected swim yesterday when a rogue wave had washed him over the rail, getting dragged by his safety harness for nearly two miles before Willa had gotten the boat stopped. As for starving—he'd awakened this morning to find it hadn't been a thick, juicy steak he'd been gnawing on in his dreams but his pillow.

He *wished* she would fire him.

"Why does the sign on the harbor master's office say Prime Point and not Keelstone Cove?" he asked.

"Because this *is* Prime Point. That storm is right on our tail, and I want the *RoseWind* on a mooring and battened down before it hits. We'd be cutting it too close to continue on to Keelstone. Check the front latches after you fix those ropes," she said, apparently hoping to hang on to her authority a while longer.

Not a chance. Sam's only focus right now was to set foot on a nonmoving surface, stuff himself until he couldn't breathe, then lay his head on a pillow that wasn't swaying. She owned the *RoseWind*; she could damn well batten down her own hatches. His conscription had ended the moment they'd gotten within swimming distance of land.

"So, how are we getting to Keelstone Cove from here?"

"*We're* not getting anywhere. I radioed a friend who lives in town, and he's giving *me* a ride home," she said, scowling when he didn't move. "A bus heading south goes through here every morning. Maybe you could stow away on *it*."

Sam turned to hide his smile. When he'd come up on deck that morning, Willa was in a bad mood, and it had gone downhill from there. He wished he'd known that telling a woman he loved her was such a turn-off; it would have saved him countless Dear Jane dinners.

He could see the main pier was crowded with trucks,

along with a small army of people hurrying to off-load their day's catch. The harbor was busier than Times Square at rush hour, and fishing boats zoomed within inches of each other. Willa blithely guided the *RoseWind* through the turmoil, and Sam scrambled to brace himself when a boat laden with lobster traps suddenly veered straight toward them.

"Willa Kent!" the man at the helm called out as he approached, causing Willa to idle to a halt. The fisherman reversed his own engine, gently inching his boat alongside the *RoseWind* with amazing precision. "I went to your factory to buy a box for Gramps yesterday, but they told me you were in New York City. You gonna be back at work this afternoon? Funeral's day after tomorrow."

Sam's jaw dropped. This guy had stopped them in the middle of the harbor to buy a casket? He was pushing sixty; how the hell old was his grandfather?

"I'm sorry to hear Gramps died, Cyrus," Willa said, walking to the rail. "I'm going to miss his outrageous stories."

"Now, don't you go feeling sorry for him, girlie. Gramps went to bed every night since Grandma died praying he wouldn't wake up in the morning. He was smiling when we found him."

Willa glanced out to sea, then back at the fisherman. "Give me a couple of hours, and I'll meet you at my factory. We'll find him a really nice casket."

The fisherman crossed his heavily muscled arms over his barrel chest. "At a forty-percent discount, I reckon. Better yet, you got any seconds? Gramps wouldn't mind a few dings and scratches, if'n the deal was sweet enough."

Sam sat down on the forward doghouse. Now he was haggling over the price?

"I give a thirty-percent discount to locals," Willa said, breaking into her first smile of the day. She leaned over the rail and dropped her voice. "But I have a beautiful rock maple casket I can sell you at half-price. It was a special order, but the client's family decided to cremate him, so they never took it. I think Gramps would be right proud to be resting in Maine maple."

"Sixty percent off. If'n it was a special order, you're stuck with it. I'd be doing you a favor to get it off your factory floor."

Willa stepped back to the wheel of the *RoseWind*. "Half-price, Cyrus, and it's cash and carry."

He scowled, obviously not liking being outtraded. "I'll be there at six sharp. You ferrying this Sengatti to Emmett for repairs?" he asked, suddenly as congenial as before the negotiations. "I seen him waiting over at the public pier."

"No, the *RoseWind* belongs to me," she said, pushing on the throttle as she waved good-bye to the gaping fisherman. "See you at six, Cyrus. And bring your brothers. Rock maple is heavy," she finished, darting the *RoseWind* between two lobster boats leaving the main pier. "That mainsail is not going to tuck itself into that boot," she told Sam.

"It's going to have to," he said, staying put. "You're not paying me enough to move."

"You ate your weight in food, Sinclair."

"And I've still lost twenty pounds." He stood up when he spotted a lobster shack next to the pier. He tossed over the bumper, then grabbed the front line, which he handed to the waiting man as Willa inched the *RoseWind* against the dock. Before she had even shut off the engine, Sam scrambled over the rail, stepped onto the pier, and fell flat on his face.

"Whoa there," the man said with a laugh, helping him to his feet. "It'll take you a while to get back your land legs. How'd she run, Willa?" he asked, dismissing Sam by handing him back the rope and walking toward the stern. "Could you feel the difference in that hull design?"

"She practically sailed herself."

Sam didn't hear the rest of Willa's response, because he was already—very carefully, so he wouldn't fall again—making his way toward the lobster shack.

"Wait up, Sam." The man, who had to be in his late seventies, was loping toward him. "Where are you going?"

"As far away from Captain Bligh as I can get."

The man chuckled, then held out his hand. "Emmett Sengatti. I'm sorry for your loss. Bram was a hell of a man."

Sam shook his hand, surprised by the powerful grip—until he remembered that Emmett Sengatti used to hand-build boats for a living. "Yes, he was. Thank you."

"You're not going to help Willa secure the *RoseWind* before the storm hits?"

Sam glanced down the pier to see her tucking the mainsail into its storm boot. "Trust me, she has everything under control."

Emmett shook his head, though Sam noticed a distinct glint come into the older man's eyes. "If I was trying to persuade a girl to marry me, I sure as hell wouldn't be abandoning her when there's work to be done."

Sam stiffened. "What makes you think I'm trying to get her to marry me? For that matter, how the hell do you even know who I am?"

"Bram spent many evenings at my place these last six weeks," Emmett said without taking offense. "Our little chats usually centered on you three boys, and you look exactly like your picture. As for the marrying part, Spencer is holding money from both Bram and me—and your showing up with Willa just made me a thousand bucks poorer."

He lowered his voice. "Bram said you *might* be the one to recognize what a gem Willamina is, but he also thought Ben might go after her, since Bram knew he's more interested in Tidewater than you are. I was guessing Jesse."

"You two *bet* on which one of us would marry her?"

"No, we bet on which one of you would try." Emmett glanced over his shoulder. "I tried my damndest to talk Bram out of writing that will, but he was convinced his plan would work." He crossed his arms over his chest with a smile. "Though you have me to thank for his leaving in that loophole."

"There's a loophole?" Sam said in surprise.

"Big enough to sail a cargo ship through."

"What is it?"

"If I have to *tell* you, I reckon you don't deserve to marry anyone—especially Willa."

Sam seriously thought about shoving the man off the pier.

"The way I see it," Emmett said, "you've got three choices. You can hold that bequest over Willa's head and *make* her marry you, you can find the loophole and then pursue Willa because you really want her, or you can walk away from the entire mess. Like you're doing right now, leaving her to batten down the *RoseWind* all by herself."

Emmett eyed Sam speculatively. "Walking away might appear to be the easiest thing in the world, but it's been my experience that guilt is a hell of an anchor to drag around the rest of your life. But then, Willa would know more about that sort of thing."

Everything suddenly clicked into place. "Bram came

to Maine because of you. But why? He rarely ever mentioned your name, except when he was buying the *RoseWind*."

"If you didn't want anyone to find you, would you hide in your usual haunts? I met Abram nearly fifty years ago, when he was attending Maine Maritime Academy over in Castine. We've always kept in touch." He shrugged. "When your grandfather needed a place to run off to, he called me."

"That makes sense, I suppose. But how does Willa figure into all of this? Why was Bram renting from her instead of staying with you? And what's your relationship to Willa? Did you introduce my grandfather to her?"

Emmett shook his head. "Two ornery old men living together is the quickest way to end a friendship. Bram found Willa all on his own, when he saw her For Rent sign out by the road. As for Willa and me, I've had the privilege of watching her grow up. When she wasn't dogging her daddy's heels, she was at my boatyard dogging mine. She's the child I always wished I'd had."

"You a member of the marriage posse?"

Emmett chuckled and shook his head. "No. And I've told Willa to tell those nosy busybodies to go straight to—"

"I need a mooring, Emmett!" Willa called out.

Both men turned, and Sam saw his dry sack and Willa's gear, including her mangled suitcase, sitting on the pier. She was coiling the ropes he'd made a mess of earlier.

"My color is still the same blue it's been for the last twenty-nine years," Emmett called back to her.

Sam looked out at the harbor and saw at least a dozen empty mooring balls in several different shades of blue.

With a pointed glower at Sam, Willa released the *RoseWind*'s dock lines and idled out into the harbor.

Emmett looked back at Sam and grinned. "You must have really pissed her off. What'd you do, make a pass?" His smile widened. "No wonder you've got bruises."

Sam sighed. "I told her I loved her."

"And do you?"

"Yes."

Emmett nodded. "That's a start. Do you know what you're up against?"

"I believe it mostly has to do with her niece."

"You're in for a treat when you meet Jennifer. We could all take a few lessons from that girl." He turned serious. "Willa especially."

"And you think forcing Willa to marry and have children is magically going to fix her?"

"Nope. But there was no persuading Bram otherwise. He said if it was *you* who fell for Willa, then the two of you could fix each other."

"Fix each—I'm not broken."

"No?" Emmett's eyes glinted again. "You don't have abandonment issues when it comes to women?"

"What in hell are you talking about?"

"You don't dump your girlfriends within a few months, before they can dump you first?"

Sam spun on his heel and headed for the lobster shack.

Emmett fell into step beside him. "I'm sorely relieved to realize you don't blame your mother for abandoning you boys to travel with your dad on his business trips."

"I have no idea what you and my grandfather talked about these last six weeks," Sam ground out, "but I do know it's none of your goddamn business."

"It became my business when Bram decided to involve Willa."

"Willamina Kent is a grown woman. She doesn't need any more interfering bastards messing up her life."

"Just you?"

Sam took a calming breath. "Stay out of my way, old man. There's more at stake here than you know."

"Barry Cobb checked into the Stone's Throw Bed and Breakfast two days ago," Emmett said with equal calmness.

Sam dropped his head with a quiet expletive.

"We can be allies, or we can be adversaries," Emmett continued. "It's your choice, Sam. I love Willamina like a daughter, and I've been the only thing standing between her and outright chaos since her parents died. If you truly do love her, you have my blessing. But if you hurt her, you won't be safe hiding on the moon. Abram Sinclair didn't have fools for friends, so don't underestimate me, and don't disappoint me. And together, we just might be able to turn this mess into a miracle."

Sam stared out at the harbor in silence, watching Willa rowing a small dinghy back toward the pier, the *RoseWind* gently bobbing on a mooring the exact same color as her eyes. He looked over at Emmett, silently studied him for several seconds, then turned and walked away.

Emmett watched the oldest Sinclair grandson stride off and smiled. *Bram, you old bastard, I don't know whether to curse you or thank you for dragging me into your cockamamie scheme. But it sure is damn invigorating squaring off against a man half my age.*

"The ungrateful wretch," Willa said, coming up behind him.

Emmett turned as she dropped her gear at her feet, a scowl on her face that would turn back a shark. "I pulled him out of the ocean—twice!—and he abandons me at the first whiff of food."

"Twice?"

"The idiot jumped out of a helicopter, then pretended he was drowning so I'd fish him out of the sea. And when he got swept overboard yesterday, I had to fish him out again." She broke into a nasty smile. "After I dragged him a good quarter-mile." Then she sobered. "Please, Em, tell me you didn't have anything to do with Abram's will."

Emmett pulled her into his embrace and rocked her back and forth. "Oh, Willy Wild Child, you know me better than that."

She hugged him fiercely. "How come you didn't warn me?"

He leaned away without releasing her. "I was caught between a rock and a hard place, Willy. I owed Bram one hell of a favor, and I gave him my word. But just because I couldn't dissuade him from writing that will doesn't mean I think it's *all* bad. Everyone needs the barnacles scraped off them once in a while."

"But what am I going to do, Em?"

He hugged her again. "I've been thinking about that ever since you called and told me you were sailing the *RoseWind* home." He tightened his grip. "I believe the wisest thing for you to do, at least for now, is nothing."

"Nothing?"

Emmett hid his amusement. "You've got three whole months. Why not sit back and see how this plays out? If it hasn't solved itself by then, then we'll use the loophole and end this farce."

"There's a loophole?"

"There's never been a contract written that didn't

have a back door to sneak out of." He gave her a reassuring smile. "Sam seems like a bright boy; he'll figure it out. Just give him some time, Willy."

"I am *not* sitting around waiting for Samuel Sinclair to rescue me."

"You're not the only injured party here, Willy. Abram blindsided his grandsons, too. You can let Warren Cobb have Tidewater and still walk away a very wealthy woman, but those boys will have lost everything."

"They're young and capable; they can go out and build their own empires."

Emmett sighed and stepped back. "I know you're angry at everyone named Sinclair right now, but you'd never be able to live with yourself if Cobb destroyed Tidewater International. You're going to have to play this game to the end." He gave her a crooked grin. "Why not consider it an adventure? It's not every day a woman has a wealthy, handsome man chasing after her."

She picked up her bags, and heading down the pier. "Let's go. It's starting to rain."

"What about Sam's gear?"

"The seagulls can have it, for all I care."

"Did you make a pass at him, Willy?" Emmett narrowed his eyes at her. "You did, didn't you?" He pointed at her. "I know how your wild child takes over when you're feeling the salt wind on your face. You've gotten your panties in a twist, little girl, because he up and turned you down, didn't he?"

She continued down the pier, stalking past Sam sitting at a picnic table, stuffing a lobster roll into his mouth. Emmett picked up Sam's bag and sauntered after her. Willa stopped a truck leaving the fishing pier, spoke to the driver, then climbed in on the passenger side. Emmett dropped the dry sack beside the picnic table, stepped up to the window, and ordered a lobster roll for himself.

"I thought Willa called *you* to take her home?" Sam said around a mouthful of lobster.

"She's got her shorts in a twist right now."

Sam snorted.

Emmett took his plate from the vendor and sat down. "You open to a bit of advice, Sam?"

The younger man gave a grunt as he chewed.

Emmett took a bite of his own roll, watching the solid sheet of rain sweep into the harbor as heavy drops began drumming on the canopy over their heads.

"Willa would have been on the *Cat's Tail* with her parents when it went down off St. Maarten eight years ago," he said softly. "But she'd married David Sommers that year, and it was the first time she didn't make the trip south with them." He looked over at Sam, who had stopped eating. "It's my guess Willa believes that if she'd been with them when that squall hit, they'd still be alive."

Sam said nothing.

"She was two months pregnant at the time. She miscarried about a week after we got the news," Emmett shrugged. "I don't know if it would have happened anyway or if the pain of losing her parents caused it. I just know we very nearly lost Willa with the baby." He looked back at Sam. "Willamina is the strongest person I've ever known, but even tempered steel has its breaking point."

"Then if she's witnessed so much tragedy, why would she choose to work with a bunch of old people and own a casket company?"

"For several reasons, though I think mostly because it gives her a sense of control. The pleasure of taking care of her aging parents was stolen from her, so she takes care of people who don't have any family to look after them." He sighed. "Like me, I suppose. She knows we're all knocking on death's door, and if she can't stop it, she can at least control some small part of it. The caskets are her way of making sure we meet our maker in style."

He chuckled. "She only intended to build them for the local market, but she made the mistake of putting a retired *Fortune* 500 CEO in charge of operations. I don't think Silas Payne has ever heard of a cottage industry."

"So Willa leaves all the day-to-day decisions to Payne?"

"She has to, because she's too busy saving the world one person at a time."

Sam gave Emmett the oddest look. "That's *exactly*

how I see her! She rushes around trying so damn hard to make sure everyone else is happy, she keeps tripping over her own feet."

Emmett took another bite of his roll, pleased to realize that Sinclair was just as sharp as his grandfather. Oh, yeah. Willy Wild Child had just met her match.

"You said you had some advice?" Sam said, picking up another roll and chomping down on it.

"It's my guess you intend to have your brothers tie up Bram's will in court to protect Tidewater, while you work on fixing Willa's guilt problem so she'll be free to marry you."

"You don't think that's a good plan?"

Emmett set down his food and turned in his seat. "Being men, our first instinct is to fix everything. But women don't want us fixing their problems for them. They want us to listen, get mad right along with them, and love them just the way they are."

"So I should . . . ?"

"You should forget about that damn bequest for a couple of months and sit back and see what happens. Get to know Willa by getting to know her sister, Shelby, and Jennifer and Cody. Hang around her factory, and talk to her workers. Roll up your sleeves and pitch in like Bram did. You'd be amazed at the clarity of mind you get when working with your hands."

"And Barry Cobb?"

"Folks around here will take care of Cobb, with a little prodding from me," he added with a grin. "We've sent more than one flatlander down the road talking to himself. You just concentrate on Willa. Charm her socks off her. Make her feel like a giddy young girl again."

Sam snorted and stuffed the last half of his roll into his mouth.

Emmett stood up, tossed both their plates into the trash, and took out his wallet. "You might as well come stay with me," he said, paying the vendor for both meals. "That way, folks will leave you alone."

Sam nodded to Emmett. "Thanks for dinner. But I thought you said two ornery men didn't make good housemates."

"Ornery *old* men." He stuffed the change into the tip jar, then pulled his keys out of his pocket and handed them to Sam. "I'm not worried about our rooming together, because age and treachery overcome youth and skill any day of the week. It's the blue pickup parked in the end lot," he said, nodding down the street. "And since rumor has it you don't drown easy, and I can be a treacherous old bastard sometimes, I'll wait here for you to pick me up."

Chapter Fourteen

Willa stared through the rain-blurred windshield at all the vehicles in her driveway. Was she *ever* going to be alone to think? One of the cars had New York plates, so it belonged to Abram's housekeeper, Peg. Damn, she'd forgotten all about her moving in. And even Shelby was conspiring against her, since her sister's minivan also sat in her cluttered driveway.

When had she lost control of her life?

"The real question, Willamina, is when are you going to take it back?" she muttered, her words drowned out by the wind and rain.

But it was the expensive-looking bright red SUV parked directly in front of her headlights, sporting temporary plates, that was really keeping Willa from going inside. Granted, she'd been at her factory for more than two hours with Cyrus's brothers, but surely Sam hadn't had time to go out and buy a car yet, had he?

Maybe she could sleep at her factory, just to get one night alone with her thoughts. Shelby was going to keep her up past midnight, asking her all about Abram's home, his grandsons, and the funeral. Willa smiled. If that *was* Sam's truck, then Shelby had already started the inquisition—after she'd given Sam a piece of her mind for shanghaiing her husband.

The kitchen door opened, and Jennifer stepped onto the porch, pulling on a rain slicker. "Auntie!" the girl called, skipping down the stairs. She ran limping up to the driver's side of Willa's truck. "Isn't it beautiful!" she exclaimed when Willa rolled down her window.

"What? The storm? Get in here before you drown," she said, motioning her to run around to the other side.

"No, let's sit in *my* truck," Jennifer said, running to the driver's side of the SUV and climbing in.

Willa rolled up her window, opened the door, and made a mad dash for the SUV. "*Your* truck!" she squealed, climbing into the passenger seat. She immediately slid back out. "It's a leather interior. We're going to get it all wet."

"Get in here, Auntie," Jen said with a laugh, grabbing Willa's sleeve and pulling her back inside. She slid the key into the ignition, started it up, and immediately turned down the volume on the radio. "Isn't this the greatest?" She flipped on the interior lights. "I just took my learner's permit exam two days ago, but I haven't tried driving it yet. It's got satellite radio, navigation, and even a DVD player in the back." She ran her hands lovingly over the steering wheel. "And it's all mine," she finished on a whisper.

"Oh, my God, Jen. It's beautiful." Willa turned in her seat to take it all in. "You could put an entire softball team in here."

Jen shook her head. "When I get my license, I won't be able to carry anyone who isn't family for six months. Abram picked it out especially for me, because it was big and safe." Her expression turned pained. "I'm sorry he died, Auntie. I really liked him, you know? He was a cool old guy."

"They don't make them any cooler," Willa agreed. "And I'm glad you got to know him, Jen." She chuckled so she wouldn't tear up. "Whenever he was talking to me about you, he always referred to you as 'that spitfire niece of yours,' " she said, dropping her voice to sound like Abram.

"He wrote me a letter," Jen said. "I put it in my jewelry box, and I'm going to keep it forever. Abram told me to grab the world by the tail and give it a good shake every now and then, just to see what happens."

Willa laughed, wiping her eyes.

"Look," Jen said, pointing at the floor by her feet. "They put the gas petal on the left side, so I can use my left foot instead of my right, but everything else is the same. And when it comes time for me to trade it in, the pedal can be put back on the right side with hardly any trouble." She looked over at Willa. "That was Emmett's idea, Abram said in his letter. The two of them decided I could learn to use my left foot just as easily as people learn to use their right foot for driving."

"It's perfect for you," Willa agreed. "But I noticed the temporary plate isn't handicapped. Do you have to wait until you register it to get one?"

Jen gaped at her. "I'm not getting one of those—they're for *handicapped* people. I've been trying to get Mom to get rid of the one on our van for years." She shot Willa a mischievous smile. "I'm getting a vanity plate that says CATCH ME. You know, as in 'Catch me if you can'? Abram suggested it in his letter."

Feeling about two inches tall, Willa gave her forehead a dramatic slap. "What was I thinking? Of course, you'll get a vanity plate."

They both jumped when somebody pounded on Jen's window. "Mom said if you two don't come in for supper, she's not even saving you the wishbone," Cody hollered through the window. He spun around and ran back to the house.

Jen shut off the truck. "I wish I could have thanked Abram personally. His letter also said Spencer was setting up an appointment for me in New York City to be fitted for a special prosthesis so I can do sports and stuff."

Willa patted her niece's arm. "You'll be thanking Abram every time you shake the world by its tail, Jen," she said with a laugh, opening her door.

Jen stopped her by grabbing her sleeve. "Um . . . Mom's got some news for you, Auntie. She's been worrying all week about telling you, so . . . well, try not to overreact, okay?"

The fine hairs on Willa's neck rose in alarm. "What news?"

Jen opened her own door. "Mom will tell you. Just don't take it personally, okay?" She scrunched up her pretty young face. "Like you usually do."

She was out the door and running through the rain before Willa could ask what in hell she'd meant by that. "I'll show you *personal*, you little brat," she muttered, dashing for the house. "Let's see how long it takes you to notice the 'Don't bother honking; I'm blond' sticker I'm going to put on your fancy new bumper."

Crammed to the gills with the best stuffing and gravy she'd ever eaten, Willa sat on the floor against her couch, her face bathed in firelight from the hearth, and fought to stay awake. "You fill my wineglass one more time, Shel, and I'm going to fall asleep right here."

"Fine with me," Shelby said, setting down the bottle and leaning against the couch next to her. "I wasn't looking forward to sharing a bed with you, anyway."

"The storm's not that bad. Go home; whatever you

have to tell me can wait until tomorrow. I haven't had a decent night's sleep in more than a week."

"Um . . . my bed is in your barn, along with all my other worldly possessions."

"Oh, my God," Willa whispered. "You left Richard."

"The timing was perfect, what with him being . . . out of the country. And I can't very well kick Richard out of his family homestead, can I? So I packed up all our belongings, stored everything in your barn, and the three of us have moved in with you," she finished with a smile.

"When did you decide to leave him?"

"I filed the divorce papers about a month ago."

"And you're only telling me now!"

Her sister became very busy swirling the wine in her glass. "I was afraid of how you'd react."

"How I'd react *how?*"

Shelby leaned her shoulder against the couch to face her. "You have a very bad habit of thinking you're somehow responsible for everything that happens to anyone you care about." She shrugged. "You've been nagging me to leave him for years now, and I knew once I did, you'd find a way to blame yourself for my marriage breaking up. Then you'd feel guilty, and then you'd start trying to fix *me*, just like you try to fix everyone."

"I do not!"

"Who marched over to school and gave Cody's basketball coach hell last fall?"

"That jerk was only interested in winning. He's supposed—"

"Without even telling me you were going to see him," Shelby continued forcefully, cutting Willa off. "And who keeps visiting her ex-mother-in-law because she feels guilty for divorcing her son and his moving to Montana?"

"I *like* Jean Sommers."

"My God, Willy, you even started a business to give a bunch of bored old people something to do."

"I have to earn a living."

"Then there's the diner. You're banned from ever going in there again, for heaven's sakes."

"That wasn't really my fault. Craig Watson is a—"

"And Uncle Jake's funeral? And Beverly and Clyde's wedding? Oh, and let's not forget last year's town meeting debacle. Shall I go on?"

Willa closed her mouth and stared into the fire.

"I'm getting a divorce because Richard and I barely talk to each other anymore," Shelby said softly. "I stuck it out for the kids, but I simply can't do it anymore." She laughed humorlessly. "Jen finally came right out and told me that if I didn't leave Richard, she was leaving *us*. She said she couldn't stand the tension anymore, and she'd take Cody and live with Emmett."

"Emmett? Not me?" Willa said in surprise.

Shelby wrapped her arms around Willa and gave her

a squeeze. "They love you to death but only in small doses, Willy. They don't want to be fussed over; they want to fight their own battles."

"I do not fuss over them."

"Yes, you do. You fuss over everyone—except yourself. When was the last time you went out on a date?"

"In March."

Shelby snorted. "Peter Thomas doesn't count. He's old enough to be our father, and that was a sympathy date because his wife had run off with a younger man. Let me rephrase the question: When was the last time you got laid?"

Willa scrambled to her feet and glared down at her sister. "How did this conversation get turned to my love life? We're supposed to be discussing your divorce."

Shelby also stood up. "There is nothing to discuss, Willa. Well, except for my living arrangements. It's going to take me a couple of weeks to find a place I can afford to buy, so I *had* planned to move in here with you. But there are only four bedrooms, and Peg has one of them. That leaves one for Cody, one for Jennifer, and yours." She grabbed the bottle of wine and refilled her glass. "I suppose I could stay in the cottage."

"I'll stay in the cottage. That way, you won't have to worry about my *fussing* over your kids."

"It was an observation, Willa, not a criticism. And I have no intention of kicking you out of your home. I'll move my things into the cottage tomorrow." She smiled impishly. "But I'm eating here. I've never had roast chicken that tasted so good."

Willa set her glass on the end table, strode into the kitchen, and grabbed her rain slicker. "You can have the house and the housekeeper. I'll move my stuff out of my bedroom tomorrow."

Shelby followed her into the kitchen. "Willa!"

Willa ran out the door and down the steps, holding the rain slicker over her head as she dashed for the cottage, fighting the wind howling off the ocean. A swaying branch snatched the slicker right out of her hands, and she was soaked to the skin when she finally reached the cottage.

The door was locked. Who in hell had locked the door? She ran back down the stairs, dug in the mud for the key she kept under the step, then finally stumbled into the darkened cottage and felt around for the light switch. The lights didn't come on, and she looked out the window at the main house and saw that it was also pitch black.

Feeling her bottom lip beginning to quiver, Willa stripped out of her clothes by the door, felt her way to the bedroom, crawled under the covers, and burst into tears.

"Oh, Auntie, I told you not to take it personally," Jen said with a sigh, sitting on the bed and brushing Willa's hair back off her face. "You cried all night, didn't you?"

Willa pulled the pillow over her head.

Jen snatched the pillow away and stood up. "Well, crying time is over, because you have to teach me to drive my truck on the way to school. Then you can take it to work and pick me up at three, and we can practice until supper. I can apply for my license by the end of August, which only gives me three months to get the hang of it."

Willa pulled the blankets up over her head. "You're a teenager, Jen. You're not supposed to be bright and cheery in the morning." She brought the covers down to her chin and glared at her niece. "Besides, your mother should be the one teaching you to drive."

"Are you nuts? We'd kill each other. Come on," Jen said, trying to pull the blankets off.

"Hey, I'm naked under here! Go see if the clothes fairy hung my clothes up to dry last night, would you?"

"The power's still out on your road," Jen said, heading into the main room. "You'll have to shower at work. Peg sent down clean clothes for you and milk and cereal." She walked back into the bedroom carrying a neatly folded bundle of clothes. "And she told me she was going to move into the cottage this morning, so Mom can have her bedroom. I told her I'd rather stay in the cottage."

"It's *my* cottage, and *I'm* staying in it," Willa sat up. "Jen," she said when the girl turned to leave. "I'm sorry your parents are getting divorced."

Jennifer gave her a sad smile. "I'm more sorry that

they don't love each other. But their separating will be better for all of us. Mom will start laughing again, and Dad will work fewer hours and spend more time with Cody and me."

"How did you get to be so wise?"

Jen shrugged. "You hang around Emmett long enough, I think you get it by osmosis. Hurry up, I want to get to school early, so everyone can see me driving my new truck," she said, whirling around and shutting the door on the way out.

Willa couldn't help but smile. Jennifer reminded her so much of herself at that age; she had haunted Emmett's boatyard every day, too. Willa knew he had always hoped she'd take over his business one day, since he had no children to pass it down to. It looked as if Jennifer was the new heir apparent, which pleased Willa to no end. Jen had a passion for wooden boats, and for Sengatti sloops in particular. Though only sixteen, she had already designed and built a day sailer that Emmett had proudly put into production last year.

"Is the *RoseWind* really yours, Auntie?" Jen asked through the door, her words sounding garbled.

"Abram left it to me in his will," Willa called back as she dressed. "Hey, are you eating my cereal?"

"We'll pick you up something on the way to school. Wow, do you know how much that boat cost new? It's in the seven figures! Abram must have been really rich. Was his family upset that you got it?"

Willa stared at the closed door. What was she going to tell Jennifer about Abram's will? And Shelby? Or anyone else, for that matter. She snorted and pulled her sweater over her head. She sure as heck wasn't telling them she was a multi-multi-millionaire.

Even if it *was* only for three months.

But she was keeping the *RoseWind*, no matter what happened. Sam had said none of them cared much about sailing, and she couldn't leave that beautiful sloop with anyone who couldn't appreciate what a work of art it was.

"I need a hairbrush," she said, walking into the main room.

"I think you need a hairdresser more. Emmett said the *RoseWind* is the fastest sloop he's ever built. I wish I could have sailed her here with you."

"I wish you had been with me, too. Sam Sinclair was more trouble than help." She snickered. "He can swim, though."

Jen's eyes widened, her spoonful of cereal stopped halfway to her mouth. "Sam Sinclair was with you?" she squeaked.

Willa wanted to kick herself. "That is not common knowledge, young lady. Especially don't tell your mother."

Jen set her spoon in her bowl, her breakfast forgotten. "Are Abram's grandsons as cool as Abram? Are they handsome? And single?" She shook her head.

"What am I thinking? If they're rich and handsome, of course they're already married."

"They are three confirmed bachelors, and women everywhere can be thankful for that. I came this close"— Willa held her thumb and finger an inch apart—"to tossing Sam overboard."

"So where is he?"

"With any luck, on his way back to New York City."

Jen sighed and stood up. "Too bad. I'd like to meet one of Abram's grandsons, so I could at least thank *him* for the truck. We need to get going so I won't be late. I found your rain slicker caught on the fence. Here—it's still raining a bit." She handed it to Willa as she walked out the door.

"We'll stop at the coffee shop, and you can run in and get me a muffin and coffee," Willa said, smoothing down her tangled hair as she followed.

Jen giggled, limping toward the main driveway. "I think it's cool how the coffee shop banned you."

"Cool."

"Well, yeah. It shows you're not afraid to stand up for what you believe in."

"Um . . . and at the town meeting last year?" Willa asked, watching her niece out of the corner of her eye. "Do you think that was cool, or did I act like a 'confounded female' who didn't know what in hell I was talking about?"

"No! Everyone has the right to speak out, *especially*

when their opinion runs contrary to popular sentiment. That's the whole point of democracy."

"But did you agree with me?"

"It doesn't matter. There were a lot of pros and cons to having a big-box store built in town, but nobody was voicing the cons. You should have sued them for removing you from the meeting. They completely disregarded your civil rights."

Willa merely smiled as she climbed into the passenger seat of the SUV.

"Okay," Jen said, putting the key in the ignition. "Promise to be patient with me."

"Willa!" Shelby called.

Willa look out the windshield to see her sister standing on the porch, wearing *her* bathrobe and slippers.

"We need to talk." Shelby lowered her voice to normal when Jennifer rolled down her window. "And you don't have to take Jen to school. I'll take her when I take Cody in, and she can practice driving with me this afternoon."

"I don't mind," Willa said, leaning over to talk out of Jen's window. "She *asked* for my help, so she must *want* me fussing over her."

"Oh, for the love of—Willa, Richard called last night. He's arriving home today."

Willa glanced briefly at Jen, then looked back at her sister. "And?"

"And . . . he doesn't know we've moved out," Shelby

said, also darting a glance at her daughter. "I just thought you might want to hang around here today."

Willa patted Jen's arm. "I'll be right back, kiddo. Go ahead and start her up, and get familiar with all the dials and buttons. I need to talk to your mom for a minute."

Willa scrambled out of the truck and ran onto the porch. "I'm not sure you want me here when Richard shows up," she said, keeping her back to Jennifer and her voice low. She glanced toward the door to make sure Cody wasn't within earshot, either. "When Richard brought Abram's body down to New York, he . . . well, he was really mad."

"About what?" Shelby asked.

"He claimed I talked you into asking for a divorce." Willa felt her face heat up. "And then Sam Sinclair showed up, and they got into a fight. Then the other two grandsons lugged Richard off and put him on that cargo ship headed to Italy." She shook her head. "Richard blames me, Shel. But if you want me to be here when you confront him, I'll come back after dropping Jen off."

Shelby frowned at her.

"I guess he's right to blame me. But I've missed hearing you laugh like you used to, Shel. I know you haven't been happy for a long time now. Richard's always putting you down, and you . . . you never defend yourself."

"That's because I no longer care what Richard thinks of me. But I didn't realize how it was affecting my children. Then one day last month, Cody said something to me, and I heard Richard's words coming out of his mouth. It wasn't so much *what* Cody said, it was the tone he used. That's when I knew staying for the sake of the children was actually hurting them." She reached out and touched Willa's sleeve. "I'm sorry he accused you, Willy. I told him the divorce was my idea and that you had nothing to do with it."

Willa shook her head. "Sam showed up just as I slipped and fell, trying to walk away from Richard, and he thought Richard had attacked me. You should have seen them, Shel; they were like two mad dogs going at each other."

"I'm going to be late!" Jen shouted.

Willa patted her sister's arm. "I'll check in at the factory, then come back here for the day. You can help me move my stuff into the cottage." She ran down the stairs before Shelby could respond.

"Okay, kiddo," she said, climbing into the truck and fastening her seat belt. "Let's see if we can get to school without breaking any speed records."

Chapter Fifteen

*W*illa *searched the cupboards* of her office bathroom for her hair dryer and finally found it in a box she'd brought in when she had first opened Kent Caskets. She plugged in the dryer. In four years, she'd never once showered at work.

There had been such a fuss over her having an executive bathroom when they renovated the old factory she'd bought. Her chief of operations, Silas Payne, had insisted that Willa have an entire office suite, saying she needed to present herself as a successful businesswoman. Maureen, head of casket interiors, had told Willa that Silas was so insistent because he couldn't very well have his own private bathroom if his boss didn't. Apparently, in big business, bathrooms were status symbols.

Willa hadn't envisioned Kent Caskets as a big business, but if her staff wanted to pretend it was, who was she to burst their bubble?

She frowned at herself in the mirror. So, okay, *maybe* there was a grain of truth in what Shelby had said last night. Maybe she had started up Kent Caskets to give the bored residents of Grand Point Bluff something to do. But she had to earn a living, so it was a win-win situation for everyone.

Willa turned on the blow dryer and started brushing her hair, smiling as she remembered her hair-raising ride to work that morning.

Jennifer had to be operating the forklifts and equipment at Emmett's yard; she'd driven the eight miles to school like a seasoned pro. However, Willa couldn't get the hang of driving with her left foot if her life depended on it. She must have looked like a giant jackrabbit, spastically jerking the accelerator, then slamming on the brakes.

When she'd peered into her rearview mirror after dropping Jennifer off, Willa had seen a horrified look on her niece's face. She didn't know if she was embarrassing Jen beyond redemption or if the teenager had feared her beautiful new truck would return minus some paint.

Once she'd managed to get on the road—after squealing the tires leaving the school driveway—she'd had to keep pulling over so the accumulating rush-hour traffic could pass. It was a miracle she hadn't been stopped for driving drunk, which is exactly what she must have looked like. Nevertheless, she was writing an editorial letter to the newspaper first thing tomorrow, explaining horn-honking etiquette to all the idiots who thought they owned the road.

She shut off the dryer, only to hear a knock on her office bathroom door, quickly followed by the familiar *tap-tap-tap* of Maureen's cane.

"Everyone's in the break room waiting for you, boss," Maureen said, taking the brush out of Willa's hand. She hung her cane on her arm, then started brushing the back of Willa's hair. "We want to hear all about your trip to New York. I especially want to hear about the board meeting. I hope you knocked the stuffing out of those suits."

Willa sighed to herself. Anyone who wore a tie to work was a suit to Maureen, who still held a few grudges from when she had worked in Boston four decades ago. She'd been passed over for more than one promotion, the positions going to men who were often less qualified than she was. Which was why Maureen had moved to Keelstone Cove and opened a fabric shop twenty-five years ago, having realized there were no glass ceilings for business *owners*. She had eventually sold the Quilted Lobster for a tidy sum, moved into Grand Point Bluff, and agreed to become Willa's director of casket interiors only because she would finally have a boss who wasn't a man. That didn't, however, stop Maureen from butting heads with Silas on a regular bases. There were days when Willa felt more like a referee than a business owner.

"I knocked out my own stuffing, Maureen," Willa said with a laugh. "I was so nervous I nearly killed myself getting off the elevator. Um . . . about those beautiful suits you lent me? The brown one is okay because I was wearing it, but the green one has a tear in the skirt. The elevator ate it—along with the slacks Joan lent me."

Maureen blinked at her in the mirror. "Can it be repaired?"

Willa turned to face her. "I don't think so. The elevator chewed it up pretty badly." She turned back to the mirror and started braiding her hair. "We'll get on the Internet tomorrow, and you can pick out a new suit that you like."

"It was a Pendleton, Willa. It cost me a week's wages."

Which was somewhere around a hundred and fifty bucks forty years ago, Willa figured. "You can also pick out a matching blouse and even a purse if you want." She tied off the end of her thick braid and tossed it over her shoulder. "And just between you and me," she said in a conspirator's whisper, "I had those stuffed suits shaking in their shoes by the end of the meeting. I told them I wasn't voting Abram's shares until I was good and ready. Then I told the three grandsons that they were taking me to dinner that night, and we wouldn't resume the board meeting until I was ready to vote."

Maureen's eyes widened. "I bet they didn't like that." She tapped her cane on the floor. "You did good, boss. Didn't I tell you to walk in there as if you owned the place? God, I wish I'd been there to see it. Which one of the boys did you vote for?"

"I didn't get to vote. Abram died the next morning, and my proxy died with him."

Maureen's excitement instantly vanished. "The old poop." She turned to leave. "This place isn't the same without him running around sticking his nose into everything." She stopped at the door and looked back. "Are you coming to the break room? You can at least tell us about the funeral." She smiled. "Abram looked right good in his casket, didn't he?"

"You saw him in it?" Willa asked in surprise.

"Spencer arranged a viewing for us before Abram was shipped out. We all wanted to say our good-byes. That Spencer is a really nice fellow, for a lawyer." She frowned. "Except he invited the coffee clubbers to come say good-bye, too. The mood sort of disintegrated when they walked in." She lifted her chin. "Those people are really annoying. They were acting as if Abram was *their* best friend."

"He had breakfast with them every morning, Maureen."

"Still. That Doris Ambrose tucked an angel figurine in Abram's casket, bawling like a baby. After she left, Silas shoved it down to Abram's feet so his grandsons wouldn't think we're all wacko up here. So, are you coming to the break room?"

Willa sighed. "I'll be there in a minute, and I'll tell you all about Rosebriar, the grandsons, and the funeral."

Maureen rushed off to inform the others, and Willa took her time straightening her bathroom. Before she'd left, she'd endured three days of being told how to act in a big-business board meeting, and her mentors were expecting to hear the details.

Willa stared into the mirror. She owed these sincere people so much for supporting her these past five years, and they deserved nothing but honesty from her. Besides, the majority of them were retired executives with cumulative decades of experience; surely they could help her figure a way out of the bequest.

Willa walked out of her office and down the hall, inhaling the familiar, comforting scent of hardwood resin. What had made her think that she could ever sail off into the sunset? She belonged *here*, in Keelstone Cove, in her factory, taking care of her adopted family. And Emmett. And Shelby and Jennifer and Cody. There might be times when she felt damned if she stayed, but she would surely die inside if she left.

She had just started to push open the door to the break room when she heard a familiar male voice say, "And this is where the mainsail winch took the first chunk out of me. They really should put safety guards on those things."

What was *he* doing here? Willa inched open the door and peeked inside, then immediately let it close, putting her back to the wall, her hand covering her heart. Holy hell, she'd forgotten how handsome he was. The last time she'd seen Sam, he'd had a five-day beard and more bruises than a prize fighter and had been stuffing his face like a caveman.

Damn, he cleaned up good.

He obviously had no intention of going back to New York. Did he think to pick up where Abram had left off, hoping to rally her workers to his cause? By God, she'd fire them all if they even *hinted* that Sam would make her a wonderful husband.

The door suddenly opened, and Maureen walked out, giving a surprised yelp. "Land gracious, Willa, you startled me! I was coming after you again. You'll never guess who's here." Then she frowned. "Wait, you knew Sam Sinclair was in town, because he said he sailed in on the *RoseWind* with you. How come you didn't tell me about him when I came to get you?"

"I forgot," Willa said, walking past her into the suddenly silent break room. "Carl, I sold that custom rock maple casket last night and put the sales slip on your desk." She went to the coffee pot and poured herself a cup, then turned and smiled at her crew. "I see you've all been very busy while I was away," she drawled. "Last night, when I stopped in to get Cyrus a casket for Gramps, I had to go back outside and look at the building to make sure I was in the right place. It amazes me how you can suddenly decide to remodel the reception area and get it completely done in less than ten days— all without the *owner* of the business knowing she even wanted to remodel."

Nobody said anything.

Willa kicked her smile up a notch. "And I see you've all met Abram's grandson Sam." She looked directly at him. "Thank you for stopping by on your way back to New York, to thank everyone personally for their condolences."

Sam brushed the front of his shirt, sprinkling the floor with tiny wood shavings. "Actually, I stopped by this morning looking for a job." He nodded toward Silas. "Mr. Payne was nice enough to give me a position in the planing room. I had no idea how precise woodworking is, but I hope I can get the hang of it in a few days." He glanced toward Levi, the master carpenter, and smiled. "Assuming Levi doesn't run *me* through the planer for ruining another bird's-eye maple board."

He was *working* here?

Willa's hormones started doing their little happy dance, and she firmly tamped them down. "Wonderful." She looked at Silas Payne. "Though I just got back, I have to leave for the day, I'm afraid. Shelby's moved in with me, and we have to do some house rearranging."

"Shelby left Richard!" Maureen shouted, thumping

her cane. "I knew that girl would come to her senses!"

Shelby was a regular at Kent Caskets when her kids were in school, sometimes filling in when a worker was sick and sometimes just visiting. Everyone knew she was unhappy, and in their own subtle way, all had encouraged her to leave Richard.

"But why did she move in with you?" one of the women from interiors asked. "Why didn't she kick Richard out?"

"She can't, Mabel," Willa explained. "That house has been in the Bates family for five generations."

"But that means Ida Bates will have to move back home to take care of Richard," another woman said. "We're going to lose our fourth for bridge."

"Richard Bates can damn well take care of himself," Maureen interjected. "Ida's not about to move back to that drafty old farmhouse. She loves her apartment at Grand Point."

Willa set her coffee mug in the dishwasher before heading for the door. "I have to go. Richard is getting back today, and he doesn't know Shelby moved out." She stopped in the doorway. "I promise to tell you all about New York tomorrow. Try not to remodel anything else until then, would you?"

She headed down the hall and out the back door and had just made it to Jennifer's truck when Sam called out, "Wait up, Willa. I want to talk to you."

Willa turned to watch Sam loping toward her. She

turned and eyed Jennifer's truck. She smiled, reaching into her pocket for the keys and tossing them to Sam.

"If you want to talk to me, you'll have to drive me home," she said, walking around to the passenger side. "That way, you can use the truck to come back to *work*." She gave him a Cheshire cat grin when he got into the driver's seat. "Levi is a tough boss. You ruin any more of his precious wood, and he'll have you sweeping floors with a toothbrush."

Before she could read his intention, Sam reached over the console, took her face in his hands, and gave her a loud kiss on the mouth.

"What did you do that for?" she snapped, glancing toward the building to see if anyone was watching. She narrowed her eyes at him. "Never mind. Just don't do it again. The voyage is over, Mr. Sinclair, and I am no longer interested."

"That kiss was for not firing me," he said with maddening calm, sliding the key into the ignition.

Willa snorted. "Fat lot of good it would do me. Silas would just hire you back."

"I thought *you* owned Kent Caskets," he said in surprise.

"I do."

"Then how could Payne hire me back if you fired me?"

Willa motioned toward her factory. "Do you like the color of my building?"

Sam gave her a quizzical look. "It's gray."

"I had the entire building painted white when I bought it, and I had the trim painted a really nice green. But then I went out of town for three days with Shel and the kids to do some shopping in Portland. When I came back, my factory was gray with blue trim." She turned in her seat to face him. "What did you think of the lobby when you walked in this morning?"

"It looks nice. I was a bit surprised to see the reception area painted in such cheery colors. I thought the collection of antique urns was a nice touch, though."

"Ten days ago, that lobby was deep green and brown, with gold leaf accents. And there was a beautiful bronze statue of a breaching whale. Now that's sitting in my office suite, under a newly installed spotlight."

Sam stared at her. "Who has the authority to sign checks on your business accounts?"

"Only me, but it doesn't matter. If I don't okay an expense, they simply use their own money. Or sometimes they pool their paychecks to buy whatever they think my business needs. My older workers are very well off, and a lot of them don't have any close family to leave their estates to. So they indulge themselves by running Kent Caskets the way *they* want to run it."

"That's actually very dangerous, Willa. If one of them dies and a relative comes out of the woodwork, you could be sued for whatever your deceased worker had contributed to your business."

"I have two retired lawyers working in sales, and they've made sure that can't happen." She shrugged. "Kent Caskets is more about people than it is about money. And if anything, they've taught me that gobs of money sitting in the bank is stagnant energy. They spent their entire lives working hard to accumulate it but found it has little value in and of itself. They claim they enjoy spending their money much more than they enjoyed earning it." She sighed. "But I think their greatest joy is doing stuff behind my back."

"You have got to be the weirdest woman I know," he said, more to himself than to her.

"Thank you," she snapped, turning to face the windshield. "Let's go. Shelby's waiting for me."

"I meant that as a compliment, Willa," he said, starting the truck. "What the—where's the gas pedal?"

"On the left side."

He looked down, touched the pedal, and revved the engine, then looked at her. "Why is it on the left?"

"This is the truck Abram bequeathed to Jennifer. She only has her learner's permit, so I let her drive to school this morning, then I drove here." She grinned smugly. "You can take her driving this afternoon. She wants to meet you anyway, to thank you in person for the truck."

"I didn't have anything to do with this truck."

Willa shrugged. "She thinks it's very nice how you Sinclair men don't mind that your grandfather gave part of your inheritance to her. Oh, and she thinks you're *really* sweet to let me keep the *RoseWind* without making a stink." She fastened her seat belt, almost giddy with anticipation. "Drive. I want to be home when Richard shows up."

"Will he cause trouble for Shelby? Maybe I should hang around your house today."

"We don't need you to protect us from Richard. He won't do anything stupid. He was angry when he brought Abram down to New York because Shel had just told him about the divorce, and he blamed me. Let's go."

Sam put his foot on the brake, pulled the shifting lever into drive, and pushed down on the accelerator with his left foot. Jennifer's brand-new truck shot out of its parking space as if it had been kicked in the ass. Willa had to brace her hand on the dash when Sam slammed on the brakes and they came to an equally abrupt halt.

"Hell," he muttered, darting a glance at the building to see if anyone was watching. He shifted in his seat and tried to reach the gas pedal with his right foot.

"I already tried that," Willa said from behind her hand, which she was using to hold in her laughter. "It doesn't work, because the brake pedal gets in the way. You *have* to use your left foot."

He turned and glared at her.

"Switching the pedal to the left was Emmett's idea, since Jennifer's right foot is a prosthesis."

"Using my right foot is so ingrained it's automatic. How did you get to work this morning without killing anyone?"

"I actually got pretty good at it after several miles. Go ahead, give it another try."

"You set me up," he growled, slowly letting his right foot off the brake, easing down on the gas pedal with his left.

"Oh, like you set me up this morning? You're supposed to be on your way back to New York—*without* telling anyone we spent the last five days together."

"They wanted to know who beat me up, and I told them you did," he said, concentrating on idling out to the road.

He looked both ways for traffic, and Willa's head slammed into the headrest when they suddenly took off. She had to grab the door handle to stay upright because they were turning at the time. "Um . . . my house is the other way."

Sam muttered something appropriately nasty.

He found a place to turn around and got them headed in the right direction, accompanied by the squeals of spinning tires. The ride eventually got less jackrabbitty as he got used to using his left foot, and they only had twenty cars behind them when they finally turned into her driveway.

Willa decided it must be a guy thing, not pulling over to let honking traffic pass.

Sam stopped the truck beside Peg's car, shut off the engine with a deep sigh, and looked around. "Nice place. I can see why it appealed to Bram."

"He stayed in that cottage over there," she said, pointing past him toward the bluff. "You can go see it if you want. I don't know if there's anything of his left in there or not; I haven't had time to look around yet."

Peg and Shelby came out of the house and stood on the porch. Sam got out to greet Peg and introduce himself to Shelby, and Willa took her time following. Did she still own that book that explained how to wipe out bad karma, or had she foolishly donated it to the library book sale?

Chapter Sixteen

As soon as Peg got a good look at Sam, she dragged him inside and scolded him for making such a mess of himself. Willa and Shelby had to run upstairs so Sam and Peg wouldn't catch them laughing hysterically. Neither of them could decide which was more outrageous, that Peg was making such a fuss over Sam or that he was letting her.

"I thought she was going to start kissing his boo-boos," Shelby said, flopping down onto Willa's bed in laughter. "Cody runs in the opposite direction if I even ask if he's hurt."

Willa walked over to her closet and started pulling out hangers of clothes. "You should have seen Sam in my break room this morning. He was pointing out every little bruise to my workers and blaming me for each one."

Shelby sat up when Willa set an armful of clothes on the bed beside her. "My God, he's handsome. Wait—why would Sam blame you? And how *did* he get so beat up?" Then her eyes widened. "Oh, my God! He sailed down from New York with you on the *RoseWind!* That's what he meant when he told Peg you tried to drown him." She jumped up and followed Willa back to the closet. "How come you didn't tell me about Sam last night?"

"I forgot."

"You *forgot?*" She grabbed Willa's arm and swung her around. "You can't just forget to tell me you spent five days on a boat with a man. I'm your sister! You're supposed to tell me everything." Shelby dragged her back to the bed. "Okay, out with it. Did he make a pass at you?" She grinned. "Did you make a pass at *him?*"

Willa escaped back to the closet. "That's none of your business."

"Emmett doesn't call you Willy Wild Child for nothing," Shelby said, following her. "You're a completely different person when you're at sea." She grabbed the clothes out of Willa's hands and tossed them in the general direction of the bed. "Or should that be wild *woman?*" Her voice dropped. "Willa, be honest now. You're attracted to Sam, aren't you? I mean, you'd consider having an affair with him if the opportunity presented itself, wouldn't you?"

"He's ten times crazier than Abram, Shel. The man

jumped out of a helicopter in the middle of Long Island Sound, for crying out loud."

Shelby pulled her into a huge hug. "Oh, this is wonderful! It's about damn time you had a fling."

Willa pulled free and crossed her arms under her breasts. "And you think he's just the man to end my drought? Well, let me tell you something about Samuel Sinclair. Five days after meeting me, he asked me to marry him, and three days ago, he actually told me he loved me."

Shelby backed up and plopped down onto a clothes-covered chair as she gaped up at Willa.

Willa nodded. "Do you still think he's a candidate for a fling?"

"He . . . he asked you to marry him?"

"The very night of Abram's funeral."

"And . . . oh, my God, Willa, what did you say?"

"I hightailed it out of there the very next morning." Willa sat on the bed with a sigh. "It's a long story, Shel, so don't interrupt, okay? It all started when Spencer read Abram's will after the funeral." She paused, then shook her head. "No, actually, it started when the elevator door opened on the thirtieth floor of Tidewater International . . ."

Sam sat at the kitchen table, nursing a large mug of maple-syrup-laced coffee. Willa's home was a classic old New England farmhouse, surrounded by towering maple and elm trees, and the kitchen looked as if it hadn't been updated in the last fifty years. The cupboards were white bead-board that ran all the way up to the ceiling, and the counter was faded and chipped first-generation Formica. The appliances were coppertone. There was even an old cast-iron wood cookstove on one of the outside walls, looking as if it had just come out of a Montgomery Ward catalog. The floor was made of pine boards stained dark brown, and it tilted toward the inside hallway.

Something suddenly brushed up against his leg under the table, and he leaned over to find a one-eyed, semibald, wheezing gray cat that looked as old as the appliances. He extended his hand to it. "Hey there, old chump," he said, smiling when it pushed its scraggly face against his fingers. "You must be on, what, your ninth life?"

"Poor old thing's deaf," Peg said as she walked into the kitchen. She pulled a vacuum cleaner out of the closet. "Took me a while to figure that out," she continued, grabbing a dust rag, which she stuffed into her apron pocket. "I nearly sucked him up in the vacuum the second day I was here because I didn't see him sleeping under the coffee table. Cody said Willa found him on the beach, nearly starved to death, about three years ago. There's no telling how old he is. His name's Ghost."

"Cody?" Sam repeated, lifting Ghost onto his lap.

"Shelby's boy. There's Jennifer, who's sixteen, and

Cody, who's ten. They're wonderful kids. You'll get to meet them at dinner tonight."

"I'm invited to dinner? Can I bring a friend?"

Peg narrowed her eyes at him. "Male or female?"

"Male. My housemate, actually. Emmett Sengatti is a close friend of Willa's. He was kind enough to take me in when she abandoned me on the dock yesterday."

"Better the dock than the middle of the ocean," Peg returned with a laugh. She wheeled the vacuum toward the living room. "And there's always room at my table."

Sam looked down at the cat on his lap. "So, Ghost, has Willa got you building your own casket, too?"

"We have a line of pet caskets and urns coming out this fall," Willa said, walking into the kitchen, her arms laden with clothes. "But the bulk of them will likely be shipped out, since most Mainers are too thrifty to spend money on something they're going to bury in the ground."

He set the cat on the floor and stood up. "Here, let me have those," he said, reaching for the clothes. "Where are you going with them?"

"I'm moving out to the cottage so Shel can have my room," she told him, not relinquishing her load.

Sam perked up at that. "You're moving to the cottage?"

She spun away and headed for the door. "Do you honestly have the audacity to miss your first day of work?"

"I have an empathetic boss. Levi told me not to come in until I'm 'back up to snuff.' Kent Caskets is a rather laid-back company."

"You expect eighty-year-olds to be workaholics? They tell anyone with a hangnail to take the day off."

"Is your entire workforce retirees?"

She laughed at that. "Are you kidding? My production would be two caskets a year if I had to rely on my Grand Point Bluff residents. I have ten able-bodied men and women who do most of the real work."

"Yet you have at least twenty on the payroll."

"Which the older workers put right back into my business."

"Sam!" Shelby shouted from the top of the stairs. "Can you come up and carry this box down for me?"

Having figured out some time ago that Willa had a thing for his chest, Sam threw back his shoulders and puffed up, shooting her a grin. "Looks like your sister appreciates my muscles."

Willa immediately walked out of the house, muttering something about hormones.

Sam headed into the hall, ran up the stairs, and stepped into the bedroom of a teenage girl. The furniture was white, the bedspread pink and green and blue-flowered lace. Like the rest of the house, Willa's bedroom seemed to be frozen in time.

"That's the box?" he asked in surprise when Shelby

handed him a shoe box full of what looked like hair thingies.

"No. Put this in that box," she said, pointing to the bed. "And carry it over to the cottage."

"Yes, ma'am."

"Please," she quickly tacked on, her cheeks turning as pink as the curtains behind her. She sighed. "I'm sorry if I sound like a drill sergeant. With children, you either give orders or get ignored. Why did you tell my sister you love her?"

Sam stopped in mid-step. "Is directness another characteristic of motherhood?"

"Do you?" she asked, lifting her chin much as Willa did.

"Yes."

"Just like that? You know her a week, and you fall madly in love with her?"

He shrugged. "Not on purpose."

"Is that the price of love these days? A fat bankbook and a few shares of some business?"

Sam picked up the large box on the bed and walked to the door. "No," he said softly. "It's the price your sister has to be willing to pay to get back her soul."

Sam decided he rather liked Maine—at least, the area around Keelstone Cove and Prime Point, of which he was getting a firsthand and personal tour. He'd just sat down to his afternoon snack when Jennifer and Cody Bates had arrived home from school, and Jennifer had promptly thanked him for her new truck and boldly asked him to take her driving.

Even though Emmett had promised Sam he was in for a treat when he met Jennifer, the old man had failed to mention that for all of her precocious charm, the girl was also drop-dead beautiful.

Shelby had blue eyes, but Jennifer's eyes were more the startling blue of Willa's. Her long hair was less curly and a bit lighter than her aunt's and definitely more manageable. But whenever the teenager canted her head just right or glanced over her shoulder with a mischievous smile, Sam got the eerie feeling that he was looking at a younger Willa.

His gut had twisted in a knot as he'd watched Jennifer wolfing down a large piece of cake. What if Willa did marry him and they did have children? And what if they had a daughter as beautiful as Jennifer? He'd never survive her teenage years! Not if the images that came to mind were any indication when Shelby asked her about a particular boy at school. Sam had become positively outraged when Jennifer said she'd heard he was planning to ask someone else to the homecoming dance.

Was the boy an idiot? And blind?

"That kid, Steven, I think you called him," Sam said as Jennifer expertly guided her SUV down the narrow and winding road. "You can't take it personally if he doesn't ask you to the dance. Until the age of thirty, all males are self-centered idiots."

Jennifer briefly glanced over at him, then back at the road. "I rarely take anything personally. That's my aunt's infuriating habit." She sighed. "I really asked you to bring me driving so we could talk, Mr. Sinclair. I think you should know that I'm fully aware of what Abram's will said." She darted another quick glance in his direction, this time hitting him full force with her heart-stopping smile. "In fact, your being here means I won the bet. So, tell me, are you planning to find a way out of the bequest, or are you going to try to marry my aunt?"

She knew? And had even placed a bet? On *him?*

"If you're about to threaten me with bodily harm if I break your aunt's heart, you'll have to stand in line. I've already gotten this speech from Emmett and your mother, as well as from Willa's entire workforce."

She turned on her blinker and pulled down an even narrower lane to their right. "Don't underestimate Emmett. He never makes idle threats."

"Yeah, he told me that, too."

"So, am I going to get a new uncle?" She gave him a quick inspection, then smiled out the windshield again. "You'd be a vast improvement over my last one. David Sommers looked like a troll and had the personality of a billy goat."

"How old did you say you are?" Sam asked with a chuckle.

"Emmett claims I'm sixteen going on sixty. You still haven't answered my question, Mr. Sinclair."

"I might, if you call me Sam."

"Okay, Sam," she said, pulling into the parking lot of a small warehouse perched on the edge of a tiny cove. She shut off the engine and looked over at him. "Please tell me you're as astute as your grandfather and can see how much my aunt deserves to have somebody love her."

"There are no knights in shining armor in real life, Jennifer. It won't matter how much I love Willa, if she's unable to love herself."

"But that's just it. I remember how Auntie used to be. I was only eight, but when Gram and Gramps died and she lost her baby, the light inside her dimmed. Then five years ago, when we had the accident," she said, touching her right knee, "that light nearly went out completely. But a tiny spark's still there; I know it is. I see hints of it every so often, like when she and I go sailing together."

"Yeah. I saw it, too, on our trip here."

"She just needs someone to toss fuel on that spark and coax it back to life."

"And you think I'm that someone?"

"Yes."

Sam leaned against his door and studied his emphatic chauffeur. "What makes you so sure?"

"Your grandfather talked about his 'three boys' all the time, so it wasn't hard for me to figure out that of all of his grandsons, you're the most like Abram. And whenever he and Aunt Willa were together, they were like baking soda and vinegar. In the six weeks your grandfather was here, I saw Auntie's spark actually burst into flame a few times. Abram Sinclair was the first person I've seen her get that close to in years."

"You don't think she's close to you? And Emmett? And your mother and brother?"

"Of course she is, but only by default, and only because she can't very well *stop* loving us." She dropped her gaze and shook her head. "I think it was okay for Abram to die, because she knew going in that it was going to happen. But God forbid anything should happen to any of us. I'm not sure she'd survive another tragedy."

Completely forgetting that he was talking to a sixteen-year-old, Sam asked, "Then what makes you think adding a husband and child for her to worry about won't send Willa over the edge?"

Jennifer sighed. "My own parents haven't had a very . . . mutually supportive relationship, but I've had many wonderful examples of the power of true love. Emmett lost his wife, Gretchen, to cancer a little more than three years ago. What I learned from them is that when two people love each other that deeply, anything is possible, even continuing on alone. Emmett misses Gretchen immensely, but every breath he's taken since she died has been filled with her spirit."

She lifted her beautiful little chin in exact mimic of

Willa. "I don't intend to settle for anything less than that kind of love for myself. Nor will I let my aunt spend the rest of her life hiding from it. I may have lost my foot five years ago, but she's the one who was crippled." She reached out and touched his arm. "You're my only hope, Sam. Please, will you help me help her?"

Sam found himself staring into eyes as desperate as the ocean was deep and as old as the earth, and suddenly he couldn't breathe, much less speak.

"Abram gave you the most powerful tool he had, Sam. His bequest is your trump card, if you decide to play it."

"It's also my greatest obstacle, Jennifer. Willa thinks I want to marry her to get those shares and to keep our home."

He stiffened as several pieces of the puzzle unexpectedly fell into place. "My God," he whispered. "You helped Bram draft that damn will."

She looked away. "I don't know anything about that sort of legal stuff."

"No, but you know Willa. You certainly knew she'd never let Tidewater fall into the hands of a man who wants to destroy it. You helped my grandfather write his last will and testament in a way that Willa's conscience wouldn't let her ignore."

The teenager brought her gaze back to his, her expression mutinous. "She needed a swift kick in the butt! You have no idea what it's been like for me these last five years. Guilt can be contagious, you know." She thumped herself on the chest. "How in hell am I supposed to get on with my life when my aunt won't get on with hers? I can never be free until *she's* free."

Sam had never considered what Willa's self-reproach might be doing to those around her. Of course, anyone who loved her would share her pain—especially Jennifer.

"Is your aunt aware of how you feel?" he asked softly.

Jennifer shrugged, then pulled the key out of the ignition and opened her door. "I've been waiting for the right man to help her figure that out."

"Where are we going?" he asked, opening his own door and getting out.

She gave him a cheeky grin across the hood of her truck. "I thought you might want to buy some lobsters for your and Emmett's supper tomorrow night. And since we're here, I also thought I'd give you a few pointers on courting." She motioned toward the warehouse, which was a fish co-op. "Steven works here. If I want him to take me to the homecoming dance, I suppose I should ask him to, shouldn't I?"

Sam choked on a bark of laughter. He strode around the truck, slipped Jennifer's arm through his, and sauntered toward the side entrance. "I tell you what. If Steven is intelligent enough to say yes, I will fly you and your mother to New York on Tidewater's private jet and take you shopping for a dress for the dance."

"Deal!" she said with delight. She batted her eyelashes at him. "But I should warn you, I've been accused of having expensive tastes."

"No problem," Sam drawled. "I've managed to tuck away some of my paychecks over the years. And if that's not enough, I'm sure my brothers won't mind kicking in a few bucks."

Sam sat at the small, battered table, in the exact same chair his grandfather had sat in to record his good-bye video. The cottage was dark except for the moonlight coming through the windows, it was half past eleven, and he was waiting for Willa to get home from her date with Barry Cobb.

Tonight's dinner conversation in the old Kent homestead had ranged from Cody's decision to try out for next year's Odyssey of the Mind, to Emmett's new keel design he was working on, to whether Sam though the Red Sox would play the Yankees in the World Series again this season. The only thing *not* discussed was Willa's blaring absence.

Sam still couldn't believe that Barry Cobb had had the audacity to drive up to her home that afternoon and boldly ask her out to dinner. Even more surprising, Willa didn't seem to mind being seen in public not only with the enemy but with a very eligible bachelor.

The enemy part didn't worry Sam; he figured Willa had agreed to dinner out of sheer curiosity. He smiled.

And maybe also to piss him off. But what if she was seen by one of the marriage posse? The last thing he needed was for those damn busybodies to decide that Cobb was the perfect match for her.

Headlights suddenly slashed through the darkness, briefly illuminating the interior of the cottage before they swung around to the beachfront and stopped. Sam smiled again when he heard a car door immediately open and shut and footsteps scampering onto the cottage porch.

The poor bastard wasn't even getting a good-night kiss for his troubles.

The headlights repeated their arcing display in reverse as the cottage door opened. The interior lights came on, and Willa let out a scream loud enough to wake the dead.

Sam stood up. "Sorry. I didn't mean to startle you."

"What are you doing here?" She clutched her jacket to her chest.

"Waiting for you."

Her expression instantly became indignant. "Are you checking up on me?"

"Hmm?" he asked, studying her. "No, of course not. Is that dirt on your forehead?" He walked over, brushed back her hair, then dropped his gaze to hers with a sigh. "Did Cobb make you nervous tonight, or did you run into the marriage posse?"

She headed to the sink, tossing her jacket over a

chair on her way by. "Barry was a perfect gentleman."

"I would have expected no less."

She frowned at him, then turned on the water, grabbed a towel hanging next to the window, and held a corner of it under the faucet. "And nobody from town saw us, because we drove thirty miles to Ellsworth to go to dinner."

He took the towel from her and gently wiped away the mud. "That was smart. There, all clean." He led her over to the table and sat her down. "How did you get mud on your forehead and knee?" he asked, squatting down to examine her knee through the large hole in her stocking.

She pulled the hem of her wrinkled dress down. "Barry already checked me out and declared I'd live," she said, her expression daring him to comment.

He stood up. "Then I shall take the *gentleman's* word." He went to the fridge, got out the large piece of dark chocolate cake he'd brought from the house, and placed it on the table in front of her. "Did he buy you dessert?"

"Warm apple pie," she snapped, swiping her finger through the frosting and popping it into her mouth.

Sam opened several drawers and came back with a fork. He sat down across from her, pulled the plate over to his side of the table, and dug in. "You still haven't told me how you got mud on your face."

"Go home, Sam. I want to be alone."

He stopped eating, studied her for several seconds,

then quietly set down his fork, stood up, and went to the door. "Will you go to the movies with me this Friday night?"

She blinked at him, though Sam didn't know if she was surprised by his leaving or his asking her out. He took his jacket off the peg and slipped it on. "Or if you prefer, we can rent a movie and stay in."

"I want to be alone Friday night, too."

"Saturday?"

"I have to wash my hair Saturday night."

"I'll check in with you next week, then," he said, stepping onto the porch and closing the door behind him.

He pulled up his collar outside but stopped under a low-hanging tree several feet away from the cottage. Through the window, he saw Willa pull the cake over to her side of the table and put a large bite into her mouth.

A few things Jennifer had said that afternoon made Sam wonder if the secret to winning Willa's heart might not be a swift kick in the butt after all.

Fanning that little spark back to life would be fun, considering how easy it was to rile her. He'd have to take things a lot further, though, if he wanted to rid Willa of the habit of being responsible for everyone's happiness. But then, mirrors were wonderful instruments for reflecting the naked truth right back at a person.

Chapter Seventeen

Willa had spent most of the last two weeks locked in her office, trying to lose herself in her new line of pet caskets but more often staring into space as she tried to figure a way out of her dilemma. And, she admitted with a sigh as she tossed her pencil down on her sketch pad, she had also been hiding from Sam.

But mostly, she'd been forced into exile by the killer glares she'd been getting from her workers. Jennifer and Shelby and Peg weren't talking to her, either, and last Monday, Cody had announced that being around a bunch of silent women was creepy and had gone to stay with his dad.

The only person who didn't appear angry at her for going to dinner with Barry Cobb four more times was Sam. Which was confounding—shouldn't he be worried that she was cavorting with the enemy? After all, it was *his* inheritance Cobb was interested in, under the guise of being interested in her.

But Sam hadn't made any attempts to see her in the last twelve days. She'd heard he'd shortened his hours at Kent Caskets to two days a week, apparently to devote more time to hunting down every last seafood restaurant within fifty miles. He obviously loved to eat a lot more than he loved her.

She'd also heard he'd gained more than ten pounds.

And the diabolical jerk had stolen her thunder by flying Shelby and Jennifer and Cody to New York City on Tidewater's private jet. He'd treated them to two days of heavy shopping and even a helicopter tour of Manhattan. What good was having a big fat bank account if she couldn't use it to impress her family? *She* had wanted to buy Jennifer's dress for the dance.

Willa turned off her desk lamp, plunging her office into darkness. She hadn't even gotten to take Jennifer driving again, since her niece had decided that Sam was a wonderful instructor.

Well, if the girl wanted to get all gaga over the man, that was her problem. Willa had been there and done that. Samuel Sinclair was just another typical male with an agenda, and if Shelby and Jennifer and Emmett couldn't see that, then . . . then that was also their problem. She was getting sick and tired of always watching out for them, anyway. Maybe they could all use a good lesson in getting themselves out of their own messes.

She snapped the light back on, picked up the phone, and dialed Emmett's house.

"Hello," Emmett said after the third ring.

"Hi, Em. I didn't want you to be worried when you got to work tomorrow and saw the *RoseWind* wasn't on her mooring. I'm taking her out sailing for a few days."

"Well, Willy, that's going to be kind of hard, considering she's missing half her paint. I brought her into dry dock five days ago to be repainted."

"You *what?* I didn't ask you to do that."

"No, Sam did. He said he thought she should be gone over, anyway. He also asked me to check all the winches."

"Sam doesn't own the *RoseWind*, I do!"

"The jib winch was sticking, I discovered," Emmett continued, ignoring her burst of temper. "And I found a large chunk had been gouged out of the keel. You must have noticed the hull vibrating. How come you didn't mention it to me when you got in?"

"It couldn't have been that large a gouge; the boat went fine. You actually dry-docked the *RoseWind* without calling me to see if it was okay?"

"Foul weather's predicted for the next few days, anyway," Emmett said. "Say, have you spoken to Sam lately?"

"No, I'm happy to say." She picked up her pencil and started doodling on her sketch pad. "Um . . . why? You sound as if something's wrong. Are his brothers okay?"

"They're fine that I know of. It's Sam I'm worried about. Have you even seen him in passing?"

"Just from a distance," she said, sitting up. "Why?"

There was a slight pause on the line. "He's not the same man who arrived here two weeks ago, Willy."

"How's that?"

"Even as beat up as he was, Sam still appeared . . . *formidable*, if you know what I mean."

"And he's not now? What are you saying, Emmett?"

A heavy sigh came over the phone. "I can't put my finger on it, exactly. I just know Sam's been acting strangely lately."

"Compared to what? You've only known him two weeks."

"Depressed, then," he growled. "If I have to put a word on it, I'd say Sam is acting depressed."

"As in *how?*" she growled back. "Is he sleeping all day? Lying on the couch watching the Lifetime channel and munching on junk food? What?"

"Well, he does eat a lot. He's been gaining weight."

"That's not depression, that's plain old gluttony."

"And he went out and bought himself a bunch of flannel shirts, and he doesn't even bother to tuck them in."

"Oh, for the love of—"

"And he's going to the coffee shop nearly every morning." His voice dropped. "And you know how depressing that group can get sometimes."

Willa grew alarmed. "Have you tried to talk to him, Emmett? Maybe you should just come out and ask him what's bothering him."

"That's not my place."

"Are you implying it's mine? Since when did I become Sam's babysitter?"

"You're just better at that sort of thing, Willamina."

"Maybe Abram's death is just now hitting him. Maybe he's simply mourning. Remember how you were when Gretchen passed? Sorrow hits everyone differently, and how long it takes to work through it is up to the individual. Abram was like a father to Sam."

Another heavy sigh came over the phone line. "You're probably right. He's likely just realizing that he and his brothers are completely alone in the world now."

"You might suggest he stop going to the coffee shop," Willa said. "They probably keep mentioning Abram, and that will keep depressing Sam."

"I'll do that," Emmett said. "I'm sorry about the *RoseWind*, Willy. But truth be told, I couldn't wait to get my hands on her again. She was my last, you know?"

"I know, Em, and it's okay. Um . . . is Sam home?"

"He left about an hour ago and told me not to wait dinner for him." He snorted. "Not that I ever do. I usually just help myself to one of the many doggie bags he keeps sticking in the fridge."

She covered her mouth to stifle a yawn. "Okay, I'd better get on home and see what Peg's put in my own fridge. Tomorrow's Saturday. I'll come over and work on the *RoseWind* with you, if you'd like."

"I'd like that. It's been a few years since we've worked side by side."

" 'Bye, Em," she said. She shut off the light again and gazed across the dark room at nothing.

Emmett thought Sam was depressed?

His weight gain would make sense if that was the case. After her parents died and she lost the baby, she'd started feeding the emptiness inside her with whatever food she could get her hands on. She'd gained twelve pounds that year, and that had been the beginning of the end for her and David. A year later, she began to suspect he was cheating on her, and she'd gained another ten pounds.

Looking back, Willa could see she'd unconsciously been driving David away, probably because he was as emotionally supportive as seaweed.

She stood up and walked out of her office, giving the bronze whale statue a pat. Nearly two weeks had gone by, and she wasn't any closer to finding a solution to Abram's bequest. If anything, she had unwittingly added one more problem to her growing list. Barry Cobb was not only so full of himself he bored her to tears, he was becoming a pest.

Willa pulled up beside Sam's rental car, shut off the engine, and stared at the lighted windows of her cottage in dismay. Great. Just what she needed, a depressed man dropping by to depress *her*.

She looked toward the main house, figuring there was probably food up there. But there was also Shelby and Jennifer and their killer glares. Peg wasn't a glarer; she just banged pot lids around whenever Barry Cobb's name came up.

Willa looked back at her cottage, trying to decide which way lay the lesser evil. She was actually surprised, but she sort of missed Sam. At least, with him, she could glare right back without feeling guilty, because he wasn't going through a divorce.

But he *was* mourning Abram.

God, she wished Emmett hadn't dry-docked the *RoseWind*. She could be sailing toward the Bermuda Triangle right now.

Willa got out of her pickup and mounted the porch steps, thinking it was kind of nice coming home to a house that wasn't empty. She perked up a bit. Maybe Sam had brought food. She'd even settle for a doggie bag from one of his restaurant excursions.

She opened the door and immediately saw that the table was empty except for a small stack of mail. Sam hadn't even brought her flowers to apologize for avoiding her for two whole weeks. Bummer.

"Over here," he said from the corner of the room. "Wash up, and come sit down. I hope you're hungry."

Her spirits rose with renewed hope. "What are we

having?" she asked, shedding her coat as she went to the sink.

"Roasted hot dogs, potato salad, and S'mores for dessert. I also found a campfire popcorn popper at the hardware store, but we'll save that for later."

Later? Willa glanced over her shoulder in time to see him add a log to the fire he'd built in the antique parlor woodstove.

Hot dogs? He's been dining at every damn restaurant in the county, and he feeds me hot dogs and S'mores? She wiped her hands and went to sit on the love seat facing the woodstove.

Sam pulled her down onto the floor beside him. "You can't reach the fire from up there. The sticks aren't long enough."

"I have to cook my own dinner?"

He handed her a forked twig with a hot dog skewered on the end of it. "Cooking the dogs is the best part. If you do it just right, they plump up and get juicy."

Willa shoved her hot dog into the fire.

Sam immediately took hold of her hand, raising it until her hot dog was above the flame. "It's already dead. And cooked," he drawled. "You just need to sear the skin."

"It's a hot dog, not filet mignon," she said, lowering it back into the flames when he let go. "And I like mine burnt on the outside, so it splits open."

"Is it okay if I don't turn the rolls into charcoal?" he asked with a chuckle, sliding two buns onto another stick that had wider-set branches. He'd very neatly whittled the bark off the ends.

"You've put a lot of time into preparing this picnic."

"After almost poking my eye out, I decided your maple tree could use a pruning. That's when I got the idea for hot dogs." He held the rolls in front of the fire, close to the embers. "Bram and Grammy Rose used to take us boys up to the Adirondacks every summer after we came to live with them. It was just the five of us—no staff, no chauffeur, no cook. We'd fly up, and Bram had a big old rusted van he kept at the airport. We'd transfer all our gear into it and pile in, then drive to the ricketiest old cabin you've ever seen."

He turned the rolls over to toast the other side. "Grammy would assign us each a chore on the way to the cabin. My job was usually spider eradication. Ben had to lug firewood, and Jesse always helped Bram drag the old fishing boat down to the water to see if it was still seaworthy."

He glanced over at her, then back at the rolls. "We didn't have an outboard motor, just oars. It took a full week for our blisters to heal, but by the end of the summer, we all had thick calluses." He shook his head. "No electricity, no running water, and an outhouse that still gives me nightmares."

"How come Abram didn't update the cabin?"

"If we'd had all the modern conveniences, we might as well have stayed home. We were roughing it, and those summers were the best times of our lives after our parents died."

Willa jumped when her hot dog exploded and fell off the stick into the fire.

Without saying a word, Sam shoved another hot dog onto the charred tines, then held it over the flames. "We tried going to the cabin the summer after Grammy died, but we only stayed a few days. It just wasn't the same." He glanced at her. "I guess you own the cabin now."

Willa took a shuddering breath and looked down at her lap. Depression *was* contagious.

"Levi fired me yesterday."

"He did? Why?"

Sam turned her hot dog over and lowered it to start burning the skin. "He claims I'm all thumbs when it comes to working with power tools. But I think it's because he found out I've been going to the coffee shop most mornings."

She started filling the toasted rolls with ketchup and relish and mustard. "What makes you think that's why he fired you?"

Sam slid her hot dog into one of the rolls, then put another one on the stick and held it over the flames. "Keelstone Cove is in the middle of a geriatric gang war."

"A *what?*"

"There's the Grand Point Bluff gang and the coffee club gang, and they went to war when Bram died."

"Oh for the love of—these are civilized people, Sam, not gang members."

"No, it's the *away* people versus the *locals*. Most of your workers retired here from New York and Boston, didn't they? It's also the *haves* against the *have nots*. The coffee clubbers think the Grand Pointers throw their money around like confetti."

"Your grandfather went to that coffee shop *and* he was friends with my workers. And he was from away and rich. So how come the coffee clubbers let him into their club?" She eyed him suspiciously. "For that matter, how come they let *you* in? Not only are you rich and from away, but you're not even old enough to be a member."

He started to slide his hot dog into its roll but stopped. "I don't like mustard."

"Oh, just eat it," she snapped. "And answer my question. How come Levi was willing to work with Abram, but he fires you for cavorting with the enemy?"

"Because before I arrived, both gangs had the same agenda."

"And that was?"

"To see you happy."

Willa stopped with her hot dog halfway to her mouth. "See me happy? As if it's any of their damn business to begin with. But wait a minute—are you saying they don't have the same agenda now? Does one of the gangs *not* want to see me happy?"

He took a large bite of his hot dog, made a face, and swallowed. "No, they both still want you happy; they just don't agree on how that should happen." He started dishing out the potato salad. "The coffee clubbers want you to marry me, like Bram thought you should. But the Grand Pointers think you should marry a local man."

Willa gaped at him. "You're funning me, right? I know this town is filled to its eyeballs with bored senior citizens, but they can't possibly be that invested in my life. Besides, you've got it backward. If anyone would want to see me married to you, it would be the Grand Pointers. They're retired executives and would want me to marry a businessman. The locals would want me to marry a local."

"Nope." He shook his head. "Silas, Maureen, and Levi cornered me in the break room the other day and told me point-blank that if I tried blackmailing you with that bequest, I could find myself inside a burlap sack on a lobster boat on a one-way trip out to sea."

"They *threatened* you?"

"They told me not to take it personally, just seriously."

"But they *liked* Abram."

"They claim they like me, too, just not as your husband." He shrugged. "At first, they thought Bram's plan was a good one, but after he died, they started thinking over the part about forcing you to get pregnant and decided he'd taken things too far. In the five days it took you to sail home, they'd persuaded themselves that the whole thing was a bad idea. They believe you should find a nice, easygoing local man to settle down with and that if you don't want babies, you shouldn't have any."

Her workers, her *friends*, were deciding whom she should fall in love with? And marry? And not have babies with?

Sam lifted her chin with his finger. "They love you, Willa. They may be misguided in their thinking, but they love you."

"And the coffee clubbers? What's their excuse?"

He smiled. "They're equally sincere, honey. They want to see you happily married, too—just not to a local man."

"But why not?"

He slid his arm around her shoulder. "One, they'd like to have some fresh young blood move into town. And two, they told me there's not a local man within a hundred miles who would marry you. You've got a bit of a reputation for stirring up trouble. Then there's the fact that you're a wild woman at sea. There aren't many coastal men who can live with a woman who can outsail them."

Willa was shocked senseless at how everyone had an opinion about what she should and shouldn't do.

"You know what I think?" Sam asked.

She refused even to hazard a guess.

"I think I should open my own business and put the coffee clubbers on *my* payroll."

"What?" she yelped, pulling away to face him. "Are you nuts?"

"I doubt they'll put their paychecks back into my business, though. I have a feeling they could use the money. Paul Dubay needs a new lawn mower; the one he drives to coffee is on its last leg."

"Paul Dubay drives a lawn mower to the coffee shop?"

"Right down Main Street. He claims the 'damn government' wouldn't renew his license because his eyesight is bad."

"Paul Dubay is more than ninety years old! He shouldn't drive anything that goes faster than a walker. And don't kid yourself; your new best buddies are a long way from living hand-to-mouth. They simply can't bring themselves to spend any of their money, because they worked too damn hard to get it." She shook her head. "We're getting off track, Sam. You are not setting yourself up as Keelstone Cove's social welfare system, and you're not opening a business just to give the coffee clubbers something to do."

"Why not? You started Kent Caskets to give *your* people something to do."

"I needed a job. I hired them because I didn't know anything about running a business."

"You told me you had a job at Grand Point Bluff."

"I decided I wanted to be my own boss. After Levi

built a casket in the wood shop, the manager at Grand Point wouldn't let me do anything creative with the residents anymore. He made me dismantle the wood shop and turned it into a bingo parlor. So I quit."

"And the residents bankrolled Kent Caskets?"

"No. Emmett did."

"Emmett? He's your silent partner?"

"Yeah. Why are you surprised?"

"I was under the impression that Emmett had hoped to turn Sengatti Yachts over to you one day. Why would he help you start a brand-new business?"

"Because his wife had just been diagnosed with inoperable cancer, and he told me he wished he was as emotionally strong as Levi and could build Gretchen a casket, too. He tried, but he couldn't do it, so I told him I would. I was going through my divorce at the time, and I think Emmett saw my opening Kent Caskets as some sort of therapy for me. So he put up the money. He said he had as much faith in my being a success as someone had faith in him nearly fifty years ago."

She suddenly gasped, touching Sam's sleeve. "Emmett told me he owed Abram a very large favor. Your grandfather must have given him the money to start Sengatti Yachts. They met when Abram was attending Maine Maritime Academy. The timing's about right."

"That makes sense." Sam folded his arms over his chest. "So, what sort of business should I open? Something to do with food, maybe? I've been eating out a lot lately, and I've had some fantastic chowders. I should probably do something different. How about lobster cakes? You know, like crab cakes? I've rarely seen lobster cakes on any of the menus. And we could eventually ship them worldwide. That's something the clubbers could do. And I'd hire able-bodied people, like you did, to pick up the slack."

"Sam, you are not opening a business in Maine."

"Why not? In three months, I'm going to need a new job."

Willa scrambled to her feet. "But not here! You're a city boy, born and raised. And you haven't lost Tidewater yet. That company needs you."

"Even if Tidewater survives, it only needs Ben," he said, also getting to his feet. "And I may be a city boy, but I really like Maine." He frowned at her. "What's so upsetting about my opening a business here?"

"Because you're doing it for all the wrong reasons." Now that he was standing, Willa got her first good look at him. "Oh, my God. Sam, what's happened to you?"

"What?" he asked, looking down at himself, then rubbed his baggy flannel shirt over his not-so-flat belly. "This, you mean?" he asked with a grin. "I started thinking about how you got David to divorce you, and I decided you might be on to something. I figured if I gained a few pounds, women would either look right past me or take the time to know the real me. I wasn't worried about your reaction, because you wouldn't care if a man is five-foot-two, bald, and cross-eyed; if you love him, it's for real." He rubbed his belly again. "A very clever idea, Willa. Just like giving the senior citizens something to do."

She was utterly speechless.

He turned away and walked to the fridge and came back with a bottle of champagne. "It's not Dom Perignon, but I've put myself on a budget." He started unwinding the wire. "Will you toast my new adventure with me?"

"Sam," she said, covering his hand to stop him. "You don't know the first thing about making lobster cakes."

"Phil Grindle used to own a lobster shack. I'll get him to oversee that part of the operation. And Doris Ambrose is a fantastic watercolorist. She can design the labels and advertising."

"Have you even asked Phil and Doris if they want jobs?"

"Of course. They're quite excited about it. Sean Graves knows of an old warehouse over in Prime Point we can buy and renovate," he said, going to work on the wire again.

Willa stopped him again. "Sam, does this have anything to do with Abram's dying? Have you considered that you might be missing your grandfather and have substituted the coffee clubbers for him?"

He sat on the love seat and frowned up at her. "Why was it a good idea for you but not for me? Why shouldn't I open a business?"

She sat beside him, resting her hand on his knee. "You're not yourself right now, Sam. You've suddenly been cast adrift with no direction or purpose. You've lost Abram, your home, and possibly Tidewater. You're depressed, Sam, and you're trying to fill the void in your life with food and . . . and with being needed."

"That's it exactly," he said, covering her hand with his. "Not the depressed part but the purpose part. Bram needed me, and I wasn't there for him. I should have seen his health was failing, but he was such a tough old bird I assumed he'd live forever. Maybe if I'd been paying better attention, he'd still be alive."

"You can't possibly know that. Abram kept his heart condition from you precisely so you wouldn't fuss over him. You have nothing to feel guilty about." She squeezed his hand. "Don't you see, Sam? You can't take Abram's dying as having anything to do with *you*. Life happens, and so does death, and none of us has a magic wand we can wave to make everything turn out perfect."

"But we can make up for our mistakes. I wasn't there for Bram in the end, but I can be there for someone else. And it feels damn good to be totally focused on helping other people, Willa. It's almost addictive." He raised her hand and kissed her fingers. "Bram might have thought he was doing you a favor by writing that bequest, but it's my eyes he opened."

He suddenly stood up, took the champagne back to the fridge, and walked to the door and grabbed his jacket. "Will you go to dinner with me tomorrow night?"

"What about tonight's dinner?" she asked, motioning toward the woodstove.

"I just realized that I've left Emmett alone a lot lately. I don't think he eats a very balanced diet. I should take him to a place I found in Ellsworth that serves a wonderful dish of broiled Maine scallops, rice, and broccoli florets. Emmett loves scallops. Is tomorrow night good for you?"

Her head spinning, Willa nodded.

"Great. I'll pick you up at six," he said, and left.

Willa stared across the suddenly empty cottage. Emmett had it all wrong. Sam wasn't depressed, he must be on drugs!

He actually thought there was a war going on in Keelstone Cove? And that he could adopt the coffee clubbers for his new family? And move here? Permanently?

As for Emmett, just when had he become *Sam's* responsibility?

Chapter Eighteen

If Willa had been asked a week ago what she thought Keelstone Cove's greatest asset was, she would have said unequivocally that it was the town's dynamic senior-citizen population. Just consider the cumulative decades of wisdom the older folks were glad to share, from weather predictions, fishing methods, and recipes to business advice. Ask any of them a simple question, and you'd be treated to a twenty-minute lecture.

Seniors were the backbone of any society.

They were not, however, supposed to start acting like rebellious teenagers—which is exactly what her Grand Point Bluff workers were doing. She stormed into work the very next morning and shot off a memo demanding that everyone older than seventy be in her conference room at ten o'clock.

Willa sat at the head of the long mahogany table in

her office suite and glared at the expensive antique wall clock that Silas had insisted Kent Caskets needed to present an air of success. It was ten-fifteen, and she didn't recognize the lone person sitting four places down on her right.

"You said you just moved into Grand Point Bluff a month ago, Mr. Goodard?" she asked. "And that Silas hired you last week?"

Gary Goodard shot her a nervous smile. "Yes, ma'am. I originally retired to Florida, but there's so many people down there I couldn't breathe. I explained to Silas I probably should work in sales, considering I used to own a Mercedes dealership, but he told me the only opening you had was in shipping. If this is about that mix-up the other day, I'm really sorry. I don't know why they ever changed the state abbreviation system. I thought AR meant Arizona, and that's why I sent those caskets to Cedar Creek, Arizona, instead of Cedar Creek, Arkansas. I promise it won't happen again, Miss Kent."

Willa sighed. "This isn't about the mix-up, Gary, since no one told me about it, anyway. And please, call me Willa. We're very informal here. Do you know if the others got my memo?" It was twenty-five minutes past ten.

"Oh, yes," Gary said, his expression brightening. "Your secretary hand-delivered it to all the departments. Say, you must know Isobel quite well, since she's your personal secretary. Can you tell me how long she's been widowed?"

"Six or seven years, I believe."

"Would you know if she's seeing anyone?"

Willa sighed again. "I don't believe she is." She stood up. "Nor do I believe anyone else is coming to my meeting, Gary. And since it wasn't about anything involving you, why don't you head back to shipping? Oh, and welcome to Kent Caskets."

Gary had stood up when she had, his joints creaking loudly. "Thank you," he said, hobbling toward the door. "I have to say, I love getting up in the morning and having someplace to go again. Retirement's not all it's cracked up to be. I spent so many hours working to make my dealership successful I never acquired any hobbies. It's very community-minded of you to hire older citizens."

"Yes, it seems I've gotten a reputation for being very community-minded."

The door suddenly opened, and Silas, Maureen, and Levi walked in, followed by the rest of her older workers.

"Sorry we're late, Willa," Silas said, pulling out the chair on her right and standing in front of it as the others went to their usual seats. "Isobel just tracked us down. It was such a beautiful day, we decided to go over our last-quarter reports outside at the picnic tables."

"Sorry to pull you away from your important meeting, but I wanted to talk to all of you together," Willa said. She realized that for them to sit down, *she* had to sit down, so she did. The moment they sat, she stood back up.

"Is this about the new line of pet caskets?" Maureen asked. "I haven't finished the interior patterns, because Levi hasn't given me the measurements yet."

"No, this isn't about our pet line. I've called you here to talk about Sam Sinclair."

"I had to let him go, Willa," Levi said. "The man's all thumbs." He shook his head. "I should have suspected it when he first showed up, considering how beat up he was."

"He was also disruptive," Silas interjected. "He spent more time talking than working. Our production was falling behind."

"That's right," Maureen piped in. "All he had to do was walk through the sewing room, and the younger women got all a-twitter. Carol actually sewed her sleeve to the pillow she was working on." She narrowed her eyes at Willa. "Sam Sinclair is a worse flirt than his grandfather was."

Willa held up her hand. "His firing is not the reason I called this meeting. I want to talk to you about this little . . . dispute you're having with the coffee clubbers, of which Sam and I seem to be the center." She placed her hands on the table and moved her glare from one person to the next. "Butt out, people. My love life is none of your business. *If* I ever decide to get married again, I will marry whomever I damn well please." She straightened and pointed her finger at them. "If you don't stop interfering in my life, I will fire every last one of you. Except you, Gary," she quickly amended, "unless I hear that you've fallen in with these outlaws."

She glared around the table again. "Do we understand each other, ladies and gentlemen? And if any of you threaten Sam again, I will call the sheriff."

"But he's only pretending to be interested in you to get back his inheritance," Maureen cried.

"Did you know he's buying the old Ingall warehouse in Prime Point?" Silas said. "Avery Ingall has been trying to unload that place for years. I bet he takes Sinclair to the cleaners."

"Word on the street is that Sam's planning to open some sort of mail-order food plant," Levi said.

Maureen snickered. "I heard he asked Doris Ambrose to head up his marketing department. I hope he knows his labels are going to have angels on them. That's all the woman can paint."

"And Phil Grindle's supposed to be his head chef," Carl Sills, a retired lawyer in charge of her sales department, added. "Throwing lobsters into a pot of boiling water for thirty years is one hell of a résumé."

Willa was horrified. "My God, you really are all a bunch of snobs."

"What?" Silas said, his face reddening. He stood up.

"We are not. But who the hell does Sam Sinclair think he is, coming here and opening a business, hiring a bunch of coffee-swigging old people to run it?"

Willa crossed her arms. "Last time I checked, Maine was still part of the United States of America. I believe anyone can open a business wherever he desires, and that if he wants to hire retired people, he can. How is what Sam's doing any different from what I did four years ago?"

"Oh, Willa!" Maureen cried, also standing up. "You're no better than my girls in the sewing room. You've taken one look at Sam's pretty face and fat bankbook and lost your senses."

"My bankbook happens to be bigger than his at the moment," Willa shot back. "And I have not lost my senses."

"Wait a minute," Levi said, also standing up and looking at Maureen and Silas. "It might be okay if she falls in love with Sam. Now that he's opening a business here, they'd be living in Keelstone Cove. It's Barry Cobb we should be worried about."

That's what all this was about? Willa sat down hard. They weren't worried about her happiness; they were worried about their jobs! They were afraid that if she fell in love with Sam, she might sell Kent Caskets and move to New York. And they damn well knew the next owner wouldn't put up with their shenanigans.

"Willa. Willa!" Maureen said, thumping her cane to get her attention. "It's okay, then, if you marry Sam. And we're sorry we threatened him."

"And if Sam and I end up having a dozen children, is that okay, too, Maureen? And Silas?" she asked, her gaze moving down the table. "Levi? Carl? And the rest of you? Because I sure as heck wouldn't want to do anything that you don't think will make me happy."

"Now, Willa," Silas said, his face red. "Your happiness is our only concern."

She stood and silently walked out the door. Ignoring Maureen's calls to her, she continued down the hall and didn't stop until she reached her truck. She looked back at her building and decided she was going to paint it white and green again.

Sam turned down Willa's driveway, smiling in anticipation of her reaction to his purchase. His new truck was identical to Jennifer's, only black instead of red. Emmett, with his usual dry humor, had wished Sam good luck this winter trying to keep it clean once they started salting the roads.

He'd originally gone shopping for a pickup but had decided on the SUV when he remembered that his future might include a car seat and other baby paraphernalia. Not that he intended to mention that to Willa.

He frowned as he pulled up beside Willa's pickup in

front of her cottage. It was five minutes to six, but there weren't any lights on inside. All the windows of the main house were ablaze. Was she visiting her sister?

Had she forgotten their date?

He got out and noticed the smell of wood smoke as he walked up the cottage steps. He peeked into the door window and saw a fire burning in the stove in the corner, its cast-iron doors open and the screen set in place.

Willa wouldn't leave an open stove unattended. He knocked, then cupped his hands to watch through the window again, but he didn't see anyone rushing to let him in. He tried the knob and found it was unlocked, so he stepped inside.

He could just make out the silhouette of her head rising above the back of the couch. "Willa?" he said, tossing his jacket onto the table.

She didn't answer him.

"Did you fall asleep?" he asked, going to her. "I've made reservations for us at seven in Ellsworth."

"Go away."

"Honey, what's wrong?" he asked, hunching down in front of her, only to find her staring blankly at the fire. He immediately scooped her up in his arms and took her place on the couch, setting her on his lap. "What's happened? Is it one of your seniors? Is someone sick?"

She buried her face in his shirt.

"Okay, we'll just sit together for a while." He kissed her hair as he held her head to his chest.

She released a deep, shuddering sigh.

What had upset her? Or who? Sam knew it wasn't his coffee gang; he'd spent most of the day with them inspecting the warehouse.

Cobb better not have bothered Willa. He'd run into Cobb in town today, and the bastard had actually tried to strike up a conversation. Sam had nearly laughed out loud when Phil Grindle, at five-foot-four and a hundred and fifty pounds, had stepped between him and Cobb and asked Barry if he wouldn't like to go on an authentic lobster run with a young fisherman friend of his. Fearing that Phil planned it to be a one-way trip, Sam had pulled his friend away before Cobb could answer.

Had Cobb visited Kent Caskets this afternoon and said something to upset Willa? Maybe one of her workers had taken ill. Or even died?

She shuddered again, as if fighting tears.

"Grammy Rose always told me that sharing a burden shrinks it by half," he said against her hair. "Please, honey, tell me what's bothering you."

"I don't like the people I work with," she said in a ragged voice. "They're selfish, manipulative snobs who are only interested in themselves, and I don't ever want to see any of them again."

"They're people, Willa, not saints. Ordinary, flawed people, just like you and me." Her rubbed his hand soothingly up and down her arm. "And though they

might put on a happy face every morning when they
come to work, it's really a mask hiding their fear."

She tilted her head back to look at him. "What are
they afraid of?"

"Of growing old and no longer being in control.
They're actually more afraid of not being alive but still
breathing than they are of dying." He smiled sadly.
"That was Bram's biggest fear after Grammy died."

"But we're supposed to become *less* selfish as we get
older."

"What did they do to upset you?"

She settled back into the crook of his arm and stared
into the fire. "I called a meeting to tell them all to stay
out of my love life, but I might as well have been talking to the wall. They kept insisting that you were
hanging around to get your inheritance."

"And this surprises you?"

"Then they started trashing the coffee clubbers, dismissing them as simple-minded locals. And they scoffed
at the idea of you opening a business just to give a bunch
of old people something to do."

"But you agree with them about my opening a business here."

She sat up to look at him. "Not in principle, I don't.
But the real reason they don't want me marrying you is
that they're afraid I'd sell Kent Caskets and move to
New York. As soon as they realized that if you opened a

business I'd stay in Keelstone Cove, they did an about-face and decided I *should* fall in love with you."

"I see. You're afraid that more than wanting to see you happy, they really only want you sticking around?" He pulled her back against his chest and tucked her head under his chin. "So, fire the whole damn bunch of them."

"I can't," she muttered into his shirt.

Sam smiled, unsurprised. "Okay, then sell Kent Caskets, and let some new boss deal with them."

"I can't do that, either."

"Then quit. Give them the entire business—lock, stock, and caskets."

"No."

"Then I guess that leaves you only one option."

She lifted her head to look at him. "What's that?"

"You're going to have to forgive them."

"I will not."

"Then *you* tell me what you're going to do. You can't fire them, because you're too softhearted; you can't sell your business, because it's a big part of who you are; and you can't quit, because that would mean they've won."

"Forgiving them would mean they've won, too."

He tucked her back under his chin. "Hmm," he murmured. "Do you suppose that's why you've never been able to forgive yourself? Because if you did, it would mean *fate* has won?"

"What are you talking about?" She wriggled to get free.

"I was just thinking out loud, trying to work something out for myself. I'm sorry they disappointed you, Willa." He started rubbing her back in long, soothing strokes and felt her slowly relax. "So, does this mean you will support my new business venture?"

"You'll just get stabbed in the back by your workers."

"No, I won't."

She tilted her head back. "What makes you so sure?"

"Because, unlike you, I don't trust people. That way, I'm never surprised or disappointed."

"But you must trust your brothers. And Abram. Surely, you trusted your grandfather."

"If I had trusted Bram, what do you suppose my reaction would have been to his will?"

She looked thoughtful, then laid her head back on his chest.

"I trust you," he whispered into her hair.

She popped back up and blinked at him. "You do? Why?"

"Because I love you."

She tried to scramble off his lap, but Sam tightened his arms and held her against his chest. "I'm sorry if that bothers you, honey, but it seems to be one of those *fate* things I don't have any control over. I tell you what. I'll try my damndest to stop telling you I love you, if you'll try to stop seeing me as the enemy."

She muttered something, and Sam realized he had to loosen his hold so she could breathe. "What was that?" he asked with a chuckle.

She scowled at him. "I agreed to go to dinner with you tonight, didn't I? And I do not eat with my enemies."

"So, that means Barry Cobb is your new best friend?"

Her scowl intensified. "How come you never confronted me about that? I went out with him *five* times."

"Because I trust you." *And because as long as Cobb was with you, I knew exactly what he was up to.* Sam cupped her face and pulled her mouth to his, giving her a big, noisy kiss before holding her so their eyes were only inches apart. "And because your going out with him to make me jealous actually gave me hope that you *do* care."

She looked ready to smack him, so he kissed her again.

This time, she took his face between her hands and kissed him like a woman with something to prove. Sam was torn between wanting to shout hallelujah and groaning. He'd promised himself he wouldn't make love to her again until she quit seeing him as a casual fling and started seeing them as a couple.

But surely he could indulge himself a little bit. She was so soft and pliable, her body filled with promise . . . and she wanted him, dammit!

She darted her tongue into his mouth and pulled him

closer. Sam sensed the world tilting on edge, not realiz‑
ing that Willa was repositioning herself to straddle his
lap until he felt her thighs gripping his. Her feminine
heat sent shock waves coursing through him, every mus‑
cle in his body going instantly taut.

He quickly grabbed her hips, stopping her madden‑
ing movements. She broke their kiss, her mouth mov‑
ing over his jaw as her hands attacked the buttons on
his shirt. Her lips soon followed, and Sam struggled to
catch his breath against her passionate assault. She
made little impatient sounds, her hips fighting his hold,
her fingers fumbling with his buttons as she rocketed
from zero to sixty in four seconds flat.

If he didn't get her under control, he would sponta‑
neously combust. "Willa. Honey. I'm not sure we—"

He yelped when her mouth found one of his nipples.

Then she lifted her head to look him in the eyes.
"Please, Sam, make love to me."

How in hell was he supposed to hold his ground
against *please?*

He framed her face with his hands. "I can't take ad‑
vantage of you like that. Not tonight," he said, wonder‑
ing whose voice was coming out of his mouth. "You're
upset and vulnerable right now."

"No, I'm aching to feel you inside me again," she
whispered, feathering her fingers over his exposed chest.
"It feels so good when you fill me up, Sam. Please make
love to me."

He groaned softly in defeat. He wrapped his arms around her, slid off the couch, and laid her beside him on the rug in front of the fire. She immediately went to work on his belt buckle.

He captured her hands and lifted them over her head. "I believe you asked *me* to make love to *you*. That means I'm the captain on this voyage."

The woodstove was producing just enough light for him to see her expression, which went from intense desire to trepidation as she obviously remembered how she'd nearly killed him on their last voyage together.

He went to work on *her* buttons, and as each one came undone, more of her beautiful breasts came into view. Sam prayed she didn't realize the firelight was enough for him finally to see what he'd only been able to feel on the *RoseWind*.

Her skin was creamy alabaster and as soft as silk. She was wearing a lace bra that pushed her full breasts together, and as he parted the edges of her blouse, he could see her nipples straining against the lace.

She stirred restlessly, and Sam leaned down and kissed her, using his free hand to undo the zipper on her pants. He stripped her down to her bra and panties about two seconds before she realized she was completely exposed to him.

She immediately tried to hide against him.

"You're beautiful, Willa," he murmured against her mouth, and kissed her again. He gently caressed her skin above the lace of her bra, running his thumb across her raised nipple.

She responded with a sweet, feminine moan and slid one of her legs up his. Sam kissed her chin, her throat, her collarbone, then delved into her cleavage, which turned her moan into a soft shout of approval. He felt her trembling beneath him as he continued on, moving his lips over the lace to her nipple. He suckled her through the material, causing her to arch her back with another encouraging shout.

He finally released her hands so he could take off her panties and bra. She immediately attacked his shirt, pushing it down over his shoulders, growling in frustration when she couldn't get it off his arms.

"Help me, Sam. I want to touch you."

He stopped undoing the front clasp on her bra long enough to shed his shirt; by then, she had already moved on to the buckle of his belt. Sam knelt upright, watching her lick her lips as she studied his chest and undid his belt, sliding his pants down to his knees.

Her gaze dropped, her eyes widened, and the hands that had been reaching for his chest suddenly headed for his erection. Apparently, she had just discovered a major advantage of having light during lovemaking. Sam jerked his groin out of her reach, capturing her hands and raising them back over her head. He used his knees to open her legs to him, then settled between her thighs.

He smiled, seeing her trepidation return. "A bit disconcerting, is it, to find yourself lying naked under a man you took blatant advantage of a couple of weeks ago?"

"I—I fished you out of the ocean. Twice," she said tremulously. "And I always took the night watch so you could get a good night's sleep."

"I'm not talking about the sailing, sweetheart."

She gasped. "I don't remember having to tie you up to have my way with you!"

He chuckled, kissing her raised chin. "No, you just set so many rules that you might as well have." He kissed the tip of her nose, then her cheek, and finally her mouth when she tried to argue. He gently nibbled her lips awhile, then began kissing his way down her neck toward her breasts.

She squirmed, pushing her hot, damp, naked sex against his erection as she wrapped her legs around him. Sam immediately slid down her body to avoid the temptation of slipping inside her, holding her hands at her sides so his mouth could continue its downward journey.

She went perfectly still. "S-Sam?"

He ignored her, having decided they were playing by his rules tonight, and dipped his tongue into her belly button. She shivered, her fingernails digging into his wrists. He moved lower, leaving a trail of kisses and gentle nips, and was rewarded by her soft, keening whimpers.

He tucked his hands holding hers under her hips, lifting her into a most intimate kiss. She shuddered violently, her whimpers turning to cries of pleasure. Her legs pushed into his shoulders, every muscle in her body coiling. Sam continued his sweet torture until he felt her quivering on the edge of orgasm, then rose to his knees. He lifted her hips onto his thighs and, placing his thumb where his mouth had just been, slowly entered her—all the time watching her in the dancing firelight.

He was barely inside her when she started convulsing around him, her hands covering her mouth to stifle her screams. Sam took hold of her wrists and pulled them away, setting them by her head as he braced himself to thrust into her deeply.

"Let me hear you come, baby," he growled, retreating slightly, then thrusting again. "Don't hold anything back."

He'd always been a visual man, and watching Willa explode with pleasure—her skin covered with dew, her eyes locked on his as she shouted his name and screamed—sent him plummeting out of control. His own release came with the suddenness of lightning, shooting through him in bolts of searing white heat. He stilled deep inside her, letting her lingering spasms finish the job.

Their gazes met and held for several heartbeats before she looked away, and Sam saw her eyes fill with emotion so raw it appeared painful.

He sighed, lying down on the floor beside her. She immediately turned to him, burying her face in his chest. He kissed her hair. "There. That's out of the way." He smiled when she stiffened.

"Excuse me?"

He scooped her up in his arms, stood, and headed for the bedroom. "Now that we've taken the edge off, we can really get down to business."

Chapter Nineteen

Willa lay in bed with her eyes closed, moving only the muscles needed to smile. Who knew there was a *captain* lurking inside Sam Sinclair's beautiful, sexy, inexhaustible body? By the third time he'd made love to her, she'd been ready to promote him to admiral. And by the fifth? Astronaut material.

His ego was probably so puffed up now, it was a wonder he had fit through the door when he'd snuck off in the wee hours of the morning.

Willa listened to the wind howling outside, heralding the arrival of a Canadian cold front. She bet if she opened her eyes, she'd see her breath, the cottage felt so cold.

It also felt so empty she wanted to weep.

Did she have the brains of a lobster or what? No, even lobsters had an innate sense of survival. She, on the other hand, had crawled into bed with Sam almost three weeks ago, blithely risking her heart just to shut up her hormones. And last night, right there on the floor in front of the fire, she'd felt her safe little world explode into pieces as fate finally caught up with her.

She loved Sam.

She didn't want to, but there it was, in all its stark, frightening truth. What had Sam been trying to tell her last night? That life happens whether we want it to or not and that sometimes fate is simply beyond our control?

She had been controlling this particular aspect of it for years, so what in hell had gone wrong? She knew she couldn't really blame her hormones; the poor things had just been doing their job.

Abram, then. This was all his fault. That stupid, insane, outrageous bequest had started her dreaming of no longer coming home to an empty house and of someday even waking up to the patter of tiny feet.

Boy, oh, boy, had she taken the bait.

Willa pulled the pillow from under her head and pressed it over her face. It was pitiful to realize she wasn't even as smart as a lobster. Lobsters were love-them-and-leave-them creatures. *They* never had to sit home and worry that something might happen to a loved one or fret over someone else's happiness.

Willa dropped the pillow to her belly with a heavy sigh and blinked up at the ceiling. "What am I supposed to do now?" she asked the universe. "Marry Sam and let *everyone* win?" She snorted. "Except I'm not going to fulfill the baby part of Abram's bequest, which means Warren Cobb will still get Tidewater, and Sam will be stuck with a wife who was shoved down his throat."

Did she believe he loved her?

"I think he *wants* to love me. And he might even *believe* he does. Who knows how the man's mind works?"

"Who are you talking to?" Jennifer asked, walking into the bedroom.

Willa yelped and pulled the blankets up to her chin. "Ohmygod, Jen, you startled me!"

"Sorry, Auntie," she said, her smile contradicting her apology. Her eyes widened. "Are you naked again? Cool. I think I'll start doing that. I bet it feels wonderful, not getting all twisted up in a nightgown ten times a night."

"What are you doing down here so early?"

"I've come to drive you to Emmett's. He said you planned to work with him on the *RoseWind* today. But we have to stop at the store on the way, so I can pick up a few things."

"Have your mom take you. I don't know how long I'm staying at Emmett's, and you have to get ready for the dance. Besides, I thought you weren't speaking to me."

"I wasn't, until I saw Sam's new truck parked beside yours most of the night." She dropped the clothes she was holding onto the bed with a smirk. "Here. I found these scattered on the floor in front of the woodstove."

"Brat," Willa muttered when the girl turned and sauntered into the kitchen. "Did Peg send down any food with you?" she asked, sprinting to the closet to find some grubby work clothes to wear.

"Yup. Bacon and eggs and homemade toast," Jen called back, her words a bit muffled. "Because, lucky for you, she also saw Sam's truck in your driveway last night."

"Are you eating my breakfast again?"

"Just a few bites. The homecoming dance is open to adults. Why don't you and Sam come tonight, too? Mom's going with Dad."

Willa rushed to the bedroom door, pulling a paint-stained sweatshirt over her head. "Shel's going with *Richard?*"

Jen nodded, swallowing a mouthful of food. "Cody thinks it's beyond weird, but I think coming home to an empty house really scared Dad. And I think Mom only agreed to go to the dance with him for Cody's and my sake. You know, so their divorce can be amicable, so we won't feel torn in our loyalties? Dad's ashamed of what happened in New York, and he told Mom he was sorry and that he intends to apologize to you the first chance he gets."

"You know about that?" Willa squeaked.

Jen looked up, her fork halfway to her mouth, and

rolled her eyes. "It's a teenager's job to eavesdrop, Auntie. How else are we going to find out what's going on? So, will you and Sam come to the dance? I can't wait for you to see my new dress. Ben came shopping with us and helped Mom and me pick it out." She canted her head at Willa. "I'm glad Sam's the grandson who fell in love with you. Ben and Jesse are really nice, but Sam fits you better."

Willa stood in the doorway, gaping at her niece.

Jen set down her fork and folded her hands on her lap, her expression suddenly serious. "Will you please give Sam a chance, Aunt Willa?" she pleaded. "If not for yourself, then for me?"

"What has my marrying Sam got to do with you?"

Jennifer looked down at the plate in front of her. "It's really important to me that you stop blaming yourself for the accident," she said, so softly that Willa had to strain to hear her. Jen looked up, her eyes welling with moisture, her little chin raised defensively. "I feel guilty for wanting to get on with my life when you can't seem to get on with yours. I want to solo-sail a Sengatti around the world when I graduate, but I can't even dream about doing it, knowing you'd be back here being miserable."

"Oh, Jennifer," Willa cried, rushing to the table. She got down on her knees and hugged her. "I'm not miserable. And that's not fair, Jen. You can't use me as an excuse not to go after your dreams."

"But I remember what you were like before the accident," the girl said into her shoulder with a sniffle. She pulled away, wiping her eyes. "It's like you became an entirely different person. You divorced David, which was a good thing, but then you suddenly stopped *living*. And you started hiding behind your old people. They take advantage of your soft heart, and you just let them. And you build caskets! I mean, jeesh, Auntie, could anything be more morbid?"

She clutched Willa's shoulders. "I'm sorry for blasting you like this, but Sam said it wasn't fair of me to resent you without your even knowing."

"Y-you resent me?"

"Because you make me feel guilty! Oh, this is coming out all wrong!" she cried, standing up and looking down at Willa, who couldn't seem to move. "You didn't ruin my life!" the girl snapped. "And I'm not a cripple. For God's sake, my foot got mangled because you saved me from burning alive! Would you please tell me why you think that's such a god-awful sin?"

"Because I *caused* the accident, Jen," Willa whispered, so overwhelmed that she couldn't stand. "I was upset from walking in on David and that woman, and I wasn't paying attention to my driving. I never saw that car."

Jen balled her hands into fists. "Accidents happen, Aunt Willa—every day, all over the world. And sometimes bad things happen to good people for no reason. But that doesn't mean you have to spend the rest of your life safely moored in the harbor. And it sure as hell doesn't mean *we* have to stay there with you!"

"Oh, my God, Jen, you're killing me," Willa cried, clutching her belly.

"There's no need for me to do that." Jennifer's voice was devoid of emotion. "You're halfway there already."

Stark silence descended over the cottage but for the sound of Jen's footsteps. The door opened, then softly closed, and Willa heard her niece limping across the porch and down the steps.

She sat on the floor, her face on her knees, and violently sobbed. All this time since the accident, what had she been doing to Jennifer?

And Cody? And Shelby? And herself?

She'd been protecting herself, hiding deep in the cracks and crevices of life in order to survive. But not only had she gone totally overboard trying to protect herself, but she had been dragging everyone she loved overboard with her.

Willa finally blew her nose and wiped her eyes with her sleeve. "Okay, enough. It's time you started living up to your name again, Willy Wild Child."

Emmett had called her that since she was a kid, but he'd rarely done so these last few years. Except . . . he'd started again after Abram had arrived, almost as if he was trying to *remind* her who she was.

"Subtle, Emmett," she said with a snort. "You should

have just dropped a mast on my head." She sighed. "How in hell am I going to fix this?"

Sam! He could help her figure out what to do about Jen. He'd bullied his way into her life; he could damn well be available when she needed him.

"All you got to do is get her pregnant."

Sam spit his coffee back in his cup, wiping his mouth on his sleeve as he looked around to see how many of the diner patrons had heard Phil Grindle's loud suggestion.

"Excuse me?" Sam whispered, leaning forward on the table. "You mind telling me how that would help anything?"

"Phil's right," Sean Graves interjected, also leaning on the table. He, at least, had the good sense to keep his voice low. "It's a known fact that pregnancy turns even the hardest-headed woman into a lamb."

"Yeah," Phil said, scowling at Sean for elaborating on his idea. "It's got something to do with all them hormones women got racing around their bodies," he told Sam. "If you put a bun in their oven, they settle right down."

"That's because they gotta stop worrying about everything else and start nesting," Avery Ingall added.

"You get Willamina pregnant," Phil said, "and you'll see her change almost overnight." He puffed out his sunken chest. "I got my Lizzy pregnant on our honeymoon, and she stopped all her talk about working at the cannery to earn her own money. She settled right down to keeping house and raising babies, and she only spent what money *I* gave her."

Sam hung on to his patience, remembering that these men were two generations older than he was. "It's not that easy to get a woman pregnant today, since they invented contraceptives."

Sean snorted. "That's when the world went to hell in a handbasket, all right."

"And even if I did manage to do as you suggest," Sam continued, "having a baby no longer means a wedding automatically follows. The rules have changed since any of you got married."

"I still say if you want to get her to the altar, just get her pregnant," Phil asserted loudly. "It's the best thing that could happen to that girl, anyway. It's unnatural to be nearly thirty and still running around loose."

These guys talked as if it was the nineteenth century!

Paul Dubay pointed a gnarled finger at Sam. "Your grandfather knew what he was about, by God. You just gotta hold Willamina to that bequest. If'n she's your wife, she'll have to support your business, because it's the law. Wives can't publicly contradict their husbands." Paul shrugged one bony shoulder. "They might even let her start coming to the town meetings again."

"You're getting your laws mixed up, Paul." Avery chuckled. "Wives can't *testify* against their husbands.

Ain't no law about them contradicting us in public *or* private."

"It don't matter," Sean said to Avery. "Paul's still right about Abram's will. Sam just has to hold Willamina to it."

Sam sat back in his chair. How in hell had his grandfather fallen in with these throwbacks? Grammy Rose had had more power than Bram at home, and she damn well hadn't been shy about using it.

"I still say getting her pregnant would kill two birds with one stone," Phil said. "Not only will she feel obliged to marry you, but a baby will take some of that fight out of her."

"I sort of like that fight," Sam said, leaning his chair on its back two legs. "It keeps things interesting."

"Uh-oh," Sean Graves said, picking up his coffee mug. "Here comes Doris. If she hears us talking about this stuff, we'll get an earful, all right."

Sam set his chair back on its legs, and the four men suddenly got busy drinking their coffee.

"Morn'n, Doris," Sam said, standing up and pulling over a chair from a nearby table for her. "Where's Mimi this morning? She's not ill, is she?"

"Her daughter went into labor last night, and she has to babysit the other three for the next few days," Doris said, smiling at Sam as he helped her out of her coat.

"I see you've brought your sketch pad," he said when she set it down.

"I was up half the night designing our new label," Doris said excitedly, sitting down and opening her pad. "That's why I'm late this morning. I also tried to come up with a list of names for our product." She opened the pad on the table and turned it toward Sam. "I figure it should be something catchy. This label," she said, tapping the page with a pink fingernail, "is one we could use if we decide to call them Angel Cakes."

"Angel Cakes!" Phil sputtered. "Ain't nothing angelic about lobsters. They're one of the ugliest creatures God ever created." He reached over and turned the pad to see for himself. "Why, this isn't a lobster dressed like an angel, it's a kid." He pushed the pad back. "What's a half-naked, fat little kid got to do with lobster cakes?"

"He's not a kid, he's an angel. And if you weren't so tight with your dollar and would go to the doctor and get stronger glasses, you'd see that he's *eating* the lobster cakes." She flipped to the next page. "Or we could make it look like the cakes themselves are angels. See, I put wings and a halo on this one." She smiled at Sam expectantly. "What do you think of my ideas?"

Sam picked up the pad and studied the labels, flipping to the first page and then back to the second.

His first thought was that he was going to have to apologize to Willa. He could see now how her seniors had completely usurped her authority, since his own little gang had certainly taken over *his* idea to open a business.

Yesterday morning, on the way to the warehouse he hoped to buy, he'd found out that Sean Graves had already negotiated the price with Avery Ingall the night before, over beers at Avery's home. Sean probably got the property for a lot less than Sam would have, but he'd been looking forward to going up against one of these Yankee traders.

Then, yesterday afternoon at the auto dealership, Phil Grindle had grabbed Sam by the arm and dragged him away—twice—from the deal he was being offered. Who knew there was so much negotiating room in the price of an automobile?

Apparently, Phil did.

Just how was he supposed to tell an eighty-year-old grandmother he really wasn't all that enamored with angels?

"Sam. Sam!" Phil said, his voice rising along with the force of the smacks he was giving Sam's arm. "Willamina's out there pacing back and forth. If you don't want to spend the day bailing her out of jail, you better get out there before she works up the nerve to come in looking for you."

"Oh, heavens." Doris gasped. "She's not allowed in here, Sam. If she steps one foot inside that door, it'll cost her seven hundred and forty-three dollars."

"And sixty-four cents," Phil added.

Sam tore his gaze from Willa, who had stopped pacing and was now eyeing the door handle. "Why?"

"She broke a few things last time she was here," Doris said, pushing Sam to his feet. "The owner said he wouldn't press charges and she wouldn't have to pay for damages if she promised never to come in here again."

Sam headed for the front door but stopped when he saw Barry Cobb reach around Willa and open the door for her. The man then placed his hand on her back and ushered her inside, completely ignoring her protests.

Sam heard several gasps behind him, and all conversation suddenly stopped. Barry Cobb spotted Sam, and he grabbed Willa by the wrist as she tried to scurry around him and dragged her toward an empty table in the front window.

Sam walked back to his gaping seniors.

"You just gonna let her sit there with that gangster?" Phil asked in disbelief when Sam sat back down.

Sam didn't know who had started the rumor that Barry Cobb might be tied in with the mob. He picked up his cup of coffee, took a sip, then smiled at his table mates. "I'm curious to see what might happen," he said, glancing toward Willa's table.

She was standing now, darting glances toward the back of the diner, then whispering something to Cobb. Cobb still had hold of her wrist, trying to get her to sit back down.

"Here comes trouble," Avery said, and Sam followed his gaze toward the kitchen.

Trouble appeared to be a rather large man wearing a

tight white T-shirt and a dingy white apron, standing in the kitchen door, glaring at Willa. Sam took another sip of his coffee, noticing that every last person in the diner had gone silent except for Barry Cobb.

"Oh, come on, Willa," Cobb scoffed, holding her wrist. "They can't stop you from coming in here; this is a public diner." He leaned forward, still not realizing he had an audience. "Will you relax? I'm glad I ran into you this morning. I want to ask if you'll go to the dance at the high school with me tonight. We could have dinner in Ellsworth first, if you'd like." He smiled. "I'll even buy you a corsage. What color dress will you be wearing?"

Sam smiled. Whatever the color, it would definitely be wrinkled.

"Willamina Kent!" a gruff, challenging voice called from the back of the diner. "You'd better have your purse with you!"

Barry Cobb finally shut up. Willa took advantage of his being distracted by the man walking toward them and jumped to her feet to dash for the door.

Cobb also stood, blocking her way. "Excuse me?" he said to the man, pulling Willa against his side. "Is there a problem?"

The man, obviously the owner, pointed at her. "She owes me seven hundred forty-three bucks and sixty-four cents." He turned the hand he was pointing at Willa palm up. "And if she doesn't give me every last penny, in cash, in exactly one minute, I'm calling the sheriff."

"Sam, do something!" Doris hissed, pushing his arm and spilling his coffee. "You need to save her!"

He looked over at Doris. "Don't women today prefer to save themselves?"

"That is a crock of shit," she snapped. "We still want to know we can count on a man in a crisis. This is your chance to prove what a good husband you'll be."

Sam blinked at Doris. Had she just said what he thought she had? He looked back at Willa, realizing she hadn't spotted him yet. He stood up and sauntered over to stand beside the owner, who was still holding out his hand, apparently expecting it to fill up with money in the next thirty seconds.

"You carry that much cash on you, Cobb?" Sam asked, stifling a grin when Willa gasped. She tried to wriggle away from Barry again, but he merely pulled her closer.

"I'm not paying this man anything," Barry said, looking from Sam to the owner's outstretched hand.

"Not even to save your girlfriend from the sheriff?" Sam asked. "She's going to look awful funny wearing a corsage in jail."

"Butt out, Sinclair," Barry snapped.

"Ten seconds," the owner growled. "Martha!" he hollered over his shoulder. "Start dialing nine-one-one!"

Surprised that Willa still hadn't done or said anything, Sam let out a loud sigh and reached back for his wallet. "Never mind, Cobb. I'll get this one. You can bail her out of the next mess she gets herself into."

Willa went from zero to sixty in one second flat. "You're not getting one stinking dime, you greedy man! It wasn't my fault the last time, and it's not my fault this time, either!" she yelled, shoving Cobb toward the owner, making them both stagger into a nearby table. She grabbed Sam's hand and headed for the door. "Come on!" she shouted over the roaring laughter of the patrons.

Willa pulled him onto the sidewalk, then suddenly stopped, undecided which way to run. Sam headed to their right, turning the corner at the first street they came to. He reached into his pocket and pulled out his key fob, hitting the unlock button as they approached his truck.

"Hop in," he said, running to the driver's side. She climbed in beside him and snapped her seat belt. Sam quickly snapped his own belt, looked over his shoulder, and pulled out onto the narrow lane. "Which way?" he asked. "We can't go to your house. That's the first place the sheriff will look for you."

"Turn left up ahead," she said a bit breathlessly. She suddenly laughed. "Oh, my God, did you see Craig's face?"

"Craig?"

"The coffee-shop owner. Craig Watson." She snickered. "I wonder what outrageous price he's going to come up with this time. I didn't even break any dishes today. Did you see me break any dishes?" she asked, batting her lashes at him.

He smiled at the gleam in her eye, then turned left

at the first road he came to. "Nope, I didn't see you break anything. I did see Cobb bump into a table and break some dishes, though."

She giggled. "I'm trying to picture myself sitting in jail wearing a corsage." She sighed. "I guess dinner and dancing is a no-go now."

"Unless you wouldn't mind if I stood in for Cobb," he said with a smile, puffing out his chest to better his chances. "I'd be right honored, Ms. Kent, if you would let *me* take you to the dance this evening."

She giggled again, then suddenly pointed. "Here! Turn left here. This is Route One, and it'll take us toward Prime Point. I know a secluded beach we can go to."

That sounded promising. "Mind telling me why Craig Watson says you owe him seven hundred and forty-three dollars?"

"And sixty-four cents," she tacked on. "Um, a few dishes might have gotten broken the last time, but Craig started it."

"And you were just an innocent bystander? Did anyone else get banned from the diner?"

"No. I was the only one in the diner with Craig at the time. His wife, Martha, had just left for the night."

"You were alone with Watson?" The man didn't look like anyone he'd want Willa to be alone with. Ever.

"I wanted to talk to him in private."

"Why?" he asked, sensing a community-crusader story coming on.

"Craig had just purchased the diner about four months earlier, and he wasn't . . . um, he wasn't doing things the way the previous owner had."

"I don't suppose he was obliged to."

She turned in the seat to face him. "Okay. Let me tell you about Gertrude, so you'll understand. There used to be a little old lady named Gertrude Bliss who lived in town. She was ninety-four, she lived alone in her big old house, and all she had for income was a small social security check. Gertrude also had six cats. They were all the family she had, and they meant the world to her, even if she could barely afford them."

"Let me guess. You paid for their upkeep."

"I took them to the veterinarian for her and paid for the visits. And the previous diner owner always saved a small bucket of clean food scraps for them. Gertrude would walk to the diner and pick up the scraps every morning, along with her cup of hazelnut coffee. When Craig bought the diner, he started charging Gertrude for the scraps, claiming it caused him a lot of extra work to sort them out. He also charged her for the coffee."

"And you decided to have a little talk with Watson to get him to give Gertrude the food for free."

"Well, yeah. Gertrude was a very proud woman, and she didn't want anyone in town to know how destitute she was. Her husband hadn't planned properly for their retirement, likely because he hadn't expected them to

live so long. When he died five years earlier, they were
already down to just their social security. But when a
husband dies, his check stops coming, and a surviving
wife is left with only *her* check, which is usually only half
of what his was if she never worked outside the home."

"So you confronted Craig Watson about charging
Gertrude for the scraps. How did it escalate to broken
dishes?"

"When he wouldn't agree to stop charging her, I
might have threatened to tell all his customers what a
rat he was. But I was bluffing, because that would mean
embarrassing Gertrude." She gave him a furtive glance,
then looked out her window. "I accidentally knocked
over a stack of plates sitting at the edge of a shelf." She
looked at Sam, her chin raised. "I wave my hands
sometimes, when I get worked up about something."

"You knocked over seven hundred dollars' worth of
plates?"

"The plates *might* have hit a couple of turkeys he
had thawing on the counter, and they *might* have fallen
into a sink full of soapy water." She waved her hand in
the air. "I don't remember, exactly. But I'm betting
Craig still served those turkeys the next day, even
though he added them to my bill. He probably tacked
on a few other things, too. I didn't exactly stick around
to take inventory."

Sam was trying so hard not to laugh that his side

started to ache. "Okay, then," he said, forcing a straight face. "Would you like *me* to talk to Watson about the table scraps?"

"It's too late; Gertrude died six months ago. I took in her cats, but four of them died of old age soon after. The other two were fairly young, and they're living at Grand Point Bluff with Ida Bates, Shelby's mother-in-law."

"What happened to Gertrude's home, since she didn't have any family?"

"She left it to the local humane society."

"Good for her. So back to tonight. Will you do me the honor of going to the dance with me, Willamina?"

"That depends." She looked down at her lap. "If you still want to after we talk . . . then yes, I'll go to the dance with you."

Sam frowned. "What's bothering you, honey? Why did you come to the diner looking for me this morning?"

He never heard her answer, only her blood-curdling scream when an oncoming delivery truck suddenly swerved into their lane and slammed into them head-on.

Chapter Twenty

Willa refused to open her eyes. She'd spent the last hour being poked and prodded, and she couldn't remember ever hurting so much. Even her hair hurt.

"Hey, sweet thing. Open your eyes for me."

The voice was smooth and cajoling and belonged to the person who'd done most of the prodding since she'd arrived at the hospital. Willa slowly opened her eyes to glare at him and blinked against the brightness of the room.

His blurred silhouette moved over her, putting her eyes in shadow. "China blue—beautiful. I've always had a thing for blue eyes. I know you're disoriented and would probably like to tell me to go jump off a pier, but we're done messing with you for now, I promise. Let's recap, shall we?" he said, his smile bright. "I'm Dr. Zeus, and you're in my ER at Berry Bay Hospital. Can you tell me your name?"

It came rushing back to her in a vivid flash. The truck coming toward them, the deafening sound of impact, the airbag exploding in her face. Then the jolt sideways, another equally violent stop, her arm exploding in pain, her screams lost in the sounds of screeching metal and shattering glass.

She was also pretty sure she remembered telling at least three people her name, including Mr. Happy Face here. "S-Sam," she said, her throat feeling as if it was on fire.

"Sorry, wrong gender. Try again," he said. "Can you tell me your name?"

Willa strained to swallow. "Sam! *S-Sam!*"

"I believe one of the men brought in is named Sam," a female voice said to her right. "Malcolm is with him."

"I'll make a deal with you, Blue Eyes. I'll have Mary go check on your boyfriend if you tell me your name."

"Willa."

"Okay, Willa. Do you know *why* you're in my ER?"

"Car crash."

"We're on a roll. You don't look like you're actually focusing on me, though. What color are *my* eyes?"

"Green."

His smile widened. "You don't happen to have a

thing for green eyes, do you? Wait, I'll turn down these lights," he said, suddenly disappearing.

The pain in her forehead eased when the bright lights dimmed.

"You were involved in what should have been an un-survivable crash, according to what the EMTs said when they brought you in," he explained, his voice moving back toward her. "They suspect what saved you was the size of your vehicle and its extensive airbag system."

Willa concentrated on making him come into focus. "Sam?"

"Mary's checking. Ready to hear a list of your boo-boos?"

"Water."

"Definitely doable. Here, this should help your throat."

A bent straw touched her lips, and Willa took a sip, carefully swallowing several times.

"Speaking of which," he continued, "your throat hurts because your seat belt gave you quite a bruise. The belt also bruised your left breast and hip. You have a slight concussion, but it's not as worrisome as it could have been. God bless those side-impact bags.

"Your right side, most specifically your wrist, took a bad hit when a tree decided your truck had gone far enough. That's going to require a little visit to the OR, which is where you're heading in about half an hour.

We're waiting for the surgeon to arrive." His smile flipped upside down. "They don't let me play with the really sharp knives; I only get to stick you with pointy things."

"My legs hurt," she said, the water having soothed her throat enough for a complete sentence.

"I'm getting there, Willa. Your knees and especially your ankles took a beating, which is typical in head-on collisions, because you automatically brace for the impact. But you were wearing some rather heavy-duty work boots for a babe, so nothing down there is broken. You probably won't be jogging for a while, though.

"As for your insides, everything's right where it should be. You've got a couple of cracked ribs that are going to hurt like the dickens for a while, but your spleen, kidneys, liver, and other important parts all appear to be happy and healthy." He touched her hair, and his smile returned, crooked this time. "Don't scream when you look in the mirror tomorrow, okay? You're going to have one hell of a shiner, and there are cuts and other small bruises, all minor."

He straightened and took hold of her left hand, being careful of the IV in the back of it. "There is one thing that I'm a bit concerned about, so I've called in someone to have a look-see. Are you aware that you're pregnant, Willa?"

She blinked at him.

"Just barely, though. About two or three weeks, near

as I can tell," he continued. "But I'm not an expert on female plumbing, so I've called in an OB-GYN to check you out before you head up to the OR."

She couldn't have spoken if her life depended on it.

"If that handsome hunk of a man next door is yours," a female voice said, walking up to the bed on Willa's right side, "I don't blame you for calling out for him. If he were mine, I'd be shouting his name every day and twice on Sundays. I'm Mary, and I'll be your in-flight attendant until we hand you over to the OR jocks." She touched Willa's shoulder. "Sam's well enough that they're threatening to strap him down if he doesn't quit trying to come find you. I assured him you're doing just fine, but I don't think he believed me." She looked over at the doctor. "Could we let them see each other? It'll make our girl here feel better, and I know it will make Sam a whole lot easier to deal with."

"I'll go talk to Malcolm," he said, heading out of the room.

"Dr. Seuss?" Willa called out.

He stopped and turned, letting out a heavy sigh. "It's Zeus, as in the handsome, powerful god."

"Sorry," Willa said, darting a glance at Mary, then back at him. "Um, what you told me about . . . about my condition. Can we keep that just between ourselves?"

He placed his hand over his heart. "Don't worry, it'll be our little secret."

Mary lightly patted her shoulder. "Sorry, but I'm one

of the players here, too. I ran your pregnancy test." She brushed Willa's hair back. "Try not to worry, honey. I'm sure your baby is just fine. I know it's no fun being in an accident, but now you'll be able to remember this day as when you found out you were pregnant. Congratulations!"

Willa closed her eyes. "Thank you," she muttered.

Sam remained sitting on the gurney, refusing to lie down. He was so scared he was shaking and so angry he was one second away from punching Malcolm in the face. "You let me see her for a few minutes," he ground out, "and then I'll go to X-ray. I have to be with her, to calm her down. She doesn't like hospitals."

"If she was any calmer, she'd be in a coma," a man said, walking into the exam room. He came up to Sam and gave him a quick visual assessment. "Sam, I presume? I don't know why you've got all the women in a dither. You look like hell."

"Who the hell are you?"

"Dr. Zeus. I'm tending your lady friend."

"Tell this bastard to let me go see her."

Dr. Zeus looked at Malcolm. "Is there a reason you haven't stuck him with something to knock him out?"

"I did. He's overriding it."

Dr. Zeus looked back at Sam. "You are exactly why I always call first dibs on the women. I tell you what,

Sam. You give me your word to cooperate with Malcolm when we get back, and I'll take you to her."

"I want to sit with her for a while."

"She's going up to the OR in half an hour. I'll give you until then."

"She needs an *operation?*"

"Her wrist is broken. We're waiting for the surgeon to arrive." He went to the corner of the room, got a wheelchair, and brought it back. "Your word, Sam."

"You've got it," Sam said, sliding off the gurney. His knees nearly gave out on him, but he grabbed the arms of the wheelchair and gingerly sat down, stifling a groan when he thought his ribs were going to rip through his sides. "Is she awake? Does she realize where she is and what happened?"

"Nothing inside her head appears to be scrambled; she's awake and talking."

Dr. Zeus wheeled him out of the room and down the hall a short distance. The chair stopped in front of a door, and the doctor stepped around to face him. "A word of warning, Sam. She's probably feeling as bad as she looks, but you both must have had angels sitting on your shoulders during that crash. The medics showed me digital photos of your truck. But other than the wrist and a lot of bruising, she's pretty much intact. So don't flip out on me when you see her, okay?"

"I won't."

Zeus started to step around to the back of the wheel-chair, but Sam grabbed his sleeve.

"Will the operation make her wrist as good as new?"

"That will depend on whether there's nerve dam-age."

"Thank you," Sam said, resting his hands on his lap.

Zeus grabbed the back handles of the wheelchair and spun Sam around, opened the door, and backed him into the room before wheeling him up to the gur-ney Willa was lying on.

Sam smiled at her, even though he felt like crying. She looked so beat up, so *hurt*. And so very, very fragile. "Hi," he whispered, reaching out and taking her hand in his, resting them on the blanket so she wouldn't feel how badly he was trembling.

"Hi," she whispered in a raspy voice, her eyes drink-ing him in. "You don't look any worse than you did when you stepped off the *RoseWind*."

Relief bubbled up in the form of a chuckle. "My side of the truck didn't slam into a tree." He lifted her hand to his mouth and kissed her knuckles. "I'm sorry, Willa," he whispered, closing his eyes and holding her fingers against his lips. "I am so damned sorry."

"Um . . . for?"

He took hold of the rail on her gurney and stood up. He leaned over her as far as his ribs would let him and feathered his fingers over her cheek, the only place that didn't appear bruised. "I'm sorry for damn near killing you. I tried to veer right to take the blow to my side, but I wasn't quick enough."

"From what I saw, you did a smashing job, Sam," Dr. Zeus said, appearing on the other side of the gurney. "And your truck did its job protecting you. The angle of impact crumpled the front driver's side nearly to the firewall. Our girl here wouldn't have gotten a scratch if the impact hadn't pushed you into that tree."

The doctor ushered the nurse to the door. "We'll be close by. If you need anything, hit the button marked Help," he instructed, gesturing toward an array of buttons on the wall over Willa's head.

Willa lifted her left hand to touch his face. "Are you really okay? Nothing's broken?"

"It feels like everything's broken." He very carefully leaned down and kissed her lips. "Don't get mad," he whispered close to her mouth. "But I love you."

"I love you, too."

He pulled away slightly and smiled. "I know."

"You do?" she squeaked, her eyes widening. "How do you know?"

"I saw it in your eyes last night, in front of the fire. Why do you think I rushed us into the bedroom? I was afraid you'd panic and send me away, so I decided to keep you . . . um . . . occupied."

She sighed heavily, her gaze locked on his. "I didn't want to love you, but it snuck up on me when I wasn't looking."

"God, Willa," he breathed, touching his nose to hers. "I nearly lost you. I am so damn sorry you got hurt."

"Quit apologizing," she rasped. "And sit down before you fall down."

"Yes, ma'am," he said, kissing her nose before he carefully lowered himself into the wheelchair. He slid his hand, palm up, under hers lying on the blanket. "Is that why you were looking for me this morning? To tell me you love me?"

She gingerly turned her head to look at him, giving a slight wince. "I was actually coming to ask you to help me with Jennifer."

"Don't strain your neck," he told her. "I can hear you just fine when you're looking up. What's the matter with Jen? Did the boy back out of their date tonight?"

"No," she said, closing her eyes. "Jen came down to the cottage this morning, and . . . and we talked."

"About?"

"Can you reach that water on the table?"

He could reach it, but he had to stand up again to hold the straw to her mouth. The whole thing took several minutes to execute, and Sam sat back down with a sigh of relief. "Did they give you something for the pain?" he asked when he realized whatever they'd given *him* was starting to make him dizzy.

"I'm fine, Sam. I want to tell you about Jennifer before she and Shel and Emmett get here. It's important."

Sam hadn't even thought about anyone else, but he

realized next-of-kin must have been called by now. He should call his brothers, maybe while Willa was in the operating room. "What did you and Jen talk about this morning?" he asked, sliding his hand under hers again.

"About her resenting me," she said, staring up at the ceiling. Tears welled in her eyes.

"Jennifer doesn't resent you, honey."

"Yes, she does, because I've ruined her life. First by mangling her foot so badly they had to cut it off, then by making *her* feel guilty about it."

"Aw, honey." Sam stood up again to cup her face. "You did not ruin Jennifer's life. I've gotten to know her pretty well these last couple of weeks, and that girl has everything going for her."

"Except for not having a right foot," Willa whispered, more tears leaking out.

Sam brushed them away. "She doesn't seem to realize it's missing," he said, straightening to give his ribs some relief. "Jen's fine, Willa. She's okay right now, and she's going to be better than okay in the future."

"Will . . . will you help me convince her of that? I need to find a way to tell her she shouldn't feel guilty about me and that she has to go after her dreams."

"I'm not sure telling her will do anything to change her mind, honey. I think you're going to have to show her."

"But how?"

He ran his thumb across her cheek. "By forgiving

yourself, Willa," he whispered. "You can't spend the rest of your life beating yourself up with guilt and not expect it to affect everyone who loves you. I know it's hard, honey. I have a nasty case of the guilts myself right now." He took as deep a breath as his ribs would allow. "I pretty near killed you."

"The accident wasn't your fault."

"Neither was yours."

"Yes, it was. I wasn't paying attention. I was upset because I'd just walked in on David and another woman. And I had my eleven-year-old niece with me at the time. Jen saw them, too."

Sam realized she was getting upset, which was the last thing he wanted. "How about another sip of water?" he asked, picking up the plastic cup. "Damn, it's empty," he said, looking around the two-bed exam room. There must be a sink on the other side of the curtain. "I'll be right back," he said, shuffling away.

His IV tube brought him up short, and he set the cup on the wheelchair seat, then wheeled the chair around the curtain.

He had just reached the sink when he heard the door open. "Okay, Miss Kent," an unfamiliar voice said, moving toward Willa. "I'm Dr. Blaine, the OB-GYN Dr. Zeus called in."

Willa gasped, and Sam went perfectly still.

"I understand congratulations are in order," the man continued. "You just relax, and we'll see how the little tyke is doing before you head upstairs. Dr. Zeus is guessing you're only two or three weeks pregnant. Is that about right?"

Sam felt very dizzy all of a sudden and sat down in his wheelchair.

Willa was two weeks *pregnant?*

"There's been some sort of mix-up. I'm not pregnant" she said. "Sam? Sam! I'm not pregnant!"

"Sam?" Dr. Blaine repeated in alarm. The curtain was suddenly drawn back, and a man dressed in a camouflage hunting shirt glared at him. "Shit! I didn't know anyone else was here!"

Sam looked at Willa, who was staring up at the ceiling, blinking tears back furiously. "Shit," Sam echoed, standing up to go to her. His IV fetched him up again. "Damn," he yelped, and ripped it out of his hand.

"Hey!" Dr. Blaine stepped toward him just as the door opened again.

"I didn't see you head in here, Ken," Dr. Zeus said, skidding to a stop and taking in the scene. "Shit!" he said, rushing over to Willa. "I got called to Exam Room Three and didn't get a chance to warn him your boyfriend was in here," he explained. "I'm sorry, Willa. I screwed up."

"I'm not pregnant."

"My test said you are."

"I'm not pregnant!"

"Okay, okay. We'll run it again."

"I *can't* be pregnant," she said. "I had my tubes tied four years ago."

All three of them stared at her in silence.

Dr. Blaine finally cleared his throat. "Yes. Well," he said, walking over to her. "I'm afraid tubal ligations don't come with guarantees, Miss Kent. There's a one-in-two-hundred chance that your tubes might not have stayed tied. There's also a chance the pregnancy is in the fallo-pian tube, and, well, ectopic pregnancies aren't viable," he said softly. He touched her shoulder. "Let's rerun the pregnancy test, okay? Then we'll know what we're deal-ing with." He turned to Sam. "Would you be the father?"

"If she's pregnant, yes, I'm the father."

Blaine turned back to Willa. "You're too early along to see if the baby is in the uterus, but we need to know if you *are* pregnant before you go up to surgery."

"Can . . . can we have a minute alone please?" she asked.

"I'll give you the time it takes to run the pregnancy test again," Dr. Zeus said. "Because the OR team is in place now, waiting for you." He looked over at Sam. "And then I hand *you* back to Malcolm. I sure wouldn't want to be you when he sees you've pulled out your IV."

When the door closed behind them, Sam walked over to Willa. "You had your tubes tied four years ago?" he asked gently. "Why?"

"I was crazy with grief over what happened to Jen," she whispered to the ceiling. "And I was going through my divorce." She lifted her left hand to wipe her eyes and finally looked at him. "And I was so scared of ever having my own children and having something happen to them that I started searching for a doctor to tie my tubes. I went to nine before I found one in Boston who would do it. The others refused, saying they wouldn't sterilize a woman my age who hadn't had any children yet."

"Does Shelby know? And Emmett?"

"Nobody knows."

"When were you going to tell me?"

"I never said anything when the will was read, because not having children was my decision—not Abram's and not anyone else's." Her lower lip quivered, and her eyes filled with tears again. "I knew that if I loved my own child even half as much as I love Jennifer and something happened to it, I would . . . I would . . ."

"Shh," he crooned, touching his nose to hers. "Everything's going to be okay, Willa. You're not alone anymore." He pulled back just enough to see her eyes. "Remember that a burden shared is reduced by half? I have really broad shoulders, honey, and I can carry as much of your burden as you need me to, for as long as you need."

"And if the tubal ligation worked? Warren Cobb will still get Tidewater."

Sam let out a deep sigh, cupping his ribs at the sharp pain it caused. "Emmett assures me there's a loophole in Bram's will. We'll put an end to this mess. And then we'll get married because we *love* each other."

"You're willing to spend your life childless if this test comes back negative?"

"I'm not after your eggs, woman," he said with a chuckle, again having to cradle his ribs. "It's *you* I want."

She actually smiled at that, and he thought she tried to roll her eyes. "You've been hanging around Phil Grindle way too much." She turned suddenly serious again. "I suppose I might marry you," she whispered. "*If* you get me out of that stupid bequest first, so everyone, especially the seniors, will know we're doing it out of love."

"Deal."

"And *if* you agree to help me restructure Kent Caskets so I actually get to run it."

"I can do that."

"And you pay Craig Watson the seven hundred forty-three dollars I owe him."

"And sixty-four cents," he said. "Consider it done."

"And you send Barry Cobb packing."

"Happy to."

"And you stop this feud between the seniors."

"I'll lock them in a room and let them duke it out." He placed a finger over her lips. "And just what will *you* be doing while I'm running around putting out all the fires you've set?"

"And you help me straighten out Jen's thinking," she continued past his finger, apparently on a roll.

Sam sighed. "Is your list much longer? Because I think I have to sit down," he said, grabbing the rail on her gurney and eyeing his wheelchair across the room.

"We're having a baby, folks!" Dr. Zeus said as he came through the door, followed by a small parade of people. "Two positives equal a few thousand diapers and twenty years of saving for college." He took one look at Sam and laughed. "It's about time that sedative kicked in. Malcolm said he gave you enough to knock out a horse." He rolled the wheelchair up behind Sam. "Okay, people, let's get this show on the road. It's opening day of spring hunting, and I've got a plump little turkey in the orchard behind my house with my name on it."

"Turkey?" Sam said, collapsing into the chair with a laugh. "I've always been more partial to partridge, myself."

Epilogue

Rosebriar, four months later

*S*am *sat straddling the* granite bench facing Bram's and Grammy Rose's graves, his arms wrapped around Willa and his hands resting on her slightly rounded belly. They'd come to the cemetery to escape the chaos that had arrived at Rosebriar last night, and they'd been sitting in blessed silence for the last ten minutes, gazing at the bouquet of roses they'd set in front of the massive gravestone.

"A penny for your thoughts," Sam said, caressing Willa's belly through her coat.

"I'm worried about Ben," she said with a sigh. "He's been acting strange ever since we got here four days ago. He seems preoccupied." She titled her head back to look up at him. "Do you think taking over Tidewater has been too much for him, now that you're living in Maine?"

Though there hadn't been any need to use it, since Willa had married him two weeks after their accident and she definitely was pregnant, the loophole to secure Tidewater had turned out to be so simple Sam was still kicking himself for not seeing it sooner. The three grandsons had had the power for years to override Bram's vote any time they wanted. Even if Warren Cobb *had* gotten hold of their grandfather's shares of Tidewater, if Sam and Ben and Jesse had combined their own shares, they would have had complete control of the company.

That spoke volumes about how much Bram had trusted them and how they'd never once thought about combining their votes against him.

"Too much for Ben?" Sam kissed her nose, then snuggled her in the warmth of his embrace. "He loves the challenge of stepping into Bram's shoes. No, I believe something else is bothering him. Emerson told me Ben started acting funny about a week ago, around the time he received a letter. Emerson said it came here to the house, which is unusual, since Ben gets most of his mail at the office. The letter didn't have a return address, but Emerson did see it was postmarked from Maine."

"Maine?" she repeated, tilting her head back to look at him again. "From Keelstone Cove?" She smiled. "Maybe Ben turned the head of someone in town when he came up on one of his visits." She gasped. "I bet it's Doris's granddaughter! She couldn't take her eyes off Ben at our wedding."

"Emerson said it was from Medicine Gore, a small town in the northwestern mountains, not far from the Canadian border."

"Who does Ben know in Medicine Gore?"

Sam shrugged. "He spent his summer between high school and college in those mountains. He was a volunteer for the Sierra Club, doing environmental research on a dam being built up there. Maybe the letter is from someone he met back then." He rubbed his cheek against hers. "I remember Ben came home really bummed out. He wouldn't talk about it, but we all thought he'd fallen for a girl and she had broken his heart. It took him almost a year to start dating again."

Willa kissed his cheek. "Maybe she realized her mistake and finally worked up the nerve to write to him."

Sam snorted. "She's out of luck, then. Ben's too enamored with Tidewater right now to rekindle an old flame."

"But he's obviously bothered by it."

"He'll get over it. So," he said, "remind me again why having Keelstone Enterprises' board meeting at Rosebriar was such a brilliant idea?"

"Because we needed to get our seniors on neutral ground." She turned on the bench to face him. "I swear, if they all don't start getting along, we're firing every last one of them and finding some teenagers to make up our board of directors. Even two-year-olds would get along better than they do. Bringing them down here is our last resort—and their last chance."

It had been Sam's idea to combine Kent Caskets and his lobster-cake business—which they were calling Sinclair Foods until everyone could agree on a name— under the mother company of Keelstone Enterprises. They'd assembled a board of directors of both groups of seniors in hopes that it would finally bring them together, but his plan wasn't working. Sam was starting to believe the old saw that you can't teach an old dog new tricks. Hell, he couldn't even teach them that it didn't matter where at the board table they sat, that all seats but the one at the head of the table were equal. Emmett actually sat there, though he'd only agreed to chair the board while Sam was giving Shelby a crash course in business management, so she could oversee their lobster-cake business.

Willa leaned back against his chest, pulled his arms around her again, and patted his hands over her belly. "Thank God Peg agreed to come down and cook for us. But then, most of her customers are down here," she said with a snicker. "It serves Craig Watson right for not being more community-minded. Maybe a little competition will straighten him out."

When Peg's three months of working for Willa were

up, she sold her cabin on Wagon Wheel Lake and opened a coffee shop right across the street from Craig Watson's diner. The coffee clubbers had shifted their business to Peg, along with half the other residents in town.

Peg had also come up with the recipe for Sam's lobster cakes, after serving several versions in her diner and getting feedback on the perfect combination of lobster, bread crumbs, and a secret ingredient she was charging him an arm and a leg for.

Emerson had refused to leave his post at Rosebriar. He disappeared quite often, though, and Sam suspected he was hiding in his room, finally writing his book.

Ronald had also stayed, to drive for Ben. And when Sam and Willa came down for a visit, he kindly drove them around in *his* Stutz Bearcat.

Willa sighed. "I can't believe Jen preferred to stay home and work on her boat this weekend. What is *up* with that girl?"

Jennifer had gotten her driver's license just before school started and her new prosthesis a little more than three weeks ago. After being Willa's maid of honor at their wedding, the teenager had started building the definitive Sengatti sloop with Emmett, and Jen intended to sail it solo around the world next summer.

Sam and Ben and Jesse had already started trying to figure out how to have their cargo ships surreptitiously shadow her on her journey. Sam broke into a cold sweat every time he pictured Jen out on the open ocean all alone.

He tightened his hands on Willa's rounded belly. "This had better be a boy. I don't think I'd survive a daughter like Jennifer."

"But if it is a girl, can we name her Rose?" Willa asked, looking up at him.

He kissed her nose. "I suppose that would be appropriate, considering that she was conceived on the *RoseWind*, which was Bram and Grammy's private little love nest.

Then he held a finger to his lips. "Listen," he whispered. "Do you hear that?"

Willa went still, then gasped. "What is that?" she whispered back. "It sounds like . . ."

"Exactly, Mrs. Sinclair. That is definitely Bram laughing his head off!"

Letter from Lake Watch

Dear Reader,

Robbie and I are in the habit of loading the camper onto our pickup whenever the mood strikes us, and simply driving out of our dooryard. When we reach the stop sign at the main road, it's only then that we look at each other and ask, "Which way do we want to go? Right or left?"

Right takes us toward the mountains; left toward the ocean. More often than not, Robbie votes we turn right. He likes heading into the mountains, as there aren't many places to spend money in the wilderness. Whereas the coastline of Maine is awash with tourist attractions, most of which have a way of sucking the dollar bills directly from our wallets. Lobster shacks, antique shops, amusement parks, pottery and craft co-ops, and schooner rides call out as my husband tries to sneak by, his fists clenched on the steering wheel and his foot heavy on the gas as he steels himself against my softly spoken, "Oh, that looks interesting. Let's stop."

For those of you who might not know, stopping a heavy truck camper in Route One summer traffic is about as easy as bringing a 22-wheeler loaded with saw logs to a halt. But my husband of thirty years knows that *if mama ain't happy, ain't no one happy,* and he smartly finds a place to turn around and go back.

But sometimes a girl's just gotta shop. I mean, what's the point of venturing out into the big beautiful world if you can't lug some of it back home with you? Granted, when we go to the mountains I return with unusual rocks, beaver-sculpted sticks, and maybe a discarded antler or two. They're all fantastic treasures to display around the house, but so are bird feeders that look like lighthouses, wind chimes that sound like offshore buoys, and lobster trap coffee tables. And the blueberry jam from Washington County is to die for.

Robbie is loading the camper right now as I write this, and just between you and me, I already have a destination in mind. When we reach the stop sign, I'm going to strongly suggest we turn left.

"Why?" he'll ask, even as he sighs in defeat.

Because, I'll tell him, I am writing a book that takes place in KeelStone Cove, an imaginary town on the downeast coast of Maine. And everyone knows that authors must thoroughly immerse themselves in their story settings.

After all, it's been a full year since I've taken a schooner ride. I also believe we should eat lobster on the pier, just to add some authenticity to my work. And what kind of writer would I be if I didn't peruse the craft shops? How can I hope to convey the essence of KeelStone Cove if I don't hit every attraction each tiny fishing village has to offer? And I have to lug *something* home to place beside my computer, to nudge my muse when I find myself staring at a blank screen.

So I urge you to also get out and explore your own corner of the world. Lug little bits of it home with you. Leave your chores, your challenges, and your worries behind, and have fun.

Can't get away right now? Then find a good romance novel and indulge yourself in a minivacation!

Until later, from LakeWatch . . . keep reading,

Janet

And now,
turn the page
for a sneak preview of
Ben Sinclair's story!

The cold, wet forest floor seeping through her wool pants made Emma uncomfortable, but it was nothing compared to the anger she felt as she watched the deliberate desecration of the woods she loved.

Treehuggers were driving spikes into the trees. There were six men, and they didn't at all look like the fancy environmentalists who had been hounding the State House and the nightly news for the last two months. These men were grubby, disgusting jackals with their own agenda for gaining their objective.

She'd heard about the terrorist act of spiking trees, but that problem had been a distant one, usually in the northwestern forests of the country. Loggers, most of them friends of hers, would come here to harvest these trees, and be ripped to shreds when their chainsaws hit those spikes. The saws would disintegrate on contact, sending missiles of sharp, jagged chain into unprotected flesh. Innocent, hard-working men would be maimed and possibly killed.

She'd been minding her business this morning, headed for a spring she knew had the sweetest drinking water in the area, when she'd heard the echo of metal thunking against live wood. It was a distinct sound that had rattled around in the forest, and it had taken her a good twenty minutes to find the source.

Now she was wet, and cold, and getting madder and madder the longer she watched. But she couldn't just go charging in. These men were out-of-staters, and they didn't look as if they would like being discovered.

Yet she couldn't walk away, either. There was no way she could point out all the vandalized trees later, and no way the loggers could take metal detectors to every tree.

Maybe she could scare them off. Stay hidden and blast the air with birdshot, making them think the calvary had arrived.

Emma checked her shotgun, making sure both the chamber and the magazine were full, then patted her pocket to make sure she had more shells to quickly reload. She raised the butt of the gun to her shoulder, aimed it ten feet above the men's heads, and clicked off the safety.

A large, powerful hand suddenly covered hers, muffling the click of the safety being replaced. Another large hand covered her mouth as a crushing weight pinned her to the forest floor.

She usually wasn't one to panic, but Emma wildly struggled to dislodge her heavy assailant. Her shotgun was ripped from her hand and pushed away, and she was roughly grabbed by the shoulder and rolled over. Still pinned and her mouth still covered, Emma stopped struggling when she looked up into the iron-gray eyes of a very angry Benjamin Sinclair.

She didn't even squeak, she was so stunned. The face less than a foot from hers didn't belong to a city-sport or corporate executive. She was looking at a man ready for battle, who didn't intend to let her win it.

He raised off her and grabbed her shotgun and pack. He kept his other hand latched on her jacket and pulled her to her feet with one swift, powerful jerk, then started dragging her down the hill.

Unable to do anything else, Emma stumbled after him. She tried to dislodge his grip on her jacket, but Ben Sinclair didn't break stride, turn around, or even acknowledge that she had to run to keep up. He did start cursing, once they were far enough away that they couldn't be heard.

Emma gave him a few choice words in return. When he suddenly stopped, she slammed into him.

"Lady, if you don't shut up and quit struggling, I promise you won't be able to sit down for a week."

Emma snapped her mouth shut and glared back at

him. He turned and started along a brook, once more dragging her behind him.

"How you and my son have survived this long is the eighth wonder of the world."

"What are you doing here?"

He stopped again and turned to her, his scowl darkening even more. "I'm on a fool's mission." That information given, he pushed her ahead of him. "Keep going until I tell you to stop."

Emma thought about planting her feet, but he was a head taller, sixty pounds heavier, and definitely stronger than she was. So she walked.

"You were going to go charging right in there, weren't you? You were going to take on six men with a four-shot gun, and not a soul to help within twenty miles. You're more insane than your moose."

The lecture went on for a good twenty minutes, and Emma learned that she was impulsive, irresponsible, and lacking the brains of a chipmunk. She discovered she was too brave to rush in where even fools wouldn't go, and that she needed a keeper. And then he asked her again how she'd managed to raise his son to manhood without getting either of them killed.

Emma suddenly sat down on a rock beside the brook, put her chin in her fists, and scowled at the water.

Ben loomed over her.

"Are you through yet?" she asked, not looking at him.

"Not by half."

"Should I be taking notes?"

Her pack and shotgun fell to the ground with a heavy thud, and the legs standing beside her bent at the knee, bringing an even angrier face within an inch of hers. "You could have gotten killed."

Emma smiled at him. "That would have solved a lot of your problems."

He lunged for her and Emma pulled back. He caught her shoulders and followed her down off the rock. Ben was back on top of her, and Emma was starting to get more than a little angry herself. "If you don't quit manhandling me, I'm gonna make sure you never father another son."

Completely ignoring her threat, he grabbed her hands pushing against his chest and pinned them over her head with one of his own. Then he took his other hand and brushed the hair from her face ever so gently.

"Emma Sands. Such bravado. Such a scam artist."

"Get off me."

He used his knees to spread her legs, and Emma sucked in a surprised breath when she felt him nestle intimately between her thighs.

"That was the wrong direction!"

"But the safest, if I want more children."

"How did you find me?"

"Michael drew me a map."

"You're suppose to be getting to know your son, not interfering in my business."

The gentleness left his face as suddenly as it had appeared. "Someone had to interfere. You were about to let your cannon loose on those men, weren't you?"

"They were spiking the trees."

He growled a nasty word.

"If I ever get you near a bar of soap, I'm going to use it to wash out your mouth."

He suddenly grinned. "You have my permission to try."

"Are you planning to get off me anytime soon?"

He wiggled, settling himself even deeper against her. "I'm rather comfortable." His grin turned sinister. "You're nicely padded in all the right places."

"Get off—"

Emma didn't finish. Ben's hand was at her mouth again as his head snapped up and he cocked it to the side, listening.

"They're walking down the back side of the ridge," he whispered, as every muscle in his body seemed to double in size.

He didn't uncover her mouth. Did he think she was going to scream hello to the vandals? Emma bit his hand. She was rewarded with a ferocious glare as he rubbed his abused appendage on her jacket.

"I'm beginning to pity the poor bastard who ends up marrying you."

Emma tried to punch him, but he caught her fist, brought it up to his lips, and kissed it. "Don't spar with me, Emma. I'm bigger and stronger and meaner than you."

"You also have a bigger ego than God."

"I need a big one, if I want to hold my own against the Sands clan."

"I'm surprised Michael didn't draw you a map that would take you to Canada."

Ben frowned darkly. "Michael's got his own agenda, and I don't think either of us will ever fully know what it is. Are you sure Kelly gave birth to him? You didn't just find him in one of Medicine Creek's hot springs, bubbled up from hell?"

"I know he's looking more and more like his father every—"

He shut her up again, but with his mouth this time. Emma gasped at the bolt of heat that suddenly shot through her. She was wet and cold and she couldn't breathe, but she was also hot and tingly and so very confused.

Fire, of the delicious feminine kind, flared deep in

the pit of her belly. Emma couldn't stop herself from kissing him back, any more than she could stop the seasons from changing.

This was so dangerous. Her nephew's father was seducing her, and she hoped he wouldn't stop. She was setting herself up for a world of heartache, but all she could do was curse the clothes that separated them.

"Slap my face, Emma."

She used her freed hands to pull his growling mouth back down to hers.

He kissed her again, opening her mouth with his tongue and taking in the taste of her, giving back his own sweet essence. His weight was no longer crushing, it was welcome. One of his hands began roaming her body, and Emma wiggled to give him easier access.

"Stop me, Em."

She started doing a little exploring herself. He was so muscled and firm, and the canvas shirt under his jacket unbuttoned easily. The hair covering his chest sprang to life against her fingers, and Emma felt Ben take a deep, shuddering breath.

"Last chance, Emma. Stop me now."

The bellow of a huge bull moose came slamming down over the ridge, followed by the cracking of branches. Ben threw his head up in surprise. Her own breath suspended, Emma watched as he slowly looked down at her, his expression turning to horror.

Emma pushed him away. "Get off me!"

He scrambled to his feet and turned his back, his hands tugging at the front of his pants.

For a stunned second, Emma lay motionless. What an idiot she was—she'd nearly let Ben Sinclair seduce her! She had no one to blame but herself. Was this what Kelly had felt sixteen years ago? Was this how quickly, how insanely, it had happened?

"I'm . . . Emma, I'm sorry."

She didn't look up at those softly spoken words. "Forget it, Mr. Sinclair."

He lifted her chin with two gentle but insistent fingers. His face was drawn, but flags of color darkened his cheeks. Leftover passion? Embarrassment? Anger?

"This shouldn't have happened."

"Damn right, it shouldn't have."

"I wasn't thinking," he said through gritted teeth.

"Certainly not with your upper brain."

His eyes widened in shock, then he suddenly threw back his head and burst out laughing. He sat down on the ground beside her. "My God. What am I suppose to do with you, Emma Sands?"

"You can go back and get Michael and take him home."

He instantly sobered. "Now? You want me to take him away right now?"

Her throat closed tight, Emma nodded.

"While you stay out here and hide?"

She lifted her chin. "I am not hiding. Michael can call me once he gets settled."

He muttered something as he picked up her pack and shotgun and his own pack.

Then, just to make the day even more delightful, it started to rain.

"Damn. We've got to find shelter," Ben growled.

"Medicine Creek Camps is sixteen miles that way," she said, pointing behind him. "If you start walking now, you'll be there before dark."

He stood looking at her, her gun clasped in his fist, his hands on his hips, both packs slung over his shoulders, and his eyes squinted against the rain. His jacket was open and his shirt was buttoned crooked.

L.L.Bean should be here with their camera now.

"I think I'll just stick around a while, if you don't mind."

"I do mind. Go away, Mr. Sinclair."

He lifted her chin again, allowing the rain to wash over her face—and cool her blush, she hoped.

"Let me rephrase that. I am going to help you set up a shelter, and then we are going to put on some dry clothes."

"Michael didn't pack you a tent?"

He shook his head, his face thoughtful. "Do you think it was an oversight?"

Emma grabbed her backpack off his shoulder and started up the brook. "Knowing Michael, it wasn't."

Ben seemed startled she was leaving, and ran to catch up. "What's that supposed to mean?"

"It means he's paying me back for not letting him skip school for the moose hunt." She looked over her shoulder and gave him a nasty grin. "Either that, or he thinks a cold, wet night outdoors would do you good."

"He hauled me out of bed at four this morning and stuck a map in my hand. Your nephew comes by his sadistic nature quite naturally, I see."

"I'm not the one going around threatening to throttle somebody." Emma stopped and turned fully to face him. "If you ever threaten to lay a hand on me again, Mr. Sinclair, you won't live long enough to gloat about it."

He nodded, his expression serious but for his laughing eyes.

Well, that had been brilliant. Attack the woman. In the dirt, no less.

Oh, very brilliant, Sinclair.

How in hell could he have known she'd go off like a keg of gunpowder? She was supposed to be in love with another man!

On his cold, dark trek through the woods this morning, Ben had devised a plan to find out who the love of Emma's life was. He'd intended to kiss her, then she'd slap his face and tell him that her heart was already taken. She was supposed to yell the bastard's name and threaten to have him kill Ben for making advances.

Instead, the little minx had blindsided him.

Thank God that rutting bull moose had made all that noise. For one short second, Ben had known exactly how the horny beast felt.

Now Emma was mad enough to kill him. On top of nearly taking her right there on the ground, he could have gotten her pregnant. He hoped like hell there were no more Sands sisters. At this rate, he was liable to found a dynasty on them.

Ben balled up his L.L.Bean shirt and threw it across the shelter Little Miss Wonder-Guide had erected from a tarp and tree branches. It kept out the wet, but not the wind.

"Dammit. It's snowing!"

"It does that in Maine sometimes," came an equally disgruntled voice from the other side of the tarp.

He tore into his pack and pulled out another shirt, this one flannel. Ben crammed his arms in the sleeves before his shivering made the task impossible. "Are you sitting out there trying to get pneumonia, or is your stubbornness keeping you warm?"

A green rubberized poncho with a head poking out of it popped into his line of sight. "It will be a lot warmer with hot tea in our stomachs."

"Couldn't we have pitched this tarp near one of your hot springs? *Damn*, it's cold."

Two steaming cups preceded two small hands into the shelter, followed by a billowing green poncho sporting huge flakes of snow. The flakes weren't melting, because Emma's smile could freeze a penguin.

"You're welcome to move on, if you'd like. The nearest hot spring is about three thousand miles west." As angry as she obviously was, she was careful when she handed him the hot cup of tea.

Ben sighed as he blew on his tea. "Let's call a truce. This shelter is too small for a battlefield."

"I'm sure Mikey packed you a poncho, Mr. Sinclair. And if you turn that map upside down, you should be able to follow it back the way you came."

"I thought you had six cabins of moose hunters arriving today. Shouldn't you be seeing to your business?"

"Mikey will settle them in. And I'll be there early tomorrow to take them out."

"Why do you call him Mikey? It doesn't quite fit."

Although it was small, Ben got his first smile of the day from her. "To remind him that he's not a grown-up yet, and that I'm older and hopefully a bit smarter than he is."

"He calls you 'bossy lady' sometimes."

"Just when he's pissed about something."

"He called you that the night you found me."

She held her tea up near her face, letting the steam warm her. "Every so often, his confidence slips. He had never landed on anything like Smokey Bog without me being in the seat beside him."

Ben suddenly didn't need the tea for warmth, as his blood began to boil. "You put my son in a situation that could have killed him?"

"No, Mr. Sinclair. Michael really *is* an excellent pilot. I didn't have any doubts; he did." She shot him a grin. "And he forgot them once he got down to business."

"You were nervous. I saw how tense you were."

"I was worried about my plane," she shot back. "Pontoons are expensive."

He was sorely tempted to kiss her again.

Ben realized she was scowling at him, and remembered he should be scowling back. "Plane floats are more precious than a boy's life?"

She looked immensely satisfied with herself, apparently convinced she was keeping the battle lines drawn. No cold war for this woman. She would go down fighting to the bitter end.

It was a survivor's defense. One Ben imagined she had developed to survive all that she'd lost. She and Kelly had lost their mother when they were very young; then at fourteen she'd lost her father, rather violently. And at just nineteen, she had suddenly found herself alone to raise a five-year-old boy. Oh, yes. Emma Sands was definitely a survivor.

He was going to have to sneak up on her tonight.

While she slept.

While her shotgun was out of reach.

And he would not lose control this time. He would kiss her once, just to prove to himself that he could. He wouldn't jump all over her, or get lost in that luscious body that could drive a man to insanity.

Ben felt himself get hard just remembering the feel of her beneath him.

"I'm turning in for the night, Miss Sands. I'm not used to getting up at four in the morning and then walking half the day over half the mountains in the state. Good night."

He crawled into the sleeping bag Michael had packed him and zipped it up to his neck, hiding the evidence of his lustful thoughts.

The soft glow of the battery lantern cast Emma in a halo of deceptive warmth. Shadows danced beside her on the tarp, which was beginning to sag with the weight of wet snow. The forest had grown eerily quiet, and Ben imagined their little shelter looked like a cocoon of peace in these woods his son called home.

Through half-closed eyes, he watched the woman who had raised Michael. She sat motionless as she contemplated the snowflakes pooling at the entrance of their temporary lodge. Emma Sands also called this place home. She was as comfortable here in a crude shelter in the middle of a snowstorm as a squirrel was nestled in a tree of leaves and downy fur. This beautiful woman, with long, wavy, blond hair and a face angels would envy, was the most remarkable woman Ben had ever known.

Emma Sands held strong convictions about many things. If she found men driving spikes into trees, she'd try to stop them. If she found men beating up another man, she would step in with her shotgun blazing. When she loved a boy like a son, she would do anything to protect him. And if she gave herself to a man, she would give herself fully.

Would she have let him make love to her today, if he hadn't stopped?

Maybe. But why? Because of her nephew? Because Ben held the power to take the boy away from her?

He would bet his business that Emma hadn't been thinking of Michael when she'd exploded with a passion so strong, and Ben had been blinded to everything else, too.

It seemed an eternity before the cause of his lust finally crawled into her sleeping bag two feet away, and turned out the lantern. Then she set her shotgun between them, rolled over, and rested one hand on the stock—not at all worried about sharing a tent with him.

Which was the first really blatant mistake he had seen Emma Sands make.